solita

VIVIEN RAINN

BOOK 1

Solita by Vivien Rainn

© 2022, Vivien Rainn

All rights reserved.

Cover design by: @fromthemillart

This novel contains content that may be troubling to some readers, including, but not limited to: references to suicide and suicidal ideation, Catholic themes and imagery, references to parental loss, blood, violence and gore.

This is a work of fiction. Unless otherwise indicated, all names, characters, businesses, places, events and incidents in this book are either the product of the author's imagination, or used in a fictitious manner. Any resemblance to actual persons, living or dead, or actual events, is purely coincidental.

To my dad,

for always believing in my dreams

PORT CANTE, PHILIPPINES

1690

THUD.

A girl presses her ear against a wooden door, straining to hear the voice coming from the room beyond; as soft as a whisper, as solemn as a prayer.

"Burn the father."

Thud.

Holding her breath, she swears the noise sounds almost like a hammer to a nail, over and over and over. Leaning down to peer into the keyhole, she squints into the haze of the room beyond, seeing nothing but shadows in the dim.

Thud.

"Bury the son."

Furrowing her brows, she attempts to recall just how many shadows she saw slip into the old dining room at the rooster's crow.

Thud.

"Blaspheme the spirit."

It's the last of the noise, as the slow creak of unhurried footsteps makes its way directly to where she stands. Heart catching in her throat, she shoots upright, motioning to scramble back into the kitchens—but it's too late. The door pushes open, and a single friar emerges. Her heart skips a beat as she realizes; of all the shadows that entered, only one remains.

"Maid-girl—you heard everything, did you not?" he asks, his voice strained.

The girl says nothing, her tongue stiff against her teeth as she struggles to find the words to face the hard-lipped friar.

"Are you alone?"

She nods quickly, twisting her fingers together behind her back.

"Hm." He relaxes his gait, holding the door close behind him. "What is your name?"

With a hoarseness to her voice she can't quite explain, she answers, "Malaya."

"You are too curious for your own good, Malaya." The tall friar rests the palm of his hand briefly over her shoulder, and she can feel the tremor of the muscles beneath his fingertips. "But your silence redeems the fault."

Withdrawing his hand, he stands upright, only for Malaya to spot the crimson stain clinging to the linen of his robes—spatters of quick-drying ichor that can only come from a wound that isn't his.

Wide-eyed, she attempts to take a step backwards, only for her limbs to fill with lead beneath this friar's gaze.

"Here, take this." Reaching out his hand, he places something small in the palm of hers, squeezing her fist in emphasis. "You are that abularyo's daughter, aren't you? The daughter of that witch on the outskirts of town…"

Malaya feels a tide of dread rising in the pit of her stomach; every fiber of her being screams at her to run—yet she's fixed like an anchor to the hardwood beneath her feet.

"Y—yes," she stutters.

"Then there is a task of great import that only you can shoulder, Malaya." Gripping her forearm, he pulls her in closer, leaning down so that his voice is a lick of a flame against her skin. "There is a demon beneath this house, carrying out a sentence that will expire only when Judgment Day comes. Be sure he never awakens... be sure he never opens his eyes."

She draws her gaze upwards to face his, and a chill overtakes her senses at the sight that welcomes her. His eyes have changed; no longer brown—but a wicked, sparkling green. "Because, Malaya, the day he does will be the day you die."

Parting her lips in dread, he withdraws his hold of her the moment a bitter stench snakes its way into the depths of the Hacienda above their heads, hanging thick in the air.

Her stomach turns at this nauseating perfume, and she forces the question out of her to fill the silence. "The *señor*? Where is the *señor*?"

The friar says nothing, and Malaya realizes that the stench can be nothing else but scorched flesh.

"This Hacienda belongs to the church now. Forget the *señor* and his son. Your one and only master watches you from on high."

Dropping her hands to her sides, she feels her head begin to spin at the swirling miasma surrounding her. The friar steps to the side, leaving the door behind him open, the yawning dark beckoning her within. But his voice pulls her back, commanding her to listen one last time.

"And Malaya—don't ever forget this..." he watches her closely, a fire moving beneath his eyes, "He is always watching."

And with that, he disappears into the Hacienda, leaving Malaya to look down at her hand, and whatever it is he left between her fingers. Unfurling her fist, she sees a baroque pearl glinting at her with all the colors of a distant, starlit sea.

She knows what she must do.

Looking to the door containing the demon beyond, she sucks in a breath of resolve before she enters.

THE CREAK of footsteps above distracts the demon trapped

beneath the floorboards from writhing in his grave. Blood stains the wood of his sealed casket, seeping through the pores and into the rich earth beneath with every pulse of his fading heart.

His fingers feel for the open gash across his chest, the flesh split asunder by a knife's edge, nerves severed, heart punctured. Blood bubbles up from his lips, the taste coating his tongue along with the realization that this is no ordinary wound. *A curse*—that's what he tastes, *the poison of a curse.*

Yet that light footfall stops at the head of his grave, followed by the whisper of a woman's voice. His vision grows hazy at the familiar sound. She speaks not Spanish, but the native tongue, whispering a prayer, a chant, a fevered incantation.

"You will never awaken."

Sleep creeps in upon his shoulders, the cold embrace of the earth tightening around him in a bloody caress.

"As long as my blood runs. As long as my heart beats..."

The shadows of his casket pull at his vision, threatening to drag him into its depths, but it's not death that waits beyond the dark valley of his eyes, it's something else entirely.

"You will not stir. You will not wake."

It's the sea of blood wrought from his hands, beckoning out to him through the dark. This is the sum of all his sin, this damnation his penance.

A ragged breath falls from his lips as he yearns for the fire to devour his flesh like it did his father, to char his bones and incinerate all that remains of his heart and the accursed wound betwixt. But there is no fire. Here, there is only darkness, leaving him with nothing but the sinking, solemn realization of one thing —eternity.

"Your dawn will never come."

He waits for death, for his blood to take root in the soil beneath and sprout the vines of sweet release. But it never comes, as another agony washes over him entirely. The eye of a wound in his heart, across his chest, blinks closed; the flesh reforming, the nerves connecting, twisting and tangling into a monster of a scar. The earth has tasted his cursed blood, and spit him out from her womb.

But there is another voice that speaks to him from above, a voice he knows well, a voice that speaks his tongue. Quietly, softly, he hears a refrain of Spanish, as this voice quotes a verse that stirs up the ache of a past he thought long and truly gone. It's a verse the demon knows well, a verse etched into the black behind his eyelids, and he can do nothing but endure it.

"I would split open my heart
with a knife, place you
within and seal my wound,
that you might dwell there
and never inhabit another
until the resurrection and
Judgment Day—thus you
would stay in my heart
while I lived, and at my death
you too would die in the entrails of my core,
in the shadow of my tomb."

And with the low creak of footsteps, the voice disappears.

Once more he hears the native incantation, and he knows his fate is sealed.

"This house will be your prison," the woman commands, *"And this sleep, your eternal mercy. Now sleep..."* Her voice becomes a lullaby, a melody wrapped up in some ancient spell.

With heavy eyes and hoarse breath, it dawns upon him—he is alive, now, tomorrow, and until the end of time.

"Just go to sleep."

No life, no death.

Only dreams.

❦ I ❧

"DOZING OFF AGAIN, STARLING?"

A whisper jostles Sadie awake, and she jerks her head upwards only to be met with the accusing eyes of the Virgin Mary peering down at her from her pedestal at the front of the church. Blinking away the tiredness of another sleepless night, Sadie turns to see Isaiah beside her with a smirk on his lips.

"Fear. It is the one emotion that should not be forgot."

Shifting her weight upon the uncomfortable pew, Sadie straightens herself up, attempting to re-focus her attention to the ending of Father Agustin's sermon.

"To truly be a good Christian, you must embrace your love of God," he leans into the pulpit, both hands gripping the sides, "and keep your fear of the Devil. For any path away from God, is a path to the inferno."

Just on cue, he begins his closing remarks. "And to the departed... we pray for their souls."

Sadie feels the priest's eyes land on hers, and she turns away, shielding herself with a soft, pliant smile.

"Let us have a moment of prayer for Natalia Pasiona, who on this day, a year past, left this world to join Our Father in Heaven."

Sadie presses her eyes shut, retreating into that hollow in her chest where she sealed up the well for her tears long ago.

The congregation begins to pour out of the church, longing for the reprieve of the ocean breeze to slice through the thickness in the air.

Isaiah's hand comes to rest over hers, and she lets out the breath she's been holding in, focusing on the warmth of his touch instead of the anniversary of her mother's death. Drawing her gaze to his, she's met with softness in his eyes—a softness she could hardly ever resist when it came to Isaiah Riviera; best friend, confidant, the closest thing she can call a boyfriend in this sleepy seaside tourist town. He's all she really has left in the world, and he takes every opportunity to remind her of it as the pad of his thumb draws circles over her knuckles.

But this suffocating summer heat reigns over the gesture he intended, and inevitably he draws his hand away. "Don't tell me you had another rough night."

Smoothing down the broderie hem of her summer dress as her thighs stick to the pew beneath, Sadie curses this sickly humidity pressing down on her like a suit of armor that offers all of the burden, but none of the protection.

She purses her lips. "Every night is a rough night."

"Nightmares?"

"Nightmares end when you wake up." She rises from her seat, walking out ahead of him.

Isaiah says nothing, and instead his fingers find hers, squeezing them tight as they stand like ants beneath the high vaulted ceilings. But even those black wood beams keeping the roof upright seem too close for comfort.

The mid-afternoon sunlight greets them both as Sadie comes to a stop by the entrance, turning her eyes away from the crowd eager to escape the stuffiness, and onto Isaiah.

Biting the inside of her cheek, she lets her thoughts tumble out, "I just... I don't know, Sai. I'm not pulling in enough bookings to keep the place standing. There've been a few inquiries, here and there—but no one ever commits. No guest has set foot inside the Hacienda ever since mama died."

"Hey, cut yourself some slack. You weren't prepared when she..." He stops himself before continuing, starting anew, "I don't think anyone else could do a better job, given the situation."

"I just want the Hacienda to be the way she wanted it—the tourist attraction she dreamed of."

"Come on—what more could she have possibly done?"

Make it a home, Sadie wants to say, but she keeps quiet, letting him ramble on.

"I mean, have you seen the place? It's ancient. Who knows who else has lived there in the past? Maybe if you offered ghost tours, you'd see a bigger pull in sales." A grin pulls the corners of his lips upwards.

"Don't joke about that." She sighs, as he leans against the old plaster walls of the church with a look in his eyes that forces her to turn away.

"But seriously, Starling..." Isaiah interrupts her thoughts. "You need to take a break from the house. You're tired... I can tell. You need to get away, too."

"It's not that easy." Her voice goes quiet, as she clutches her bag to her chest. "Restoring the Hacienda was my parent's life's work. I can't just abandon it now they're..." she trails off.

"But you're not abandoning it, you know. Ever heard of a vacation?" She doesn't respond, and for a moment, he's silent before letting out a sigh. "You can do whatever you want. Sell it, condemn it, abandon it... You own the place."

Sadie shakes her head. "I wish I did."

"Sadie!"

Turning their heads, they see Father Agustin approach with a languid smile, in no hurry at all. The crisp white of his priest's collar stands stark against his sun browned skin, accenting the lines that have begun to creep in. But in spite of his age, his features are diffused by those endlessly sincere, brown eyes.

Isaiah tips his head up towards his uncle; the only man he could really call family ever since his father found his final comfort in the bottom of a bottle. On his tombstone read, *Juan Riviera: beloved father and brother.* But Sadie knew that the words rung hollow for both Isaiah and Agustin.

"Hello, Father," she greets him, choking the gratitude out of her throat. "Thank you for the service this morning. I really appreciate it... mom would have appreciated it."

Placing a firm hand on her shoulder, he nods in acknowledgement, his face that same warm expression that so rarely betrayed what went on beneath.

Amidst the chaos of her mother's death, at the very least, Sadie could always rely on Agustin's solemnity throughout it all. He arranged her wake, her funeral, and whatever was left of her estate. He paid it all off out of his own pocket, too—a gesture Sadie would never forget. The two of them form the only constant in her life that stayed the same before and after.

Isaiah's arm winds around her shoulder, pulling her from her thoughts.

A smile pulls up at Agustin's features, his preacher's gait softening at the sight. "Look at you two... after everything that's happened to you both, I couldn't be more grateful that you have each other."

Sadie focuses on the altar at the end of the church, and the gleaming, golden halo cast behind the statue of Christ on his crucifix. His head is bowed in agony, body pocked with the same mortal wounds that grant him immortality. *It's the suffering that makes it holy,* she tells herself, *the pain that makes it sacred.* She nods on autopilot as Isaiah squeezes her arm, leaving a numbness in his wake.

"Isaiah told me you would be joining us for dinner tonight."

The invitation takes her by surprise. "Oh—did he?"

"Come on, Sadie. It's been so long since you've dropped by."

Sadie presses her lips into a thin line before letting out an unconvincing lie. "Another time... I have a mountain of housework waiting for me. And I've been putting it off since forever."

Father Agustin peers down at her with his watching eyes before nodding. "I see. That's fine." He masks his disappointment with a smile, and Sadie can't help but want to turn away from the sight.

"I'll see you back at the house then, Isaiah. And Sadie—say a prayer for your mom. I'll be doing the same." Father Agustin squeezes her shoulder before withdrawing to disappear into the small crowd of his lingering congregation, ready to impart their praise for yet another fear-inspiring sermon.

The thought of praying feels like a wisp of smoke to a stormy sea, but she lets his words slide off her with Isaiah's voice.

"Come on. I'll take you home." Isaiah pulls her towards his pick-up, and she follows. Listless in the heat, Sadie flicks her eyes upwards to the façade of the church—one of the oldest in the Philippines, a shining example of Spanish architecture built by the *conquistas* centuries ago. Their rule is long gone, yet their presence lingers in the faith they brought with them from across the sea, a faith as strong, as prevalent, as pervasive as that first wooden cross Magellan staked into the heart of these remote lands.

The church stands an amalgamation of their conquest; the brick bell tower the only surviving remnant of the original structure as it rises tall over the baroque façade of the main building. Yet in all its solemnity, the façade is comprised of a baby blue plaster that almost renders it soft, perhaps even inviting—but inviting isn't quite the word Sadie would use to describe it.

The car ride back is a silent one, the blur of Port Cante passing by in the blink of an eye, those streaks of civilization disappearing as the road twists into the lush jungle that leads back to the only place Sadie can call home.

The moment Isaiah parks his pick-up beside the plumeria tree at end of the driveway leading up to the Hacienda's front steps, she wishes that she could sink down into the depths between the cracked leather seats, amidst the spare change and lost pieces of trash—*anything would be better than coming back to an empty house.*

But she climbs out of the pick-up, gathering her bag up in her hands.

"Hey!" he calls out after her, and she stops in her tracks.

She turns to him, running her eyes over his face with a lingering gaze. "Mm?"

"Are you sure you want to be alone, Starling?" He leans over the steering wheel. "Something's bugging you. I can tell. I always can."

A lazy half-smile pulls up at his lips, and she concedes. Making her way over to his car door, she leans against his rolled down window.

"You really wanna know?"

He scoffs. "Of course I do."

Letting out a sigh, she concedes, "I had that same dream... about Italy."

"That same old dream again?" He raises an eyebrow.

Sadie goes quiet, her voice barely above a whisper. "It's where... it's where mom said she'd take me on my twentieth."

And how did your twentieth go? Alone on the floor of mom's bedroom sobbing, exasperated and breathless.

"Oh." Concern colors his eyes. "I didn't know."

There's so much of her grief that she never shared with Isaiah, so much she never had the inclination to reveal—not when sentiment is something he'd closed himself off to years ago.

She turns away, shifting back onto her feet.

Taking the cue, he hops out of the car, hands in the pockets of his denim jeans. A breeze whistles through the shady canopy of trees hiding the Hacienda away from the rest of Port Cante, and for a moment the light dances over Isaiah's eyes in a way that makes them look like balls of flame.

"Come on. At least let me walk you in."

She wants to fight, she wants to resist, but she simply can't. Not today, not now, not beneath the eyes of the Hacienda. Nodding, she turns with him in tow as the monster she calls a home peers down at her from between the overhanging canopy of the jungle slowly reclaiming the land stolen from it.

Hacienda Espinosa.

The Hacienda boasts an exterior façade lovingly restored to its original Spanish colonial *bahay na bato* style by Sadie's parents, with stone brick work comprising the first floor, and near-black mulawin wood making up the second floor. *Ventanillas,* floor length Spanish-style windows, set in gleaming capiz shell peek out from every wall of the second floor, allowing the cool air inside during the hottest months of the year. Sadie's gaze lingers as the sun catches every pearlescent shimmer of shell, giving the effect of lifeless eyes staring back at her in the daylight.

Isaiah hums as he walks on ahead, leaving Sadie beneath the shadow of the overgrown plumeria tree, its leaves rustling against a hard wind.

'An echo of the past,' is how Sadie's mother described it—every piece of architecture, every feature, addition and renovation over the years is just another verse, another refrain to a song that stretches back for hundreds of years.

Built on the remains of a sprawling cacao plantation pioneered by the friars, the foundation of the house was laid out sometime in the middle of the 1600s. Whichever Spaniard saw that the local huts were built elevated from the earth followed suit—dictating that the Hacienda be built with an ample crawlspace to avoid the damp from claiming the supports. It's because of him that the house still stands on a foundation that hasn't ever needed to change.

The Spanish, the Americans, the Japanese came and went, each leaving their marks upon a house that has kept all of their bloodied secrets—secrets that have soaked through the wood, countless whispers entwined with the intricately carved wall panels, voices woven into the very woodgrain of every vast, empty room. All of them traces of the past that began to fade away over the decades as the house was left abandoned after WWII, that is until the house caught the eye of Enrique Pasiona, Sadie's father, who sought about restoring the dilapidated shell to its former glory.

The rest is history, another verse in a song that haunts Sadie's every waking moment, every sleepless night.

"Hey!" Isaiah calls out, "As much as I love just waiting around for you, I have other places to be."

Sadie strides over to the front doors—double doors cast in the same mulawin wood, carved panels of orange blossoms creeping across either side. Raking through the contents of her bag to search for the house key, she shoves aside the pamphlet for her mother's memorial service and a half-melted stick of ChapStick, finally retrieving the key with a sigh.

Pulling at the wrought iron handle, the dark interior of the Hacienda stares back at them both. They say every house has its ghosts; but the Hacienda has only one—and she re-enters her domain like a tide of melancholy against a beaten down shore.

Wordlessly, Sadie and Isaiah enter the foyer, his shoes clicking over the umber tiles as he throws open the shutters to let in some fresh air.

"That's better." Isaiah smirks as a flood of light falls over the grand staircase. "Come here..." He saunters over to Sadie, cast in a halo of languid afternoon sunlight.

She can't help but soften as he nears, melting into his chest as he wraps his arms tightly around her. Allowing herself a single moment, she buries her face into the fabric of his shirt, fighting back the reality that awaits her once he leaves. Because he always leaves, and at the end of the day, she's always alone.

The faint scent of motor oil and sea spray lingers on his shirt, and she breathes him in like a breath of fresh air in a house full of swirling dust motes. If there was one thing she could always count on Isaiah for, it's *this*—easy comfort, and fast-fading words.

"Everything will be okay," he assures her, pressing his lips to the top of her forehead.

All she does is screw her eyes shut tight in response—there's nothing to say, nothing to affirm, until they both hear a near-deafening noise.

Thud.

A loud, distinctive thud yanks their attentions towards the kitchen down the hall to their left.

"What the...?" Isaiah pulls away, leaving Sadie at the base of the stairs.

Searching her mind for any possible explanation as to what the noise could've been, she follows after him. "Wait!"

Isaiah is already standing at the boarded up door at the end of the hallway, one finger pressed to his lips as he listens for what lays beyond.

Silence.

"What's behind here?" he asks in a whisper as Sadie listens beside him.

She hesitates for a moment, recalling that the first thing her mom did when she pulled herself out of her grief was to continue with dad's conservation work. She plunged herself into it head first, drafting up plans to have the ground floor transformed into some sort of walk in museum—a time capsule of how the house was before the wars, before the revolution, before everything changed.

It was a suggestion that her mom always shot down; *I don't want strangers in our family home,* she'd always say. But things changed. Without the money her dad brought in to fund the conservation work, her mom knew that keeping the Hacienda sealed up to the public would be a death wish. And the plans were going full speed ahead until those last few weeks leading up to her death. She seemed so withdrawn then, so afraid—so unlike the mother who raised her.

That's just what grief does, doesn't it?

"Nothing but dirt." Sadie swallows the lump in her throat.

"They were in the middle of re-doing the floors... until they just stopped."

"Is there any way inside?" he asks, testing the boards sealing the door, only to find they're hammered in as securely as humanely possible.

"Through the courtyard out back. But I think it's locked." Sadie twists her fingers together.

"Come on," is all he says, turning towards the front door. "Let's go check it out."

"I don't think it's—"

"—What? A good idea?" He smirks with a playful glint in his eyes, "This is *your* house isn't it?" He shoots her a wink before leading the way forward, Sadie trailing behind with a knot in her stomach.

Not even the soft cascade of sunlight into the central courtyard can penetrate her inexplicable nerves as Isaiah positions himself in front of the door in question. Rubbing his hands together, he pulls hard at the door handle but to no avail—the lock remains staunchly in place.

"There you go." Isaiah raises his hands in defeat. "Guess there's no one to chase out."

"Very funny."

Thud.

Sadie's heart jumps in her chest, whipping her head around to the source of the noise.

A smear of crimson sits streaked against a window on the second floor, her eyes trailing downwards to a black shape laying at the base of the courtyard. Rushing over, she's greeted by a bird that's a mass of glossy plumage, feathers soaked through with droplets of blood—but beneath the opened gash is a movement, a rise and fall. A pulse.

He's still alive.

Dropping to her knees, she balls up the hem of her dress between her fingers, tearing a strip of white cotton clean off.

"What are you doing?" Isaiah's voice peeks over her shoulder.

Bundling up the bleeding bird as gently as she can, she takes him into her arms, his heartbeat rapid under her touch.

"She okay?" Isaiah asks, peering down at the bundle in her arms.

"*He,*" Sadie corrects him, casting her eyes over the iridescent green plumage that adorns his ebony black body, his eyes two pinpricks of vivid crimson. "He's a starling."

"Right," Isaiah nods. "Of course it is."

She knows it as the Asian glossy starling, her father having taught her early on of its scientific name, *aplonis panayensis,* while her mother referred to the bird simply as *kulansiyang.* Nonetheless, the bird in her hands is her namesake, the reason for her middle name, her parent's first gift—and here it lays wounded before her in what must be a symbol, a remembrance, some kind of twisted sign.

"I'm going to stitch him up..." she whispers, motioning to side-step Isaiah, only for his voice to stop her.

"Let me just put him out of his misery, Sadie. It's the right thing to do."

She frowns, grip on the bundle in her arms tightening ever so slightly. "*No,*" she insists, "He's going to make it."

Isaiah shoots her an incredulous look before stepping out of her way.

"I'm going to make sure he will."

With quick steps, Sadie makes her way back to the front of the house, stopping for a brief moment at the corner. Casting her eyes back to the locked door in the courtyard, she can't help but feel an echo of dread pinch at the back of her neck; like a whisper of darkness against the shell of her ear.

But she continues onwards, the Hacienda opening up to Sadie and her starling with welcoming arms, leaving Isaiah behind at the threshold.

He hesitates for a moment before scuffing the toe of his shoe against the doorframe. "I should, uh, head back."

She turns to face him, plucked from the heartbeat of the bird between her fingers for but a moment. "Okay, Sai." She smiles.

He searches her face for a moment, looking for a way in—but it's a dead end. "Okay." Shoving his hands into his pockets, he turns to leave, calling out over his shoulder, "I'll see you tomorrow!"

"What's tomorrow?" she calls back, watching him hop into the driver's seat of his pick-up.

He grins. "A surprise. Something to take your mind off things."

And with a wave he's gone.

Sadie shuts the door behind him, taking no time in heading for the first aid kit in the kitchen. Setting the immobile starling down on the kitchen table, she teases apart the blood-matted feathers until she sees the wound—a horizontal gash right in the center of his ebony breast.

Preparing the suture and thread feels just like diving back into the needlework that used to fill her days before her mother died, her projects ranging from intricate embroidery to creating floral swirls on the hems of her dresses. Yet all of it lays forgotten, shoved unceremoniously into a box in the depths of her closet where she can't fathom bringing it out to see the light of day.

Here and now, all she has to stitch is flesh and feather.

Holding her breath, she makes quick work of the suture and thread, tying off the now closed gash with a single tight knot before clipping it and cleaning away as much of the blood she can.

"There you go," she whispers, a soft smile on her lips. Digging out a shallow banana box from the depths of the pantry, she lines it with an old towel before nestling the little black bird into its center. Taking the box in both her hands, she exits the kitchen, stopping at the center of the foyer. She watches the sunlight filter in through the trees from outside the window, spilling over the stairs, in dancing, vibrant hues.

The rumble of Isaiah's engine soon grows faint, overtaken by the bird song in the trees above and the bird's pulse between her fingers. Shaking her mind from its haze, she makes the ascent up the stairs to her bedroom. Running her fingers over the old bannister, the polish of the narra wood floors greets her at the top of the steps, every empty chair and rattan couch taunting her with their emptiness, with the promise of life that simply isn't there.

The hallway of the second floor stretches out endlessly before her, her grip on the box between her fingers tightening instinctively as she stares at the door at the end of the hallway, allowing herself just this day to surrender to the pull from the other side.

Dropping her shoulders, she stops outside the dark double doors of her parents' old bedroom, pulling the memorial service pamphlet out of her bag.

Natalia Pasiona, in memoriam

She runs her eyes over the letters, a dull ache pulsing through her. She turns the handle, and the door opens with a slow groan. Sadie enters without a thought, setting the now slumbering starling down gently on the bedside table before falling onto the sheets, where the scent of her mom's perfume lingers only faintly now.

The light of the setting sun fills the room in a golden glow, as it sinks into the horizon, sucking all the light from this little island sitting on the edge of the world. Stretching her hand out to stroke the starling at the bedside, she lets the bird's heartbeat and the day's fatigue lull her to sleep, Sadie drifting into a dream that she knows all too well. A nightmare that's come to plague her every night since that fateful day a year ago.

A nightmare of the day she died.

The sting of the typhoon winds against her skin is piercing as she makes it up the winding path that leads to the top of the limestone cliffs, the ocean opening up around the bay like a raging, storming beast. She sees her up ahead, standing at the precipice, battered by the rains.

Taking a step forward, she reaches out to touch her, to feel the woman who abandoned her. A thousand questions course through her veins, rage-fueled and adrenalin-set, and she hopes the moment she touches her she'll find the answer to that melancholy *why?*

But just like every night, she's too late.

Her mom takes that fatal step forward, her grief stricken heart the anchor that drowns her in the sea below.

The winds press hard against Sadie's body, urging her forwards, to join her mother, but the warmth of her tears is the only thing that tethers her back to this world.

That, and a faint *thud.*

It must be another bird—another starling dashed against the walls of the Hacienda. One more death claimed by this old house. Another blood stain to scrub, another being to bury.

Thud.

There it is again—what is that?

Thud.

But like every other night since her mother died, Sadie simply screws her eyes shut tight, willing herself to return to those cliffs and that storming, raging sea.

2

SADIE DOESN'T REMEMBER SHUTTING her eyes, but a bright beam of sunlight streaming in from the open windows elicits a blinding headache that can only mean it's morning. The chirp of birdsong from the jungle canopy flits in from the open windows, along with a breeze that catches the muslin bed curtains.

Weird.

She doesn't remember ever opening the windows.

But tiredness pulls at her bones, an ache, a restlessness that curled up deep inside her the day of her mother's funeral that hasn't left since. Raking her hands over her face, she longs to sink back into deep, dreamless sleep, only to be pulled back into the waking world by the box on the nightstand.

She turns to see the starling still curled up against the old towel. With a gentle finger she strokes his ebony feathers, lifting his broken wing ever so slightly to see the stitches still intact—no sign of fresh bleeding. Satisfied, she feels the ache inside her finally begin to ebb as she settles into the sight of her parent's empty bedroom, a bedroom that they'll never inhabit again save for the phantoms of their memories. She lets her shoulders loose, only for the loud buzz of her phone to slice through the quiet. She reaches out for her phone to see a single message lighting up her screen.

Isaiah: Almost there

The words sink in slowly—but when they do, her heart skips a beat.

She rips the sheets off her body, taking the starling and making her way back to her own bedroom, where she settles him down atop her dresser.

Running through the shower, she lets the cold water run over her, hoping it will be enough to wash away tell-tale signs of yet another nightmare-fueled sleep.

Drying off, she slips into a faded blue summer dress, padding around the room in a whirlwind of mascara and a hint of cherry red blush, anything to bring the life that's so sorely missing back to her cheeks. She runs a brush through her tangled hair before the sound of wheels against the scorch-dry dirt driveway pulls at her attention.

Shit.

She barely has the time to stop in front of her mirror and smooth out the wrinkles of her cotton dress before her phone buzzes again. She reaches over to read it.

Isaiah: We're here

"We?"

The sound of Isaiah killing the engine of his beaten-up truck resounds from below, and Sadie looks at herself for a final time in the mirror. Sweeping her silk-black hair over her shoulders in an attempt to fend off this heat, she casts her eyes across the reflection, taking in the features that so mournfully come from her mother. Echoes of her memory dance in the rich dark of her earth brown eyes and golden ochre skin, down to the short stature that she wished she inherited from her father instead.

Sadie's arms subconsciously wrap around herself in an attempt to hide away her figure, a nasty habit she'd developed long ago in the hopes of not being noticed, not being remarked upon, or the worst of all—being seen.

It was always easier this way.

Thanking God for the wonders a dab of concealer can do, she lets out a sigh, the thought of Isaiah's *surprise* like a needle pricking at the pink matter in her skull. *A surprise date? A trip to a resort? A restaurant?* The possibilities flutter in the pit of her stomach, a tiny bloom of hope sprouting at the thought of Isaiah for the first time proving that this is more than just a relationship born from convenience, from comfort, from something monstrous and colored with grief.

But the sound of laughter pulls her back, killing that hope dead as it's followed by a quick rap at the door. It's a melodious lilt that sounds as familiar as it does forgotten.

"I'm coming!" she calls out, voice hoarse with the embrace of solitude as she makes a swift descent into the foyer and towards the front doors. Her fingers come to wrap around the handles, ready to pull until a woman's voice speaks on the other side.

"Do you think she'll remember me?"

And with a sinking heart, she throws the double doors open wide, where she's met not only with Isaiah's face, but with a girl taller than she, unfamiliar green eyes beaming through her long, dark lashes.

"Sadie!" she shrieks, pulling her into a bear hug that's almost suffocating.

"Odette...?" Sadie's voice drips with disbelief as she takes in the sight of her childhood best friend standing on her door step.

"The very same." Odette strikes a pose, the grin on her face accentuating her dimpled cheeks. "I just got off the ferry, and I couldn't wait to see you, so here I am."

Odette had always been the lighter-skinned, sharper-nosed of the two, her features always the point of comparison between them both. *"If you pinch your nose, Sadie, it won't be as flat."* One old grandmother wisely suggested while another one would echo, *"Papaya soap will make your skin as light as Odette's!"*

Odette's biological father was a foreign sailor of the European variety, her half-blood and light skin making her instantly worthy of being the next Miss Philippines, at least in the eyes of every gossipy aunty and overbearing grandmother of Port Cante. But no one ever gossiped about the fact that her father docked and sailed away without so much as a word, leaving Odette's mother with nothing but a baby in her belly.

That, no one talked about.

Why would they? Sadie thinks to herself, not when it's so much easier to just wash it all away with that sickly-scented papaya soap that she still feels burning on her skin.

"It's been so long. I didn't know you were coming." Sadie forces a smile.

Odette had only grown more beautiful since the last time she laid eyes on her. Her natural black hair is forgotten beneath a wash of light brown dye, her skin a shade of tan that can only come from beneath a Spanish sun, her modelesque figure wrapped up in the mustard yellow rayon of a maxi dress, green contacts set into her eyes that don't quite conceal the brown irises beneath.

Isaiah lets out a chuckle, standing beside Odette with her suitcase in one hand. Sadie raises an eyebrow, eyeing the faded travel stickers covering every inch of her suitcase, "And I didn't know you were staying either..."

Odette bats her eyelashes, pouting her lips. "Oh please, Sadie! It'll just be for a few days, I promise."

"I... I don't know what to say." Sadie crosses her arms against her chest, attempting to come up with some sort of excuse—but she knows anything she says against the idea will be nothing more than a feeble attempt to prolong this loneliness. Drawing her eyes back up to Odette's cat eyes, she can't help but give. "I can make up a room for you."

Odette's lips pull up into a grin as she leaps forward to wrap her arms around Sadie again.

"Thanks so much Sadie, I knew I could count on you!"

Sadie smiles softly. "But don't expect the hotel experience you're used to. This place is old—and hot. And there's no wi-fi."

"Oh it's fine, I'm just glad to be back." She waves her hand dismissively. "I need to freshen up. I'm exhausted." Odette peers into the empty house beside her and Sadie's hands instinctively stiffen around the door, suddenly aware of the fact that it's only ever been Isaiah who's set foot inside the house since her mother died.

"Um—of course." Sadie opens the door wider, gesturing the two of them to enter. "I'm sorry, Odette, you just caught me off guard. Go ahead—you remember where the bathroom is, don't you?"

Odette nods with a smile, squeezing her shoulder. "If anyone should be sorry, it's me." She sticks her tongue out as she pads off towards the bathroom, the mustard rayon of her maxi dress the only splash of vivid color against the black wood walls and all the Hacienda's earthen trappings. Sadie's eyes follow Odette until she and Isaiah are alone.

He clears his throat.

"So... This is the *surprise?*"

He nods, a smirk on his lips. "Come on, just think of it as the perfect opportunity to be a good hostess—just like your mom was."

Sadie says nothing, the words ringing hollow in her ears. Narrowing her eyes, she lowers her voice to a whisper, "What did she do this time?"

Isaiah mirrors her volume, "The usual, I think. Pissed off her dad. That's all she told me, anyway."

Odette's adopted father, Dominic Arias, is practically Sadie's uncle—if not by blood then at the very least by association. If it weren't for Dominic's endlessly deep pockets, Sadie's father never would have been able to restore the Hacienda back to its former glory. *Whatever that is.*

The two men's friendship stretched all the way back to their youth, where they met between the dusty bookshelves of the University of Barcelona's Library, Dominic studying Theology with plans to enter the seminary, and her father studying Conservation and Spanish history.

But their friendship ended shortly with the completion of the Hacienda. Life happened and so they fell out. Dominic adopted Odette after her mother up and left, promptly deciding to take her with him back to Spain. Then she was only fourteen, Sadie only twelve. Dominic conjured up some excuse about Odette needing a *real education*—meaning one that wasn't here. That was the last Sadie saw of Odette and the father that whisked her away.

"Dominic *angry?* I don't think I'd ever want to see that." Sadie crosses her arms over her chest. "Well, I guess it must be bad if she went straight here."

Isaiah shrugs, making his way into the house to set Odette's suitcase down on the floor beside the lounge set.

"I mean, if this is what it takes to see her—then that's fine with me." Sadie leans against the back of the sofa, flicking her hair over her shoulder. Isaiah smiles, his eyes following the movement of her hair.

"Say..." He scratches the back of his neck. "You wanna come with us to the beachfront later tonight? She said she wanted to catch up with what's changed since she left."

Sadie scoffs, "That's going to be a very short trip."

"Well, you wanna come with?"

Sadie looks up at him, a strange sincerity in his eyes that rarely ever came to visit.

"I'd love to—but I have..." Sadie flounders in yet another lie, the sting of not hearing a single word from Odette over the years a pain she can't ignore.

Isaiah raises an eyebrow, "No more excuses—you're coming with. No backing out."

"I have a life, Sai. I have a house to look after and all the chores that come with it." She purses her lips.

"What's your problem?" He narrows his eyes, his tone taking on that edge that's all too familiar. "Just because you became an orphan and she stopped being one—that's no reason to take it out on her."

Sadie's ears ring, and there's nothing left for her to say.

Isaiah's eyes are piercing, and Sadie casts her eyes away as he lowers his voice, "You should take a lesson from Odette, you know. She knows how to relax."

And before he has the chance to salt the wound any further, in saunters Odette.

"Thanks for dropping me off, Sai." She takes her luggage in hand, giving him a one-armed hug.

"No problem."

He turns to leave, and Sadie shoots him a final look beneath the archway of the entrance.

"Tonight. No excuses." He gives her a wink before scuttling down the front steps and back into his pick-up. "I'll swing by around seven, alright?"

"Alright." Sadie and Odette reply in unison.

"Try to keep her out of trouble!" he yells out, before he disappears down the winding road leading back into town.

Sadie shuts and locks the door behind her with a sigh, turning to Odette who has another yawn on her lips.

"You must be tired. Come on, you can just sleep in my bed while I work on setting your room up."

Odette pulls her into an appreciative hug before leading her up the staircase, down the hall and towards Sadie's bedroom, arms linked.

"You won't regret having me here, Sadie." Odette squeezes her arm before collapsing onto the plush of Sadie's bed. As Sadie wraps her fingers around the door knob to leave her, Odette's voice calls her back. "It's nice to see you again."

Sadie turns to face her, giving her a soft smile. "It is."

And with that, she shuts the door and leaves her to rest.

The hallway stretches out before her like an ebony snake, its scales the hardwood, its gleaming eyes the long unopened guest room at the far end of the Hacienda.

It's been long enough, she thinks to herself as she stops before the wooden slat door, pushing it open with a creak.

Specters of white greet her from every corner of the room. The white sheets her mother draped over the antique narra wood furniture remains just as she left it—to keep it from the dust, from the elements, from the living.

But it's time to peel back the veil.

Steeling herself to clean, she's armed with a mop, a duster and the unyielding determination to be as good a hostess as her mother was. The day passes in a haze of sickly summer heat, marked only by the scent of wood polish and endless motes of dust as Sadie cleans up a storm, readying the sheets, polishing every visible wooden surface and beating out the carpets over the open windows.

Once she's cleaned enough to put a five star hotel to shame, she makes her way back out into the hallway. Odette's soft snores drift through the slats of her bedroom door as Sadie inevitably makes her way back to her parents' old room, curling up in the cool of those sheets like she did the night before.

She holds her breath, simply waiting for the sound of the front door to creak open, for the sound of her mother's footsteps to pad down the hallway, for the look on her face as she sets eyes on her only daughter—the only family she had left, the only family she decided to abandon.

Gazing into the picture frame by the bedside table, Sadie sees a phantom of the past, her father with his arm draped across her mother's shoulder. She's dressed in traditional costume for the Port Cante's annual *Our Lady of Sorrows* Festival—a hand-made Maria Clara with a delicate lace fan between her fingertips, her eyes like two stars peeking out from the handwoven eyelets, the inky necklace of traditional *batok* tattoos draped across her collarbones. She's wearing the only family heirloom she inherited, a pearl pendant she never took off—a pearl pendant that probably lays at the bottom of Infanta Bay.

Remembering the story mama used to tell, she described it as the present dad used to propose to her. *"It was more a peace offering,"* he would tell Sadie with a chuckle as he hoisted her up into the air. How her father was able to get her grandmother's blessing in receiving that heirloom of a pearl, she'll never know—all Sadie remembers thinking is that she had never set eyes on something so beautiful before, the way the pendant gleamed in the light, reflecting what seemed like each color of the rainbow all at once. She remembers telling her mother that she wished she could have something as beautiful one day, to which she replied:

"It's yours when you're twenty-one."

But twenty-one came and went, with nothing to show for it.

Turning away from the picture and onto her side, her eyes scan the room to see everything is exactly how she left it—from the clothes hanging in her closet, to the boxes upon boxes of dad's heritage notes she sealed up, strands of hair still entwined with the teeth of her hairbrush, to the sharp indentation of the last note she tore off on the notepad sitting atop her nightstand.

Sadie's voice is but a trembling whisper as she asks, "Why did you have to go?" A thousand words rise and fall on the valley of her tongue. Rage for her abandonment, despair at her absence—yet all of it nothing compared to her only company. An inescapable, looming, loneliness.

She wishes her mother would answer for her sin of a betrayal, but there's only silence.

With an ache settling into her shoulders from dusting and scrubbing the far and tall corners of the guest room, she feels her eyes grow heavy.

Curling up against the pillows, Sadie feels herself plunge into the same dark dream that's come to plague her every night since that fateful day a year ago.

The dream of the cliffs.

But this time, it's different.

The woman she reaches out for at the precipice is nothing like her mother—it's not just sadness that radiates from her silhouette; but heartache. Heartache for something lost.

The winds urge her forward, beckoning her to join the woman standing on the edge, but a sound from the waking world pulls her from slumber.

Footsteps.

It's the sound of footsteps that plucks her from that nightmarish sea, hurling her back to the reality to which she belongs.

Her eyes shoot open as she props herself up, exasperated, "Mama?"

Living under the Hacienda's roof came with its fair share of history, and strange happenings weren't just expected—it came with the territory. And hearing footsteps and whispers of voices while utterly alone was something Sadie had resigned herself to accepting years ago. For the sake of her own sanity, at least.

Thud.

There it is again. Yet it doesn't sound like something breaking apart. It sounds like something longing to break free.

Night has well and truly enveloped the little town of Port Cante, casting the Hacienda in an impenetrable veil of darkness. Propping herself up to feel for the lamp switch on the nightstand, she lets out a sigh when the warm glow of lamplight floods her parent's bedroom—only for a flutter of movement to capture her attention.

Sitting on the rim of the lamp shade is an earth-brown moth, attracted to the light that flickers once, twice—and then it dies.

Just what I needed, she thinks to herself, *another brown out.* Waiting for the sound of the wind to confirm it's nothing but the loose shutters in her bedroom, she waits, yet all she hears is the cicada song of the jungle. There's not a lick of wind to rustle the canopy, no reason for that discordant, dread-soaked noise.

Thud.

Peeling the sheets from her skin, a momentary break in the clouds allows the light of the moon to guide her way through the dark. That, and the flutter of the moth as it flies before her and towards the door—not quite fast enough to escape her, but not slow enough to be hiding.

It's almost as if it's guiding her forwards.

Thud.

Sadie's heart quickens in her chest as a sinking feeling grips her, but she attempts to swallow her fear as she twists the door open, the moth flittering out into the dark of the hallway.

Following the beat of those brown-gray wings, Sadie descends into the darkness, stopping momentarily at the threshold of her bedroom. Holding her breath, she can hear Odette's sleep murmurs from behind the door, whispers of a nightmare rising through the air.

Pressing her lips together, Sadie can't help herself from wondering if it's truly her grief that spins her nightmares—*perhaps it's this house, instead.*

But that same thud reverberates through her bones once more, gripping her heart and commanding her thoughts completely. Stopping at the top of the staircase, Sadie looks downwards into the inky black below. The moth lingers at the top banister, just long enough for her to catch up as it flits its way down into the foyer.

The Hacienda always takes on a different aura at night, the old bones of the house assuming the skin of a living, still-breathing beast in its own right, where Sadie is nothing more than a pest in its maw of a belly. The deathly stillness is punctuated only by the sharp staccato of Sadie's heartbeat as she descends the steps, following the *thud* like a beckoning melody.

Come on, Sadie. It's nothing.

There's no need to check where it's coming from—she already knows.

She slips on a pair of sun-faded sneakers before grabbing the flashlight hanging by the front door. Twisting the handle, she steps out into the cool of the night, the cicada song a chorus to the rhythm drawing her out as she makes her way to the courtyard out back.

With those ashen wings illuminated by the moon and her flashlight, the moth continues onwards, knowing exactly where to go.

It was a sunlit dining room, once upon a time. But her parent's extensive renovation of the kitchen rendered its function near useless, and it fell through the cracks of the never-ending list of conservation work needed to restore this old house.

That is, until her father died, and her mother plunged herself into restoring this room in a desperate attempt to band-aid over the gaping wound of her grief.

The wind rustles through the treetops, and Sadie points her flashlight up ahead to see that same dark door peering back at her. She passes by the dirt streaked windows, keeping her light on that fluttering moth before it stops to rest on the aged, bronze handle.

Thud.

The fear spills out of her in a gasp, as she takes in the sight of the door Isaiah tried just hours before, expecting—hoping for the resistance of the lock.

But for her, the door opens.

The moth flutters inside, devoured by the darkness stretching out to take her. There's only one way to know what it is that lurks beyond—and with a deep breath she lets herself be consumed by the shadows.

3

Only the beam of the flashlight can slice through the dark, illuminating the fluttering moth and the dust motes beyond. Adjusting her eyes, Sadie lets her shoulders drop the moment she sees exactly what she pictured. A sprawling, vacuous room stretches out before her, the floor comprised of nothing more than dry dirt and twisted tangles of wood propped up against the walls. Squinting into the dim, she sees countless piles of the old narra wood floorboards lining the length of this vast space.

Scanning the room for any dark figures lurking in the corners, she releases the tension in her shoulders when she sees it's just as empty as she hoped it would be.

Below the door sits a set of three makeshift steps, caked in dust. Testing the first step before descending, she lets out a breath as she searches for that little, guiding moth—only to find it's disappeared, along with that discordant *thud*.

Yet the silence is just as unnerving.

She lands onto the soft dirt underfoot, drawing her eyes over the cob web laden walls and corners, examining every piece of old flooring left behind, all of it abandoned in a rush.

A hard wind rattles the Hacienda's windows, and for the

briefest of moments Sadie can swear she can smell the faint scent of her mother's perfume wrap tight around her in an embrace that rends the breath from her lungs. Pressing her eyes shut tight, she finds the strength to continue onwards, into the dark.

Recalling the construction crew's plans to rip up the old narra floorboards and replace them with a modern equivalent, memories of the day they suddenly stopped filter in through the dim. Packing up in a flurry of disappointment and awkwardness, the fragments of a shouting match between her mom and the head contractor play out in her mind as she takes in the half-renovated room, the light of the flashlight her only guiding star.

The grief must have been too much, the heartache too strong—why would she continue to build upon a dream that belonged to a man who would never see it done?

Running her light over the ground, Sadie spies mounds of upturned earth all around her. With cautious steps, she navigates carefully between them, inhaling the smell of old wood and dust. But the toe of her shoe meets a hollow in the ground, and she shines her light into the dark before her.

It's a cavity in the dirt floor. Below the crawlspace, deep into the foundation—it's a hole in the ground that's been there as long as the Hacienda has been standing.

She leans down, peering into the black, the pulse of her heart the only sound in this vacant, forgotten room. But there's something in the cavity, a shimmer embedded in its dark embrace.

It's an opalescent glint from between the strange shapes, smooth and untainted by dirt.

No... it can't be.

Furrowing her brows, she drops to her knees at the cavity's edge, setting the flashlight down beside her. Reaching down into the darkness, she feels for something hard, wrapping her fingers around the first thing she can dig her nails into.

Her fingers find purchase against something solid, something hard—a mess of old wood.

It must be the discarded flooring.

There's a hole in the deteriorated wood where she can see it glimmer once more, but it's too small for her to fit her fingers through. Leaning deeper into the cavity, she feels for a give in the wood below, wrapping her fingers tight against the edges of what feels like a smooth panel.

With a groan she pulls as hard as she can, only to be met with a resistance that only drives her to pull harder.

Finally there's a creak of wood, and several rusted nails fly up into the air as Sadie lands backwards on her rear, alongside splinters and fragments of dry dark earth.

Crawling onto her hands and knees, she reaches deep into the pit, wrapping her fingers around what she thinks is lying in wait dark below. It's unmistakably smooth in her palm, the dull glint of a gold chain shining back at her.

It's not possible...

Unfurling her palm, she parts her lips as the sight of what lays in her hand only erases all doubt.

Mama's pearl necklace.

A necklace she never took off under any circumstances. A necklace she should have died with, that should be at the bottom of the ocean, tied to her bones.

A necklace that shouldn't be here.

An itch forms at the tip of her nose—it's the moth, fluttering mere inches away from her face. With every fervent beat of those ash-like wings, her presence becomes less of a random encounter and more of a deadly, desperate warning.

Sadie sets her eyes on the smooth panel she hauled up and out of the pit below, her heart sinking in realization as the beam of the flashlight falls over the smooth wooden panel—it's no discarded flooring, but a lid.

The lid of a casket.

And this pit is the grave that houses it.

Dread washes like a king tide over her, her heart beginning to pace frantically out of control as whatever stirs within leaves gooseflesh over her skin. "Mama?" Sadie whispers, regretting it the moment the word leaves her lips.

Terror sets into her veins, snatching her breath as a lick of fire snakes around her wrist, plunging her downwards into the black below.

Breathless and afraid, she falls.

The earth stretches open to take her into its black embrace, Sadie refusing to relinquish her grip around her mother's pearl necklace as she lands atop the contents of the casket.

Feeling around in the dark, her pulse is achingly loud as she feels no cold beneath her, but warmth. Wide-eyed, she rakes her gaze over to her wrist, where it's not bone digging into her skin— but fingers. Flesh and blood.

With a gasp she whips forward towards the head of the casket, where she sees the unmistakable contours of a man's face.

He's no corpse, no skeleton, no withered remains. He's living, breathing, impossibly alive. He's a man marked in grave-dirt and deathly decay, lost in a dream beneath a house older than time itself.

And those eyes—*his* eyes. Twin oceans of abyssal black, with two pinpricks of reflective light for pupils piercing into the very depths of her.

Time slips from her grasp as she falls beneath his gaze. And it's as mesmerizing, as devastating, as inescapable as the pull of the grave wrapped around them both.

His lips part to speak, his voice a deep timbre of old Spanish.

"Ha llegado el amanecer."

Her vision swims, senses a haze as her eyes roll back into the dark of her skull. Slowly, almost sweetly, the meaning of his words come to her.

Dawn has come.

And all goes black.

Sadie awakes with a gasp, heat-soaked and tangled up in her sheets.

Chest heaving, she darts her eyes over a familiar scene—her parents' bedroom. Wind whips against the open windows, rattling the capiz shell panels as Sadie screws her eyes shut tight. *It was just a dream,* she tells herself, rubbing circles over her temples, willing her pulse to normalcy, it *was just a bad nightmare.*

Opening her eyes, she sees her fingers are stained with the mark of the grave. Dirt clings to the very fibers of her cotton dress, beneath her fingernails, embedded into the blood rushing quick through her veins—dirt staining the pearl pendant in the palm of her hand, its chain tangled up between her trembling fingers.

Yet above them all rises the overpowering stench of death.

It was real—as real as the creak of the floorboards at the foot of the bed, rupturing the illusion that she's not alone in this house.

With a deafening heartbeat, she draws her gaze upwards as the weight of an unwanted presence sinks into the very woodgrain beneath. Wide-eyed, she pulls her gaze up higher, her vision becoming clear—the wind outside dying with a choke as Sadie attempts to make sense of what stands before her.

A figure in black.

A man.

Her pulse is achingly loud in her ears, and all she can do is stare into the void of his face, struggling to make out the features, as if a cloud of smoke billows over his skin, veiling him in the dark he comes from.

Rags of decayed fabric hang from his body like twisting vines as he looms over her, voice hoarse, wrapped up in centuries of sleep.

"How long has it been?" he dictates the question in English, yet the answer clings like tar to the inside of her throat.

"I—I—" she sputters on her words as she rakes her eyes downwards to the center of his chest, where the mark of an angry scar peers up at her from between the tatters of fabric.

"How. Long."

Her blood swooshes as she attempts to draw backwards, sitting up stick-straight against her headboard, turning her head to the side to escape his gaze. She clutches the sheets tight around her in a vain attempt to regain control, but it's useless when his eyes alone peer back at her with all the promise of death incarnate.

He parts his lips to repeat himself, but he finds the answer written plain in the fear of her eyes. "So it's been that long... All that time in a dream."

His shadow stretches out further as he looms over her, his gaze stopping at the pendant between her fingers.

"And you—do you know what you have done?"

His voice echoes hollow when he speaks, his words a lick of candle flame against her skin as he leans down, outstretching his hand and motioning to touch the pearl in her palm. His fingers hover just above hers, her heart beating wildly in her chest as she feels his shadowy figure encroaching closer and closer upon the edge of her bed.

"Do you know what you have unleashed?"

She turns to face him, instantly transfixed to the hollows of his eyes where a light smolders deep beneath the surface.

"W—what are you?"

"There are many names for what I am..." The longer she holds his gaze, the sooner she realizes it's not a light she sees, nor only a fire—but an inferno. "Yet in your tongue and mine, I am one and the same."

She parts her lips to speak, but the dread of his voice wraps tight around her heart, holding her tongue still as he delivers the final blow.

"*Demonio,*" he answers, Sadie's heart recoiling.

A demon, she blinks frantically, *he's a demon.*

"And here you lay, in this bed...." The shadows of the room move in unison with his movements, as if he's as much a fixture of the house as the wooden beams that hold it upright, "In this room..." she dares meet his gaze, a wicked smile pulling the corners of his lips upwards, "In my house."

A cold wind brings with it a break in the clouds, enough for the moon to filter in from the windows at Sadie's bedside, casting him in a halo of pale moonlight that pulls at his attention. The moon shines brighter, stripping him bare of his shadows as he turns towards the open windows, sweeping across the room in an ocean of darkness as he stops to take in the splendor of the light, the sky, the pearlescent moon.

For the first time she can see him through the veil of the dark, his pale skin marked with the color of the grave, his features hard, weathered by centuries of a life long gone. His eyes are near black beneath thick brows, etched with a weariness she can see also written beneath his broad, towering frame that it seems even he doesn't know how to carry.

Unable to help herself, she draws her eyes over him as her heart pulses out of control. Whatever remains of his clothing hangs in ribbons of rot from his wide shoulders, every remaining sliver of fabric clinging desperately to the hard muscles of his arms. His linen undershirt, once white, is now frayed the color of earth, wrapped up in black fingers of brocade clinging limply to his frame.

Yet as tattered as the fabric may be, Sadie can still trace the faint glimmer of silver thread woven into the brocade—the echo of a pattern that once was, the echo of a different time, a different Philippines.

Pressing herself up and onto her knees, Sadie gains resolve as the light finds purchase over the dark. "Whoever you are..." her voice comes out a desperate whisper, "Whoever you *were*... Please. Just go back to where you belong."

The stars, the sky, the night, converge across the planes of his face as he allows himself to take it all in, his expression contorting into something almost pained. Silence passes, Sadie transfixed to his profile as his jaw clenches. He answers simply, "This *is* where I belong."

He turns to face her, and in a blink of an eye her resolve melts away. "What's your name?"

The moon plunges back behind the clouds, letting the darkness and the demon who commands it reign once more.

"Silas," he answers, the faintest trace of hesitation lacing his tone, "Silas Espinosa."

And the room begins to spin.

The Hacienda Espinosa—it was named after him, it was his home, *his*. And he was buried under it, left to rot; left to be forgotten. Until she opened his grave.

He's standing flush close now, his shadow spilling over the edge of the mattress, his towering frame filling her vision completely. His mere presence forces her head to tilt backwards, hair spilling across her sheets in a cascade of night as he takes her in—reading her features as if she's a book spread open beneath his gaze.

"And your name is Sara..." His voice is both a whisper and tremor; like the deep rumble of distant thunder. Sadie's breath hitches in her throat as she stares up at him, less of a shadow with each passing second and more of a human; more of a man. "It is your true name."

"I—I..." her words fumble from her lips. "Yes."

The question *how do you know* rises on her tongue, yet he never needs to hear it said as he answers, "I have seen the dreams of all the dreamers beneath this roof. And you are just one of many in the long list of the living who have occupied this house."

Sadie's mind surges with the thought of just how long he's spent under the floorboards. *The Japanese, the Americans—the Spanish;* he's been alive through them all. Her mind unravels, yet his voice anchors her back to his abyssal eyes.

"And how alive you are," whispers the demon, as he draws his fingers up towards her face, inches away from her cheeks. The longer she stays still, the more the tremble in her hands takes over, and it all comes crumbling down the moment she feels his fiery skin meet the flush of her cheeks. "So human."

Her pulse is wild against her ribcage, and she screws her eyes shut tight in response as his fingers trail across the skin of her jaw with all the softness of a knife's edge slicing through flesh.

"Yet there is something about you. Something that belongs to the grave..." He stops, pulling away, leaving her with one final word. "*Soñadora*."

And as the clouds suffocate all trace of the moon, the shadows reclaim him once more, the demon disappearing into the dark recesses of the Hacienda. And once again, Sadie is alone.

The meaning of his words linger like smoke, finally rising to the tip of her tongue as she pieces it together. *Soñadora—it means dreamer.*

Footsteps in the night, Sadie could handle, the nightmares, the odd voices—but this—*not this*. This certainly did *not* come with the territory.

Letting her shoulders fall, she casts her eyes downwards, unfurling her palm to see her mother's dirt flecked necklace between her fingers.

Cleaning it off with the skirt of her dress, she lets out a sigh as she runs her fingers over the opalescent freshwater pearl, its luster returning after God knows how long in his grave.

A demon's grave.

"No..." Sadie tries to choke it out, "I'm alone in this house." Her words are a clumsy jumble from her lips as she attempts to ground herself back to reality, "It's just me, it's just me, it's just—" she screws her eyes shut tight, "...me."

Focusing all her energy into willing truth into her words, Sadie lets out a breath as she slowly regains control of her senses. Throwing the sheets off her body, her feet find the floor, only for the sound of footsteps in the hallway to threaten her nerves once more.

"Sadie?" A softer voice calls out, this time coming from the other side of door.

"I—I'm coming." Sadie chokes out, swiftly crossing the room to peek through the door. It's Odette, now awake—hair an effortless mess as she stands barefoot in a silk robe, running a hairbrush through her hair. "Who were you talking to?"

Wide-eyed, Sadie swallows before replying, the scent of death wrapping her voice up in a hoarse whisper. "I was just dreaming."

Odette's eyes linger for a second longer before she continues fiddling with her hair. "Isaiah will be here soon—I'm just getting ready. And, uh..." Odette raises an arched brow. "Have you been rolling around in the dirt?" she smirks, casting her eyes over her earth-marked dress.

It must have been real, his grave, his death, his touch.

And for it, Sadie shivers—for it must have been *him* who took her back up into her parents' bedroom. Yet the fear sits frozen on her tongue as she realizes he didn't kill her when he had the chance, when it would have been so easy. Dread sinks into her bones as the thought of what he could want from her *alive* reigns loose upon her mind.

"I... I fell asleep after cleaning," she lies through her teeth before scrambling to change the topic. "But your room is ready, now. You can sleep there tonight."

"Thanks again, Sadie." Odette smiles, lingering briefly before motioning to turn away and continue the rest of her routine. That is, until Sadie reaches out for her silk-draped arm. "Wait—"

"Mm?"

"I—I'm coming with you."

Odette's lips pull up into a wide grin. "What made you change your mind?"

The hope that there's still some sanity left inside me, Sadie thinks to herself as she clasps her mother's long lost necklace around her collarbones.

"It doesn't matter..." She shakes her head. "I just need to get out of this goddamned house."

SADIE'S NERVES hardly have the time to settle by the time Isaiah pulls into the grass-patch-turned-parking-lot overlooking the beach. The steam of the shower and a change of clothes can only scrub away so much, and that dark distinct scent of the grave clings to the very pores of her skin—a scent she does her best to shake from her thoughts.

Odette's already hopped out of the backseat, perched on the sand with her expensive-looking camera out and pointed at the mesmeric twinkle of the stars overhead, a smile plastered across her lips at the view, drowning in nostalgia. Yet for all Odette's excitement, Sadie lingers.

Even beneath the shade of night, the white sands of Infanta Bay beach glimmers in the darkness, the crashing of those pitch black waves the only tell-tale sign that there's an entire ocean stretching endlessly out around them. Up ahead there's a sudden glow, and Sadie turns to see a haze of lights switched on—dozens of paper lanterns cast in jewel tones are strung up around the porch hugging the bar up ahead, which can only mean one thing. It's happy hour at the Taverna.

The Taverna proudly calls itself Port Cante's busiest hotspot after dark, straddling a dense thicket of palm trees and the pristine white sands of Infanta Bay.

The pick-up door clicks open, and she looks up to see Isaiah leaning against the side of the truck, peering down at her with a raised brow.

"When was the last time you came here and it wasn't for work?"

The wind rushes past him, and she soaks in the scent of sea spray, the salty air filling her with the desire to get away—but she bites her tongue, attempting to drown out the thought of what awaits her at the Hacienda. "Too long ago," she answers, shrugging past him to hop out of the truck and onto the grass underfoot.

"Hm." He leans in, arms crossed against his chest as he follows her over to the hood. She can feel his watching eyes on her, trying to dig beneath the surface, the usual refrain of *are you okay* sitting on the tip of his tongue, but she never gives him the chance to say it.

"Come on," she murmurs, drawing her hair over her shoulder in a movement that Isaiah lingers on. "Let's go."

"Funny how this place feels just like how I remembered." Odette's strides are languid beside the two as she takes in the endless crashing waves of the crystalline sea.

"I'm surprised you still remembered," Sadie whispers under her breath before she legs it up the stairs of the Taverna.

Isaiah holds the door open for the two girls, Odette entering first, no doubt eager to take the edge off a long journey. Sadie follows behind, breathing in the warmth and noise of the crowded bar, and of course the mingling scent of booze, cheap cologne and cigarette smoke. It smells nothing like the Hacienda, and Sadie inhales deeply, savoring the fact.

Isaiah tips his head up at the familiar faces that call out to greet him, those same faces silenced almost immediately by the sight of the solemn girl he leads inside.

Has it really been that long?

No one could politely recall the last time anyone in Port Cante had seen Sadie on the other side of the bar top, nor the last time she entered through the front doors instead of the back, let alone bring it up without expecting a fiery glare thrown their way.

The feeling of their whispers, their eyes roaming over her face; studying, watching—it sends her hands up to her side, wrapping her arms around herself in a motion she knows all too well, a motion that does nothing to hide the cracks they can see so clearly.

The night draws on with a tight smile painted on Sadie's face, her cheeks strained with the weight of holding up a façade that everything's okay. *There isn't a grave beneath the house,* her knuckles tighten white around an untouched bottle of San Miguel Odette placed between her fingers, *and it wasn't a demon that came out of it.*

She watches as Maria de la Rosa, her boss, sits in the corner, fanning herself and her swollen belly to keep the heat at bay, while her husband Hector—of whom she is also the boss—moves quickly to point an electric fan in her direction.

For the length of a year and a blink of an eye, Sadie has worked the bar at the Taverna, more at the insistence of Maria over anything else. *You can't be alone,* she demanded, *working here will be the distraction you need to heal.* Distraction it's been, but heal is anything it's achieved.

A voice booms from behind the counter, "And now it's time for the main event!" A few seconds later, Hector is hauling out a karaoke machine most likely older than time itself.

Odette's eyes light up, growing two sizes bigger and three sizes tipsier. "Sing with me, Sadie!"

Her smile is infectious, but her enthusiasm for singing in front of a crowd not so much. Shaking her head, Sadie squeezes Odette's fingers. "Not tonight, Odette... I'm exhausted. You go ahead."

"Fine." Odette raises an eyebrow before practically bouncing off towards the make-shift stage to the right of the bar, taking the mic with that effortless grace that always made her seem untouchable in Sadie's eyes.

Isaiah's voice captures her attention as Maria slides him another drink from across the bar. "What's the matter?" He takes a swig. "Not in the mood again?"

The lights of the bar dim as the karaoke machine springs to life, filling the Taverna with that strange, not-quite-right electro melody that's nothing more than a cheap imitation of the usual classic pop ballads.

She replies, "I'm here for her. Not for me." A feigned smile pulls up at her lips as she draws her gaze to his.

Isaiah's eyes have abandoned their usual honey brown richness —instead, beneath the dim lights, they're almost black.

"Hm," he scoffs, taking another swig, more this time. "You're doing that thing you do."

She sighs. "What is that supposed to mean?"

"That thing you do when you want to say something, but you don't. You're an open book, you know." He polishes off the bottle, setting it down on the table with a loud clink.

Sadie presses her lips into a thin line, focusing on a half-moon indentation staring back at her from the faded countertop. "Maybe I am."

Isaiah leans in closer, Sadie drawing her gaze down to his fingers brushing against hers.

"It's about Sunday, isn't it? The memorial mass... your mom."

Sadie says nothing.

"She wouldn't want you to dwell on it, Sadie. Believe me. All she'd want for you is to live your life as normal and—"

"—*normal?*" Sadie whips around to face him, pushing the bottle of San Miguel away as heat creeps up beneath her cheeks, "You think it's that easy?"

"You're wearing her necklace," he remarks, his eyes flicking down to the pearl hanging between her collarbones. "To me, that's a sign of moving on."

And just like that, the fire burning on her tongue is extinguished as she toys with the pearl between her fingers, her thoughts dancing around the shape of the grave she plucked it out from.

"The past is the past." He squeezes her hand with a half-smile before pressing his lips to her forehead. "Let it rest, okay?"

How can I? She wants to say, but before she has the chance to say it, a familiar voice begins to sing, rendering the room silent. It almost knocks the wind out of her in the way Odette's voice always did, but this time she can't help but notice in her periphery Isaiah's eyes no longer on hers, but on the blinding stage lights illuminating Odette.

She can't help but linger on his profile as he watches Odette sing. Him and his brown eyes, sun kissed skin; his calloused fingers, the cuts on his knuckles, the way he smells so much of the sea.

Sadie loved the sea, once. It reminded her of everything that once was, of everything *before*—just as Isaiah does.

"Isaiah..." She so wants to be the reason for the smile that pulls up his lips, wanting for once not to be another burden; another echo of a past that simply isn't there. Whether it's out of naiveté or desperation, Sadie doesn't know what it is that urges her to reach out and close the distance between them, wanting him near, near enough for her to forget how much this all hurts. "I'm sorry for—"

"—Isaiah! This is a duet, and I'm not singing without you." But the present comes calling, and Odette's voice slices through the space between them.

A light shines on Isaiah, momentarily blinding him.

Odette beckons him forth, with all the promise of the sun's boisterous warmth to winter wet skin. *Why wouldn't he join her?*

The distance between them becomes a cavernous divide once more when he leaves her side with barely a passing glance, leaving her heart with a rapid pulse she tries to drown in the melody of this next song. All the noise, the music, the song fades into silence as Sadie turns her head away from the two of her closest friends on the stage, focusing instead on the shelf behind the bar.

Amidst the glistening bottles of liquor and twinkling spirits,

Sadie's eyes skim over the multitude of colors in an attempt to escape from her own mind—but a darker shade of black pulls her back to reality. Her reality.

There's a man.

He's sitting in the far corner, silhouetted by the neon red of a beer sign behind him. She can make out his features, the very same she saw at the Hacienda, but only this time shrouded in nothing but the clarity of a crimson light as he sits in waiting, the bar patrons moving past him as if there were no one there at all.

Of course, she realizes, *they can't see him.*

Only she can—and she takes in the sight of him, his hair falling in waves of black, stopping just above his shoulders. The paler shade of his skin and the hardness of his features telling of his life beneath a different sun, a different time. Yet for however old he must be, there's a timelessness in the sculptural quality of his features—something reminiscent of those anguished statues that hold up the weight of those gilded European Cathedrals on their shoulders, something otherworldly, something simply mesmerizing.

She realizes too late that she's been staring, and when his lips pull up into a smile, her heart stops.

He sees me.

Feeling her insides begin to twist, she pushes herself away from the bar top, rising to her feet, almost stumbling forwards towards the rest room.

The sticky heat swirls around Sadie, growing tighter and tighter around her body as she makes her way to the back of the bar, away from the song, away from the voices, away from the melody. Pushing open the bathroom door, she beelines for the sink, gripping the cold porcelain in an attempt to regain control over her heart.

I need to go home.

With a deep breath she makes her way out of the restroom, her heart catching in her throat as she's met with a dark figure standing at the end of the narrow hallway. His eyes are one and the same with the shadows, those two, piercing pinpricks of reflective light he calls pupils staring back at her the way an animal watches from the undergrowth.

"Please just leave me alone!" Sadie presses her fingers against her temples, but as she draws her eyes upwards, she stiffens when it's not the demon named Silas peering back at her. Sadie squints into the dark, catching a shadow of familiarity written in his features, but she swallows her paranoia. *Paranoia,* yes—that's what it is. "I—I'm sorry. I thought you were someone else."

The man simply smiles at her, his tall frame almost blocking out the light of the *EXIT* sign that taunts Sadie with each passing second. His skin is a deep shade of tan, lean and broad-shouldered, with an authority to his presence that she can't quite explain.

She wants to turn away, but his voice keeps her attention.

"Your name. It's Sara, isn't it?"

A knot pulls at her stomach.

"I—"

"—And you own that old Hacienda on the edge of town, don't you?"

There's no trace of the usual American accent tourists brought with them to Port Cante—instead he speaks with a lilt to his words that gives him the air of being from another place and time entirely. In another light he'd be the perfect picture of a vintage Hollywood hero if it weren't for the mark of modernity snaking out from beneath the collar of his button up shirt, a tattoo of an emerald viper with eyes blacker than sin.

He must be her senior in the way he expects her to fold at his feet, but there's not a sign of age on his hard, angular features. Well-dressed and groomed to perfection, perhaps he'd be handsome in another light, charming, even—if it weren't for this cloak of darkness that he wears like a second skin.

There's something about him that sends Sadie's hairs on end, prompting her to ask, "And who are you, exactly?"

He laughs—an unsettling ripple of amusement. "No need to

worry." He crosses his arms over his chest in a languid motion that only tightens the knot in the pit of her stomach. "I'm not going to hurt you."

Sadie lets out the breath she's been holding, motioning to leave —but his voice reaches around her to keep her where she stands.

"That's something I leave to *him*." The shadows soak through his voice, his tone growing dark as he asks, "He's here, isn't he?" It's a question that sounds more like a threat, shattering all pretense the moment he says that name, "Silas is finally awake."

Wide-eyed, Sadie scrambles to fill the silence. "I... I don't know who that is." Her heart beats wildly as she seizes the chance to make an escape, briskly making her way past him until the green glow of the *EXIT* sign envelopes her, only for his fingers to wrap tightly around her wrist.

"Don't lie to me." His knuckles are white as he grips her forearm tight. "I can smell him on you..." he trails off as his eyes flick down to the pearl at her neck, and in a heartbeat his eyes flash a darker shade.

"Let me go!" Sadie wrenches her arm away from his grip, backing herself up against the door that leads out into the crowded main room. In the dim of the hallway she looks up at the figure standing tall before her, his presence stretching out around her like rays of a black sun. All-consuming, and inescapable.

But light floods in from the door that opens and shuts behind her, the sight of whatever it is that now occupies the narrow hallway forcing the stranger backwards—blinded momentarily by the light, and the abyssal shadow that follows.

In her periphery she can see a black silhouette towering tall behind her, yet she dares not turn to face him—her body frozen between both men. The scent of grave dirt clings tightly to the tatters of fabric hanging from his shoulders. *It's him,* she lets out an inaudible gasp, *the demon*—Silas.

"Sara." Silas' voice is a tremble of thunder, the sound of her name from his lips a mercy that spares her the wrath of the other man.

Silas' heavy hand comes to rest upon her shoulder, moving her to the side as he steps forward between them both. Sadie's stomach tangles with dread as the din of the Taverna on the other side of the door fades from her senses. It's nothing but the ebb of a distant world, lapping at the shadows of this crossroads meeting. *Make a run for it,* the voice in her head screams at her—but she stays glued to where she stands, transfixed to the simmering rage in the air and the ghost of their shared past lurking between them both.

"It seems even centuries of time have done nothing to change you, Silas. Here is another one of your play things, another toy... Just what I expected from you, *hermano.*"

Hermano? Brother?

Silas takes a step closer, cornering the other man against the opposite wall, his jaw clenched. "Why are you here, Lorenzo?"

The other man—Lorenzo—grits his teeth. "I'm simply here to make sure there are no..." his eyes land on Sadie, raking over her body in a way that makes her skin crawl, "Distractions."

"Distraction from what?"

"Our Father's will." Lorenzo swipes his tongue across his teeth, the mention of their father eliciting a dark fire from his brother as he closes the distance between them in a single stride. Silas' fist wraps around the fabric of Lorenzo's shirt, pinning him up against the wall with all the ease of a wind gust to a sand dune. As sharp-tongued as Lorenzo is, acting the wolf in sheep's clothing, Silas is every bit the beast in both imposing stature and size.

"Father is dead, Lorenzo." Shadows drip from his every word, "I saw him burn... and I can still smell the char of his skin. His plan, his will, is nothing more than ash."

"*His* will is all that we have left of this family, of this name. Don't you understand?!" Lorenzo bares his teeth, "You are an Espinosa, same as I. We share the burden, no matter how much you try to escape the fact."

Silas slams his brother hard against the wall, words a violent hiss. "I was *buried* for this name, brother. Cursed to spend an eternity alive, alone in the dark, my fate to lie in slumber until the day of Judgment. Do not talk to me of escape." His grip on his brother loosens, "You know nothing of what I endured…"

Lorenzo finds his footing, his black eyes as unwavering as they are wicked. "Hm," he narrows his eyes, searching for any trace of a weakness. "I am here now. That is all that matters."

"Your presence changes nothing," Silas replies.

A wicked grin erupts over Lorenzo's features. Whatever he was searching for, he found it. "You're wrong, brother… It changes everything."

Sadie lets out a breath as Lorenzo digs his hand into the chink in Silas' armor—that scar in the center of his chest. "You're weak, Silas." Lorenzo presses his fist to his brother's chest with a force that Sadie can feel ripple through the air, drawing a gasp from her lips.

Silas shows no hesitation in bringing his fingers up to his brother's neck, wrapping tight around his jugular. A pulse passes and the muscles of Silas' arm contract, his fingers gripping his brother's flesh tighter and tighter, those dark eyes flaring deep red. He holds him up higher against the wall, the veins in his throat beginning to bulge, his brimming rage boiling over.

"Yet you've always been weaker." Vitriol drips from his words, and Sadie feels herself suffocating in the miasma of their past, their burden, the weight of the name *Espinosa*.

Silas tightens his grip until a whimper of a breath escapes Lorenzo's lips—he concedes. Silas lets him drop to the ground, where he slumps over, clutching at his neck where blue-black bruises snake across his tattooed skin. But in spite of his mortal mark, there's an air of knowing that clings to his features. As if he knows so much more than those dark eyes belie. "Remember your name, *hermano*… And don't forget—no distractions." His voice is hoarse yet taunting, the shadowy hallway encasing his body as he makes his retreat into the dark, "Or I will make sure of it myself."

Odette's laughter resounds from beyond the hallway, momentarily cutting through the tension hanging thick in the air. The shadows twist and writhe, reclaiming Lorenzo limb by limb. With a sordid grin, he leaves her with a final whisper, "And you, girl. How unfortunate you are, to be born into a spider's web..." Lorenzo chuckles darkly. "Let's hope you are not just a little fly."

And with that, he's gone.

Yet there's still the demon behind her.

She attempts to step backwards, as far as she can away from this unholy reunion she never should have witnessed. *A play thing,* Lorenzo's words linger at the shell of her ear, *a toy,* one last warning as she backs up, eyes fixed to the demon before her, his back turned. Fear clambers up the sides of her throat, rendering her unable to speak in the sudden silence that follows Lorenzo's absence.

Yet Silas is the first to break it, his voice low. "Tell me, Sara..." he turns his head, profile illuminated by green light. "To which God do you pledge your devotion?"

He turns to face her, and she steps back.

"For Him, would you bleed?"

Feeling the wall behind her, there's nowhere to run as he draws closer, his eyes distant, brimming with black. "For Him, would you bend? For him would you *break?*"

Her hair fans out against the bulletin board behind her, tangling with the pushpins and faded advertisements as he stops arm's width away from her.

"I—is that what you're going to do to me?"

Splaying his one hand out against the board behind her, he bows his head low, his breath flush close against hers.

"Hm." A smile forms and falters on his lips. "Unlike Him," his voice softens, a pained expression settling over his features, "I do not feed on the innocent."

Innocent.

The word leaves a bitter sting on the tip of her tongue, a sting she attempts to rectify as she resists against it. "I don't... I don't believe. Not in Him."

Panic sets into her nerves as she scolds herself for speaking. She should have held her tongue, bitten down on it until she tasted blood—yet there's something about him that draws the truth out of her in a way that should feel like violation. But how can it? How can it be violation when the admission is of her own doing, her answer nothing but the truth?

Curiosity colors his features, as he drinks in the fear that falls from her lips in an exhale, as if the taste were sweeter than any wine.

"I stopped believing in Him the day my mom killed herself."

He peers deep inside her soul, finding the shadow of a flaw in her words, taking it in his palm, and into his demon's grip. "No. You lie. Your faith is not dead, but changed," his other hand comes to rest over the center of his chest, his knuckles white-hot. "There is devotion inside you, but it is not for His suffering..." A trickle of black drips from between his fingers, "It is for your own."

Sadie flicks her eyes downwards, where a droplet of his blood falls to the floor, its scent wrapped up in smoke.

He's hurt.

With no chance to ponder, Silas lurches forwards, catching himself against the poster board behind her. A black mass stains the shreds of fabric hanging over his chest, nothing but a small tell of the agonizing wound beneath.

A flush of courage rises to her tongue at the sight of his blood, his fallibility, and she asks, "How are you here? How can you follow me?"

He answers simply, "There is a curse upon my soul—a binding." With head still bowed, he lets out a labored breath before he draws his gaze upwards to face the poster board. "Yet it is not the Hacienda I am bound to..."

Slipping out from beneath his gaze, she steps behind him, where she can see his dark eyes in the glossy reflection.

"It is you. And you must tell me why."

Sadie draws further backwards, "I—I don't know why."

"Then you will find out..." He straightens himself up, forcing his breath to normality.

"And why would I do that?!" Sadie grits her teeth.

"You have no living blood... no family. No parents."

Sadie swears his voice is laced with a tone that almost feels like he's mocking her, but fire erupts from her tongue when she realizes it's nothing but the plain, simple truth.

Clenching her fists at her sides she lets out a hiss, "And what does that mean!?"

His eyes brim black, voice a monotone that slices straight through her, "You have nothing left to lose."

Her heart catches in her throat, but before Sadie has the chance to speak, she turns towards the sound of footsteps heading straight for the hallway, that distinct footfall rising above the singing and electro-melody of the karaoke machine blaring from behind the door. Whipping her head towards Silas, she sees his gaze no longer locked on hers through the reflection of the poster board, but instead on its contents.

Inside is a tourist advertisement boasting a businessman clad in a suit and tie, stepping out onto a sandy beach, where alleged paradise awaits.

Straightening himself up, a shroud of smoke envelopes his body and in the blink of an eye the tatters of fabric hanging from his shoulders are all but gone. He's conjured himself up a suit akin to the one in the ad; although it's a shade darker than black, all crisp and tailored to perfection, giving him the air of the otherworldly that she can't help but find entrancing.

As the hallway door swings open, Sadie instinctively steps in front of Silas, as if she could shield the beast of a man with her smaller-than-average frame. Nonetheless, she tries her best as she locks eyes with Isaiah standing at the door with questioning eyes.

"Sadie..." Isaiah calls out, doing nothing to mask his disdain at the sight of the man towering over her. "Who's this?"

With her breath caught in her throat, she scrambles to form words. "H—he's staying at the Hacienda. He's a guest."

What the hell, Sadie? She wants nothing more than to clamp her hand over her mouth, to take it all back—but it's too late. All she can do is run with it. "He was just telling me how his um, flight was delayed. He just got here on the last bus... It's been a long journey and when he stopped by at the Hacienda, no one was there! So he came here, and what a coincidence—here I am."

Breathless from blubbering, the scream that wants to rip through her throat never does as she glances quickly at Silas, who wears something resembling an amused smile for the briefest of moments. There's not a hint of a tremble in his gait, nor a hint of the blood she saw dripping to the floor—the illusion of his normalcy, his humanity, a potent one.

Isaiah gives him a onceover, sizing him up as if he's intruding on a piece of territory that belongs to him. The thought of it sends pinpricks of irritation through Sadie, yet she presses on with the lie, "He's having fun here, so he's going take a cab back to the Hacienda tonight."

"Fun?" Isaiah raises an eyebrow at Silas' solemn expression.

"He's European. It's how they are." Sadie waves him off.

Isaiah's eyes remain fixed squarely on Silas. "What's your name?"

Ever the picture of old world formality in his conjured-up suit, he answers simply, "Silas."

"Isaiah."

And Sadie just about feels on the verge of imploding as she makes her way down the hallway, away from the demon, and towards the familiarity of the Taverna. "Isaiah." His name almost fumbles from her lips, "I think I'm ready to head home. Can you go get Odette?"

She dares not look back into Silas' eyes, afraid of what she'll see.

"What's the matter?" Isaiah peers cautiously into her eyes as they walk back into the thick of the noise, the blaring music and singing all but drowning out all traces of the demon who calls himself Silas Espinosa.

"You look like you've seen a ghost." He prods again, the half-smile on his lips quickly fading away as he sees a seriousness etched into her eyes.

"No... I'm fine. I just—I'm tired."

Isaiah simply nods, "Come on." With a hand on her lower back, he leads her towards the exit, and she follows along with stiff shoulders as he whispers, "I'm staying over tonight." And it's more of a command than a question.

Looking up into his dark eyes, she wills herself to move in a motion that mimics a nod, "Okay."

"I'll go get Odette." Isaiah leaves her beneath the covered front steps of the Taverna, swaying in the night breeze with only the deafening cicada song to keep her company. Yet as the waves crash over Infanta Bay up ahead, Sadie feels a shadow wrap around the lightbulb overhead. It flickers once, twice, in unison with a voice that murmurs against the shell of her ear.

It's Silas—yet this time, she's sure only she can hear his voice.

"I'll see you in your dreams."

Her heart skips a beat as she realizes she's not alone; not anymore, not as long as there's a dream left in her body.

THE CLOCK STRIKES ELEVEN THIRTY, and sleep evades the girl laying restlessly beside her boyfriend. *If that's what you can call what we are*, she thinks to herself, letting out a heat soaked breath not even the turn of the box fan in the corner can pierce through. The hallmarks of a relationship are all there; envy, possessiveness—and of course the ever present reminder that there's no one else out there who could possibly understand her the way he does, the way he has, the way he always will.

All that's missing is that binding label of officiality—the only label that matters under the eyes of God and to Father Agustin, the thought of disappointing the latter evoking a profound guilt that staring up at Port Cante's crucifix never could quite inspire.

But the weight of Isaiah's arm draped around her suffocates her thoughts the longer she's sleepless, and she turns to her side to be rid of the feeling and of the thought.

With her hair falling over the mattress' edge, Sadie's gaze lands on the chain of her mom's pearl pendant laying across her collarbones, the baroque pearl shimmering with all the ghosts of a distant past. It's the only reprieve she has and she holds onto it with all she has left.

Facing the door, she stares at the space between the floor and the foot of the door, illuminated by the moonlight streaming in from outside. Sadie holds her breath, listening over the sound of the rickety fan.

I'll see you in your dreams.

His voice rings loud in her ears, but she continues to stare unblinkingly at the line of white light—*not if I stay awake,* she tells herself. But it's futile. The moment she closes her eyes, the feeling of his pupils burning against her skin is an image she just can't blink away.

The silence of the house amplifies the sound of her footsteps as she presses herself up and out of bed, the oversized t-shirt that once belonged to her father now hanging threadbare, stopping mid-thigh. Quietly, she slips her satin robe around her shoulders before peering into the box on her dresser. The starling is asleep, just as she left him earlier. Gently, she strokes the sleeping bird's smooth feathers, the thrum of his heartbeat beneath her fingertips a moment of relief.

Fetching a small saucer from the bathroom, she fills it with cold water and sets it by the starling's nest of towels before making her way towards the door. Wincing as a floorboard creaks underfoot, she looks back from beneath the doorway, only to see Isaiah hasn't moved an inch.

Satisfied, she steps out into the dark hallway, briefly hearing Odette's sleep babble as she passes by her room, and farther behind, the creak of her bedframe as Isaiah fills up the empty space she left behind across the sheets.

Darkness wraps around her as she walks onwards, towards the only door left in the Hacienda that's been left unopened for far too long. Twisting her fingers around the sleek blue satin of her robe, Sadie comes to a stop at the door sitting at the end of the hallway, the door that leads to her dad's old study. Lingering on the memory of her mother's unfinished work in turning his study into another guest room, Sadie fights against the memory of her mother's endless tears as she packed up box after box after box.

She waits for a moment, holding her breath—and when she hears nothing, she urges forward, into this memory of the past.

Everything is just how it was the last time she was inside; and her heart aches the more for it. An antique narra wood four poster bed sits in the center of the room, with a sprawling ceiling-length shelf running across the entirety of the far wall. The shelf is brimming with her parents' extensive collection, from her father's history books and academic journals, to her mother's countless fiction. In between his and hers, sits Sadie's favorite collection of poetry—a paperback dog-eared and sun worn, boasting the faded author's name: *Edna St Vincent Millay*. She could recite her favorite poems from memory, much to the pride and joy of her father—but now the thought of picking up that same book leaves her with nothing but the dull ache of loss.

The rest of the room is comprised of her father's belongings; his desk, his record player, and an ancient T.V. set are pressed up tight against the opposite wall.

She would have expected that a lifetime of being home schooled by her father in this very room would have ignited a passion for history and the world beyond her doorstep, but all it did was the very opposite the day he died.

A brain aneurysm was the culprit, during a Spanish history lesson. One minute he was reading aloud tales of the Inquisition, the next he was lying on the floor. Her mother rushed in, screaming bloody murder—but all Sadie could hear was the deafening chorus of the starlings outside, thinking of how much better it is to stay right where she is, where it's simply so much quieter.

But now, there's not a hint of birdsong ahead, and Sadie inhales a sharp breath before bee lining to the closet and throwing its doors open. Greeted by boxes upon boxes of papers and old journals, Sadie runs her eyes over the sum of a lifetime of conservation and heritage work, pinpricks of melancholy stabbing at her chest. Pressing her lips together in focus, she begins to dig through the boxes, stopping the moment she feels fabric beneath her fingers, the fabric of something that shouldn't be here.

It's a dress.

Not just any dress, it's her mother's hand-made Maria Clara. The one she wore in the photo on her nightstand, shoved unceremoniously into a box of her father's notes. She fights hard against the tears that prick at her eyes at the thought of her mother throwing this memory into a dusty old box to be sealed away, where it can die along with the memory of her father and everything else she once had. Carefully, she re-folds the dress, not allowing herself to linger over a piece of the past that doesn't belong to her. Neatly, she places it back in the closet along with her un-shed tears.

Focusing back on the box before her, she spies *Hacienda Espinosa* labelled on its side. The words peer back at her with a magnetic pull, and she scoops it up in her arms and lays it down on the floor. Positioning the lamp beside her, the room is bathed in a soft glow as she thumbs through countless spines—on each of them is labelled simply:

Enrique Pasiona.

Sadie wastes no time diving into the stack, finding them filled mostly with illegible conservation notes, endless scrawlings in the margins, unreadable to anyone except the owner—until she sees the word *Espinosa.*

Scanning her eyes over the page, she drinks it in:

Hacienda Espinosa. Estate built by Spaniard Salbador Espinosa, c. 1670s.

A wealthy nobleman based in Seville, Espinosa became invested in the Manilla Galleon trade and migrated to the Philippines to capitalize on the bustling trade route. Hacienda Espinosa is the sum of his accomplishments; with no expense spared in the construction of the estate. From imported mahogany furnishings to carpetry from Malaga, Espinosa readily commissioned local artisans to craft the mulawin wood panels and the narra wood furniture.

After a house fire that killed him and his son, the Hacienda was bequeathed to the will of the local church.

Underneath it is the word *family,* yet all Sadie sees is one name:

Survived by one; Lorenzo Espinosa.

Furrowing her brows, she flicks through the rest of the notebook in an attempt to find the missing pieces—but that name is all she gets.

"Lorenzo..." Her mind wanders to that dark hallway at the Taverna beneath the sordid dark of his piercing eyes. "The only survivor...?" she whispers to herself, knowing that there's more to this family than the history suggests. *It was no house fire that sealed Silas up in that grave,* she thinks to herself. But that's all that's written; Sadie finding nothing more on the Espinosas—yet there's something more between the pages, just as there was something more beneath the floorboards.

There's a Polaroid poking out of the notebook. Furrowing her brows, she pulls it out from between the pages, and immediately Sadie recognizes her dad sitting side by side with Odette's father Dominic behind the bar top of the Taverna, shot glasses framing the table they're sat at. Dominic's arm is resting lazily over dad's shoulder in a way that undermines everything mama used to say about him.

A horrible, horrible man, she would mutter under her breath whenever his name inevitably popped up on the news for his acts of charity. But this image doesn't scream *horrible*—instead it shows the years of friendship required for two men to invest in a venture so involved as restoring an abandoned heritage site.

The moment she's done examining the photo, she leafs through the rest of the box's contents, finding nothing else but irrelevant journals filled with history notes of places she's only ever dreamed of seeing.

A wave of tiredness washes over her as the day finally catches up to her body. Her head bobs as she begins to nod off, resting her chin on her knuckles. Sleep is finally in her grasp, the world around her melting away into a haze of warmth, of softness—until she hears a sound.

It could just be the wind, or the bones of the old structure settling, but for a girl who's spent sleepless nights alone beneath the creaking whispers and low groans of the Hacienda; she knows exactly what that sound is.

Knocking—and it's desperate.

It's him.

Pressing herself quickly up to her feet, she rushes out into the hallway, down the grand staircase and into the main foyer. There's an unmistakable chill in the air, the cold caressing her bare legs as she suddenly becomes all too aware of her less than ideal state of dress. But there's no chance to dwell as the knocking begins again.

Sadie glances over her shoulder, and to her relief, there's not a single movement in the rooms above, meaning whatever she opens the door to now will only be for her eyes to see.

With a rapid-fire pulse, she unlatches the lock on the front door with a click, hesitating for a moment before pulling the door open—letting a shadow spill across the tiled floors.

"Silas..." she lets his name leave her lips in a breath as she takes him in; his hair awry, that illusion of a suit now fading fast, back into the smoke and shadow he conjured it up from.

He's upright for only a moment before staggering forward, his fingers curling around the doorframe. Sadie draws her eyes up to his face, fixated on the weariness etched into the hard line of his jaw as he attempts to contain the agony brimming over deep within.

"Let me in..." he groans, his voice a ripple of pain. Traces of smoke cling to the fabric of his clothes, and Sadie grimaces at the scent as her eyes begin to travel downward... And then she sees it.

No longer a droplet, nor a trickle, but a palm-sized black stain clinging to the fabric of his white undershirt, growing larger in size with every passing pulse.

"*Dyios...*" Sadie's lips part, the Lord's name tumbling out, spilling onto the floor where demon's blood meets it. Pulling her robe from her shoulders, she bundles it up and presses it into his chest to soak up the fast falling ichor. Silas clutches the satin hard against the gash in his chest as he lurches forward, her fingers around the door handle turning limp. Sadie throws the door open, allowing him inside. A few steps forward, he stops at the foot of the staircase, casting his dark eyes on the girl still standing with the front door in one hand, a desperation in the dark of his eyes that almost feels like a plea.

In all of Father Agustin's warnings against the evil, temptation and sin a demon can trail in their wake, Sadie never for once thought they could bleed just like she can.

And it dawns upon her, *he's at your mercy.*

The realization urges her to shut and lock the door behind her, rushing to his side with a whisper on her lips, "Come with me."

Brushing her hair back behind her ears, she steps past him and makes her way up the steps, the sound of his footsteps following her in the dark a steady rhythm that matches the pulse of her heart. The last unoccupied guest bedroom is her father's old office, and with knotted nerves, she leads him in with no other choice.

"Quickly," she whispers, opening the door to a room she'd rarely ever set foot since her father's death—all to give it away to *him,* an injured demon—her guest.

Sadie enters first, the lamp still on where she left it.

His shadow follows him in from the dark of the hallway, as towering, as all-encompassing as he himself. Silas shows no hesitation in entering, and in three long strides his one hand is gripping one of the four bedposts, his knuckles white hot, threatening to snap the wood beneath his fingers. But he composes himself, turning before sinking into the edge of the bed like a wounded animal, head bowed, elbows over his knees in an attempt to hide the hurt.

With no other thought in her mind, she stops just arm's length away from where he sits, wide-eyed and mesmerized at the sight. Her satin robe is all but soaked through with the stain of his blood, her heartbeat loud in her skull as she reaches her hand out, palm upturned, "Let me help..."

A groan escapes his lips, his fingers fumbling with the unfamiliar fastenings, those pesky buttons of his conjured up illusion nothing more than another restraint. His eyes flicker crimson, forcing Sadie to move quickly—she closes the distance between them, fingers deftly undoing the buttons until he simply can't take any more.

Twisting the fabric beneath his clenched fists, he rips the shirt apart in a single swift movement, the loud tear forcing her to back away. Silas' chest heaves as he tears away the crimson stained rags that remain hanging over his opened, bloodied chest.

Sadie drags her eyes over the width of him, his body marbled like the Roman statues she'd always dreamed of seeing in the museums of Italy, his skin the closest shade to death there is. Yet in the center, is a glaring imperfection in the stone, a monstrous fracture where his heart lays beneath. A hollowed eye stares up at her—an opened scar, oozing black blood, and Sadie can't help herself from staring back.

It must be from his reunion with his brother back at the Taverna, Lorenzo's fingers digging into the flesh of his heart, the exertion too much for even a demon awoken from God knows how long in the dirt.

The gash is grotesque, tendrils of pink skin radiating from the wound in the center like the flaming heart the Virgin Mary holds above the altar of Port Cante's church—and beneath its gaze she feels the inexplicable need to fall to her knees in veneration.

But he snaps his eyes upwards, those two pinpricks of light now stained through with a vivid red, pinning her to where she stands.

Her breath hitches at the sight, but he leans forward, sending her thoughts in a spiral. He's too close, those demon eyes too much, too piercing—all Sadie wants is to draw away, to run, but the baritone of his voice pulls her ever closer.

"Give me..." His voice is hoarse, almost as if he's a man starved, as he wills himself to stay upright, "Give me your hand."

"W—What?" Even with his blood on her fingers, she feels her hand is too much of an intimacy, a closeness, a sacred touch that she simply can't afford to give. "My hand?"

"I have spent centuries beneath the earth—parched." He swallows, his throat thick, voice dry. "I must drink."

Twisting her fingers around the necklace at the base of her throat, Sadie fans the fear enveloping her thoughts as she thinks of her blood against his lips, her neck beneath his teeth. "My... my blood?"

He shakes his head sharply, "No, *soñadora*. Your blood is our binding..." he winces as the wound seems to move of its own accord, the stinging pain etched into his features, his voice strained. "It is the tether that chains me to you, and it is strongest beneath this roof. Outside this house, I have not yet regained the strength I once did. But it is not your blood I need..."

Sadie's mind brews like a monsoon sea, her stomach turning as she quickly becomes all too aware of what a demon could possibly want from a human girl. If it's not in her death, in the spilling of her blood and feasting of her heart—then what more can he possibly want?

"*Sara,*" his voice is a strike of lightning, "You wish to be rid of me, do you not?"

Desperately, she nods.

"Then give me your hand!" His breathing grows more desperate with each passing moment the wound writhes across his chest—but Sadie resists, the embers of a slumbering fire stoked by the crimson of a demon's eyes.

"On one condition," she says, her tongue stiff against her teeth as she touches her pearl necklace.

"W—what is it?"

She feeds her fear to the flame as she dictates, "This necklace, *her* necklace. I found it in your grave. And it shouldn't have been there."

"And!?" His voice is a crackle of fire.

"Tell me what you know about my mom!" she demands, her voice a wound as raw as his.

He goes quiet, peering up at her for a moment too long before he clutches at his chest in an attempt to stop the bleeding, to close the wound.

And he falls backwards.

Shit.

With panic setting into her nerves, Sadie crawls onto the sheets beside him, perched on her hands and knees, fingers tentatively raised above his monstrous wound. She leans down to hear for a sign of life, gaze fixed to his pale lips as he blinks, once, twice —silence.

Ever closer, she leans down, her hair spilling across her shoulders to form a curtain of black around his face as she listens with bated breath. For a moment in this stillness she believes truly that he's slipped away, but the red flare of his eyes as they shoot open tells her she's oh so wrong.

Spanish leaves his lips in a fierce whisper, "*Dame tu angustia.*"

And he never allows the words to sink in as he reaches over to wrap his blood soaked fingers around her wrist, and like a tremor of thunder he pulls her down into him, pressing the flat of her palm against his open, bleeding pulse.

With a gasp, she seizes up, a wall of darkness rushing over her vision as she feels herself plunge into the depths of his wound; into the abyss where his veins run infernal red. Sadie sinks into him, through his tangled nerves, his muscle and sinew, deeper and deeper until she sees the cage of bone that encases his heart, a heart that beats accursed black.

In its center is a knifepoint—a dagger's tip.

She's suspended in the darkness, yet there's something that pulls her towards the fatal organ, and she stretches her fingers to reach for it. An echo lingers at the shell of her ear—the voice of a demon woven through the strands of her hair, lapping at her thoughts in unceasing tide.

Dame tu angustia, he commands, and her body responds.

Tears brim her eyes for a reason she can't discern, her mind devoid of all reason as her heart beats tirelessly with all the force of a storming sea. Fighting against her surging emotions, she presses on through the darkness, reaching out endlessly until she makes contact.

His heart is in her hands, and a wicked cold erupts from her fingertips.

A sea of sin has swallowed her up, all she can hear is the weight of the ocean currents swirling around her body, threatening to crush her in its dark embrace, just like it did her mother. She can taste her mother's fear, her grief, her agony along with the sting of the salt water that stripped her of her skin and wrought her bones to the abyssal sea floor.

And it tastes just like her own.

Tears fall fast from her cheeks as a year's worth of emotions come surging through every valve of her cobwebbed heart. Vaguely, faintly—the meaning of Silas' words come to sink into her psyche, acting the anchor that plunges her back to reality.

Give me your suffering.

She opens her eyes to see two pinpricks of light staring back at her—his eyes. No longer blood-red, no longer brimming with torturous pain. On his face are droplets of tears wetting his face, staining his lips.

His hand remains at her wrist in a languid grip as he swipes his tongue to capture the essence of a tear between his lips. "How sweet you taste," he whispers, breath hot against Sadie's cheek as she becomes all too aware that her body is entwined with his—just as it was when she fell into his grave.

Immediately she pulls her hand away from his, clambering off the bed and the demon within it until she's on her feet, desperately fighting the flush of her wet cheeks at this unholy intimacy between them.

She touches her cheeks, staining them with his blood—only to realize in horror she'd been crying, those tears on his tongue belonging to *her.* There's no doubt he saw it all, her grief, her pain, everything she's tried so hard to keep buried, but to no avail. Just like him, it's all been unearthed.

And it lays between them both in the shape of a gaping wound.

She clutches her hand to her necklace, watching awestruck as his bleeding stops, the gash closing over. Entranced, she can only stare as the broken tissue stitches itself back together, wisps of flesh twining in an intricate spider's web until there's nothing left but that initial, furious scar.

It's over now, and Silas lets out a deep breath.

The aftermath of blood spatters his skin, flecks soaked through the ivory sheets upon which his palms are upturned, the rise and fall of his chest proof enough that miracles exist.

Those devoted martyrs Father Agustin preached of embraced death openly—but Silas, on the other hand, cheats it with every breath, with every pulse of his cursed heart. And she never for once thought that cheating death could look like this.

So beautiful, so holy, so saint-like.

He's a demon, she chides herself, *a monster.*

Yet Sadie remembers that the brightest star amongst the Heavens fell to earth too, and she denies herself the chance to linger on the thought.

"Now you see..." he murmurs, his pallor returning, his voice ebbing back to its same deep cadence. He shuts his eyes closed for a moment, satiated.

Looking down at her blood smeared fingers, she feels no trace of fear, not when she's seen inside him, from the pattern of his veins to the thrumming tissue of his heart. Demon he may be, he has a pulse that bleeds, *just like mine.*

Sadie sits at the mattress' edge, arm's length beside him, mind racing. "Of course..." The wind whistles through the Hacienda, rustling the trees surrounding the estate, bowing their trunks to the demon within as the realization dawns over her. "Suffering," she whispers, her heart beginning to still as she closes her parted lips. "Suffering is what keeps you alive."

Shadows dance over the dark of his eyes as he runs a weary hand through his jet black hair. "Sane more than alive," he answers, sitting upright. "This curse in my heart is what keeps me from death, and your suffering is my nourishment. Without it, I would cease to be all that I am. My memories, my past... all of it gone."

"So all those years this house was abandoned, you—"

"—Starved." He runs his fingers over the scar yawning over his chest, pressing his eyes closed as if to will the pain away. "I have fed upon the agonies of all that have dreamed in this house... But all those years with nothing to feast upon has brought upon me a deprivation that has eaten away at my memory... robbed me of that face who struck my heart and began this eternal damnation of mine."

"Your brother, Lorenzo... What if it was him?"

Silas leans his head back against the headboard. "No..." his eyes grow distant, "It wasn't him. That I am sure of."

"How can you be sure?"

"He is my brother," his eyes lock onto hers, the embers of an old fire stoked with every word. "I know him best."

She wants to press further, to ensure he's not lying—but she's rendered speechless as she's caught beneath his gaze, beneath his piercing eyes, like a leaf under a rolling, raging current. Spent beneath his eyes, she has only one question left inside her, and she surrenders to it.

There's nothing else to do, not when she's already held his cursed heart in her hands, and he already feasted from the well of her tears.

"What does it taste like?" she asks. "My suffering?"

He tilts his head, not expecting her question. "Your suffering...?" he mulls it over for a moment before letting his gaze fall back to hers. "It tastes like saltwater." A dark smile pulls up at his lips, "And it's sweeter than sin."

She's silent under the weight of a distant sea, its tide her tears, its currents her heartache.

"You must go." He releases her from his spell, her attention turning from the taste of saltwater to the color of his blood against her skin. "I believe you are missed."

Sadie nods, body heavy as she wills herself to turn away and make her way to the door. She stops with her fingers wrapped around the handle, turning to face him again. He's watching her, perfectly motionless in the soft glow of the lamp light and the darkness encasing it.

She forces the words out of her—the need to play hostess overriding the coal-smoke scent of his blood on her hands. "Goodnight, Silas."

"Goodnight, Sara." He whispers, and she steps out into the dark of the hallway, shutting the door softly behind her.

She presses her eyes shut tight at the sting of hearing her name from his lips. *Sara,* a name reserved only for her family to call her, a name that's written on the dotted line of her birth certificate, and nowhere else. And the fact that he knows it, that he's dredged it up from the depths of her dreams and nightmares, feels too much like being seen, or worst of all, being known.

In a daze, she heads for the bathroom, not daring to look at her reflection in the mirror. The cold water washes the flecks of blood and tears from her fingers and cheeks, and once her wrists are red raw from scrubbing, she makes her descent back to reality.

The walk back to her bedroom is a stillness that eludes the

raging storm of her thoughts. Thoughts she must push aside as she softly opens her bedroom door.

Isaiah is awake—she can feel his eyes on her in the dark. And when she climbs back into bed, even in the shadows she can clearly see the faint outline of a frown on his lips.

"Why are you up?" he asks, voice lacking the luster of sleep.

"Silas came back. I had to open the door for him."

She says nothing else, turning onto her side and letting her gaze rest on the door and the light coming from beneath it.

"I don't trust him."

"Why do you say that?" Her voice is a deadpan, already knowing the answer.

"It doesn't matter why," he scoffs. "All that matters is that I'm here."

She furrows her brows, letting him continue.

"I mean, you don't have to worry as long as I'm here."

Annoyance ticks in the back of her throat, but she's too tired to protest.

He rakes his fingers through his hair with a deep sigh, the moonlight filtering in from the windows giving him a silhouette that's almost jagged.

"Sadie..." he calls out, his voice softer. "I'm sorry. I didn't mean it like that. "I just... care. That's all." He brushes his fingers against her arm, but she doesn't let up. "Someone has to, after all."

She presses her eyes closed, her heart beating loudly in her ears, blood swooshing between her temples. *He's right.*

Like he always is.

Once the silence nestles into the space between them, he rolls back to his side of the bed. "Goodnight."

"Night, Sai."

And soon after, she's alone once more. The sound of his breath, the constant *in* and *out* just another reminder that there's no use waking him, not when all he'll do is roll over back to sleep with that usual refrain under his breath, *you're safe with me.*

She turns back to face the sliver of light under her door, breathing beginning to slow, heartbeat steadying as the tension wringing her shoulders releases its grip over her—yet when she presses her eyes closed, she doesn't dare open them again until dawn breaks.

🎐 6 🎐

WHEN SADIE OPENS HER EYES, a beam of morning sun yanks her out from the haze of sleep and into the waking world. Turning away from the light, and onto her side, Sadie finds the bed beside her empty. Judging from the brightness of the sunshine filtering in through the lace bed curtains, Isaiah must have left for work at the Port long ago.

Sadie sits up in bed, hugging her knees to her chest.

At least he doesn't have to see me like this.

The mornings were always hardest; and that's why he never stuck around for them.

Wanting nothing more than to sink back into the depths beneath her sheets, she lets out a deep breath, mustering up the resolve to face whatever awaits beyond her bedroom door. Rising to her feet, she brushes out her tangled hair, spotting droplets of demon blood spattered across the hem of her shirt—another firm reminder that last night was no mere fever dream. Slipping into a fresh white summer dress, Sadie slips on a loose cardigan across her shoulders before making her way down to the kitchen, constantly fighting the urge to check over her shoulder for the door at the end of the hall.

The kitchen is dead silent as she starts off breakfast, her eyes darting up far too often at the hands of the clock strung up above the fridge.

Her heart pulses with each tick of the clock, her fingers fidgeting with the apron tied around her waist as she strikes the match to light the stove. Autopilot takes over as she cracks the umpteenth egg into an oiled pan, the hiss of heat a familiarity she settles into as she cooks up a frenzy. By the time she's cleaned up the last of the pots and pans, Sadie lets out a breath as she sets the kettle on the stovetop before leaning back against the counter.

Drawing her hand up to her necklace, she twirls the baroque pearl between her fingers as she lets her mind wander to the thought of the demon sprawled out over the sheets in the guest bedroom upstairs. She can see him so clearly in her mind's eye, the length of his body laid out across the linen, skin shrouded in his own dark blood like a constellation of crimson against an ivory night sky. Her thoughts wander to that furious scar set in the center of his chest, twining tight around the feeling of it beneath her palm, how it closed with nothing more than her touch and her tears.

It's all he needs, she tells herself—still unsure of what she would rather have him feast upon; her corpse, or her suffering. Yet it feels all too much like the same horror bound up in one... a horror that doesn't quite instill the fear that it should.

The high pitched whistle of the kettle and the sound of a knock against the wooden archway sends her plummeting back to reality.

"That smells a-mazing!"

It's Odette, her hair up in a twist, clad in a sunset orange tank top and blue jeans, not hesitating to seat herself at the breakfast nook. "But don't you think you overdid it a little?"

"What do you mean?" Sadie begins to awaken from her daze as she sets the pot of *champorado* rice pudding onto the wooden place setting in the middle of the table, the full array of food hitting her senses. Looking down at the kitchen table and the lavish breakfast spread out before her, twelve eggs sunny-side up, a pot of garlic fried rice and a serving plate brimming with bacon, *longganisa* sausages and cucumber slices stare up at her as she lets out a sigh. "Oh." She wipes her hands on her apron. "I guess I got carried away."

Odette only laughs, taking a seat at the table, not hesitating to scoop up some eggs and garlic fried rice onto her plate. "I'm not complaining—and besides, now you'll have leftovers for days." Odette grins, leaning over the table to slide the windows open as Sadie sets down two coffee mugs.

"I missed this view!" Odette sing-songs, a longing written in her eyes as she gazes out beyond the capiz shell windows. Miles of jungle stretch out around the Hacienda, the canopy looming high above, housing a perpetual chorus of birdsong.

Sadie joins her at the table, willing herself to lift her fork and spear a piece of egg, but her appetite is marred by the memory of smoke-stained blood. Thankfully, Odette never gives her the chance to taste it. "Hey. Can I ask a question?"

She lowers her fork. "Sure."

"Remember when we used to daydream about all the places we'd go to? All the places we said we'd travel to together?"

Pressing her lips together, a strange pang rises in the pit of Sadie's stomach, not nostalgia, but dread.

"*Remember,* Sadie?" Odette smiles, her eyes persistently searching for a piece of the past Sadie so desperately doesn't want her to find. "I always wanted to go to France. See the Eiffel Tower and stuff my face with all the pastries from every pâtisserie in Paris. And that's exactly where my dad took me for my twenty-first." She giggles to herself at the memory. "But you... you always wanted to go to Italy—I remember now. You said you wanted to throw a coin into the Trevi Fountain."

Her voice is quiet, as the memory is upturned, spread out across her plate like a cadaver ready to be dissected. "I remember."

"Come on, Sadie. You were *fixated*—practically obsessed! You still have that coin, don't you? The one you said you'd wish on?"

"I don't think we remember it the same way." With her appetite gone, she pushes her plate away. "And yes... I still have the coin. Somewhere in the depths of my jewelry box, I think."

Odette pouts, "Hmph. You should fish it out. I got to live my dream. I want to help you live yours."

Sadie shoots her an incredulous look, rising to her feet and plucking the kettle from the stove.

"Easier said than done, Odette." She pours them each some coffee in an effort to quiet her thoughts, yet Odette persists.

"We could go travelling together just like we said we would." Odette's hand comes to rest on Sadie's, forcing them to lock eyes. "Just like we dreamed..."

There's a softness in Odette's eyes that so rarely ever showed, but the time and space between them has simply grown too cavernous. "As much as I'd love to, I can't just pack up and take a vacation whenever I want when there's the house to look after... And I'm the only one left who can."

"I'm sure it will still be standing when we get back. We can go sightseeing and exploring and oh don't even get me started on the shopping. It'll be so much fun just us girls against the—"

"—Odette!" Sadie rips her hand away.

Odette stops, her smile faltering.

"I'm sorry..." With a sigh, Sadie drops her shoulders, "I'll think about it, okay?" Sadie concedes, "I promise."

Satisfied, Odette sets down her fork and folds her hands over the rattan placemat. If there was one thing Sadie could count on Odette for, it was always her ability to keep the conversation as light as air; no matter the weight of the past. She smiles, letting it go. "Good. That's all I want." Helping herself to another portion, Odette pushes her shoulders back and her perfectly curled hair along with it. "Moving onto the next order of business—how did you sleep?"

Clearing her throat, Sadie scrapes her fork against the plate before answering, "Fine."

"Are you sure? Because I heard a whole lot of moving around last night. Who's the lucky guy, Sadie?" Odette smirks, a mischievous glint dancing in her eyes.

"What? I don't know what you're talking about," Sadie's shoulders fall at the terrible lie. Quickly she adds, "I don't sleep with the guests, you know."

"So he's a *guest* is he?" Odette raises her brow in accusation

"Yes." Sadie stares her down, carefully tip-toeing around every word. "You saw... him?"

Odette doesn't let up as she leans across the table, drumming her fingers over the table. "I caught a glimpse of him at the Taverna last night while you were talking to Isaiah..." A grin pulls up at her lips and Sadie looks away. "But oh boy, he sure is *some—*"

"*Shh!*" Sadie hisses, casting her eyes to the archway, where she's almost certain he'll materialize out of thin air.

"Oh please. No one's listening." Odette smiles.

She's right—there's no demon that emerges at the summoning of his name, and Sadie lets out the breath she's been holding.

"Now tell me why I saw you up and about late in the wee hours of the night, running from that guest bedroom back to your own?"

Sadie exhales sharply before conceding. "His name is Silas. He just came home late, and I showed him to his room. I was *not* in his room doing God knows whatever you're thinking."

Odette rolls her eyes, and Sadie presses her lips together, feeling a warmth descend upon her cheeks.

"Come on, that's all you're going to give me?" Odette shoots her a side-glance. With threatening gusto, she points her spoon in Sadie's direction, "If you're hiding something from me, you know I'll get to the truth sooner or later."

Rolling her eyes, Sadie pushes a piece of egg around with a butter knife, head in hand. "You really think there's anything going on in my life that's worth hiding? And besides..." Sadie casts her eyes down to her plate. "I'm with Sai."

Odette pauses, "Oh." She brings a finger to her rosy lips to wipe away a crumb that isn't there before continuing her sentence, "You and Sai."

Sadie lets the silence speak for her, knowing that Odette and Isaiah had always been closer. Closer in age, closer in personality, closer in every way Sadie could never be.

"When did you...?"

"After his dad died."

A sad smile pulls at the corners of Odette's lips, yet it doesn't seem to reach her eyes. "It's nice you have each other."

"We're all we have." Sadie drums her fingers over the table before turning to Odette, whose gaze is fixed to the trees beyond the window, the color of the sky reflected in her eyes.

Taking a sip of her coffee, Odette comes back out of her reverie with that same playfulness from earlier dancing over her features. Sadie brings her hands to her knees, thanking the fact that Odette isn't the kind to linger.

"Anyway," Odette rests her arms on the table, clearing her plate. "I'm going into town. I don't have anything to wear for the Festival."

Shit—the Festival.

Port Cante's annual Festival of *Our Lady* fast approaches. It honors the discovery of the town's revered relic of the Virgin Mary, falling right on the cusp of the rainy season. Before the downpour begins, Port Cante would parade the centuries-old wooden statue through town in traditional costume and colorful pageantry. It's a solemn procession, a sea of candles that takes the relic back to the spot she was fished from out of a nearby lagoon in reenactment of a miracle that occurred centuries ago.

"Neither." Sadie bites her lip, only for an idea to surface—her mother's Maria Clara would fit her with a few simple adjustments, but she shakes her head at the thought, cramming the idea back into the same box where it belongs. Untouched, unused, waiting for its owner to return.

"Well, all I was planning to do today was to go for a walk along the beachfront. Maybe you want to join?"

"I'd love to but—"

"—Spare me your excuses." Odette purses her lips, "I just thought I'd offer. I didn't want you to be alone in the house with such a beast of a *'guest'*. That's what friends are for, right?" She winks. "Unless, that's what you want."

"I have *work,* Odette." Sadie side steps her last remark, "We can go to Louisa's tomorrow."

"She's still running the tailor shop?

"Who else would?"

"I thought maybe you would've taken over by now," she laughs. "But this house has kept you busy it seems. And don't sweat it, I'll get out and stretch my legs without you." Odette concedes, "I'm just making sure you'll be okay here on your own."

"Of course I am." Sadie forces a smile. "Go ahead to the beach. I'll see you when I finish my shift, alright?"

"Sure thing," Odette chirps, taking both their plates to the kitchen sink.

By the time Sadie waves off the cab that whisks Odette away, that same, creeping dread comes back to nip at her thoughts. It's not a few minutes later when she's standing in front of the kitchen table, shoveling a portion of breakfast onto a plate and into a breakfast tray. Without giving herself time to back out, Sadie lets the thumping in her chest take the reins over her senses as she heads back up the stairs and down the empty hall in a flurry of silence. Only stopping to re-balance the breakfast tray, she finds herself standing alone outside her guest's door—*his* door. She knocks once.

"Hello...?"

Nothing.

"Hello?" Again she knocks, calling out a little louder before pressing her ear against the door, straining to hear any semblance of a noise within. Clearing her throat, she begins again, "I made breakfast... I don't know if you even eat... Do you?" She holds her breath, almost giving up when she hears a noise.

It's the sound of the door clicking, and with a phantom breeze it opens before her with a long creak. Peering into the stillness of the room, her gaze is caught on the billowing curtains and the striking blue of the morning sky beyond.

And then she sees him.

He's stretched out against the sheets, still bloodied and bare-chested, eyes pressed closed. He's almost exactly where she left him just the night before, only now the blood has set, the stains darkened, her satin robe hanging from the chair beside the nightstand, ruined beyond repair.

Letting out the breath she's been holding, she steps quietly towards the nightstand, setting the breakfast tray down as quietly as she can—but the rattle of cutlery gives her trembling fingers away. Heart seizing up, she turns to see a pair of tired eyes peering back at her from between the sheets.

"I—um, made breakfast..." she mutters, standing upright, twisting her fingers together. *What a great host you are,* Sadie curses her fumbling tongue. "It's still hot if you want to eat."

If it wasn't for the rise and fall of his chest, it would almost look like she's serving a corpse.

Letting out a sigh, Sadie turns on her heel to leave him be—that is until his voice calls her back.

"Wait."

And she does.

"Come here," he commands, his voice softened by the veil of sleep.

She obliges him, coming to a stop at his bedside. Though it's mid-morning, this room is a well of darkness, shadows swirling around the demon who inhabits it, the demon who sits up against the headboard with unreadable, watching eyes. He gestures to the chair, "Sit."

Taking in a deep breath, Sadie takes her bloodied robe from the chair's back, balling the ruined fabric up between her fingers in an attempt to keep her twisted nerves at bay before taking a seat beside him.

He turns his gaze away from hers, shutting his eyes closed once more, as if a great invisible chain keeps pulling him back to the lull of endless sleep. She can't help her eyes from wandering, something about his figure harkening back to those marble statues of antiquity, their once vivid colors stripped away from centuries of weathering, those paint flecks nothing more than a distant dream as they stand only in the marble they were born from.

Silas is as much a sculpture as any of those museum-pieces, forged by time, and cursed with immortality.

"What is it on your mind?" He opens his eyes, forcing her to meet him halfway. Drawing her eyes upwards, he's gazing back at her with an indiscernible emotion swirling in the dark behind his pupils. The question catches her off guard, and her breath is stuck in her throat as he stares straight into the depths of her, searching for the answers he draws to the surface. "I can see the questions burning on your tongue. Let them loose, spare me this silence. It's all I've had for company beneath the ground."

Sadie turns her eyes to her hands, clenching her fists around the ruined satin draped across her lap. She snaps herself out of this spell, forcing her knotted tongue to move. "Your scar... does it hurt?"

"Once healed, it's the same as any other scar. Wrought open— it's a pain like none other I've felt."

Sadie nods, shifting in her seat as quiet settles into the space between them once more.

"You have no reason to be afraid," he says, voice a richness that sends a shiver up her spine. "I have no need to cause any more suffering to a girl already consumed by it."

He's right, Sadie hates that it's the truth, hates that all he needs to do is catch the tears she can no longer contain to be sated.

"Silas..." she says his name, testing it out on her tongue, the taste as foreign as it is reminiscent of coal smoke. "How... how old are you?" Sadie asks, a strange mix of curiosity and dread brewing in the pit of her stomach.

"I was born in Seville, under the reign of Isabella and Ferdinand."

"Isabella and Ferdinand..." Sadie whispers, the memories of her father's history lessons stirring in her mind. "That—that must have been the 1400s... *Dyios,*" Sadie curses, taking in a deep breath, fighting to wrestle control of her thoughts. "You're over 600 years old."

"So I am."

The weight of time presses down upon her shoulders, his age, his life, his past—all of it a scorching desert to the grain of sand that is her paltry twenty-two years of existence.

"You must have seen so much of the world..." she whispers in quiet wonderment.

"I saw too much." Something dark passes behind the film of his eyes, and Sadie doesn't for a second claim to understand what it is as she continues onwards, curiosity filling her as she teeters on the edge of her seat.

The thought of who he was exactly sparks a thousand more questions—but she resolves to ask just one more. "What about your brother, Lorenzo?"

The muscle stretching out across his jaw stiffens almost imperceptibly—but Sadie catches it, the dark of his voice suffocating whatever curiosity that arose from his answers. "What of him?"

"W—what does he want from you?"

He contemplates the answer for a moment, as if even speaking the words is an act of summoning. "Nothing he hasn't already taken."

A thorn-tipped silence settles between them, and Sadie doesn't press any further in fear of opening up any other old wounds. Taking a breath, Sadie opts instead to steer the silence towards last night.

"Our deal..." She pulls him back to the present, to this Hacienda, to her. "Tell me what you know about my mom."

He casts his eyes around the room, taking it in—the sights, the sounds, the smells of the waking world. "She unearthed me," he begins, sitting up against the head board. "For a brief moment I saw her standing over my grave, that necklace in her hand. And when she placed it against my chest, I returned to the darkness. There must have been some enchantment on it, some kind of seal to put me back to sleep."

Sadie bites down on the inside of her cheek, stewing over his words in an attempt to fight away the memories of her mother, to fight away the thought of *why*.

"And when I found you—when I took her necklace back, I broke it?"

He stays silent, and Sadie takes it for affirmation. With her mind beginning to fog, Sadie twists her fingers in her lap. "You said you saw her—what did you see, exactly?"

"I remember one thing. The winds rattling the Hacienda's walls... A storm was brewing."

A storm—Sadie's heart beats faster.

"That was the day she died, it must have been." Whipping around to face him, she fumbles over her words, "What else did you see? I need to know."

"I told you," his voice is an even calm. "She woke me, only to put me back under. And all I remember next is you. That is all."

With a deep sigh, Sadie releases the tension from her shoulders. She can't help but feel he's telling the truth. But this moment of quiet is broken by the sound of his voice. "Now for my side of the deal..."

She furrows her brows. "I did what you told me to. The deal is done."

"Not quite." He swings his legs over the side of the bed, leaning forward to close the distance between them. "This wound is just a symptom."

She falters at the sudden closeness between them, forcing the words out through her teeth, "And what does that mean?"

"The deal is not complete until you find the cure."

Shaking her head, she fights against the swirling shadows closing in on her as he draws ever closer. "I can't cure a scar."

"Then you can help me learn who inflicted it."

He's but a hair's width away, and in the quiet she can hear his breath, his pulse, the sound of his heart. And it's soon joined by the feeling of phantom fingers around her chin, tilting her gaze upwards with a gentility that can only be the wind.

"How could I possibly do that?" His closeness is intoxicating, the summer heat her only sobriety.

"It's simple..." He peers into the very depths of her, searching for her darkest shadows, her deepest depths. "Just let me drink."

He wants your tears.

"Until I have recovered... until I have had enough."

Sadie screws her eyes shut tight, attempting to avert her gaze from his, but it's too late. The darkness behind his eyes has already seared the very soul sleeping within her bones. Sadie's voice is nothing but a whisper, "And how much is enough?"

"Until there's not a tear left in those eyes." The beginnings of a wicked smile pulls up at his lips—the words so gentle yet their meaning wrapped up in everything she'd been taught to fear, to run from, to spite. But it's so difficult to see Hell in his eyes when all Sadie can see is her reflection.

As clear, as plain, as simple as day.

She shudders at his touch, and the moment he senses this, he withdraws, leaving her with a gasp of a breath on her lips as the cold fills his stead.

"Only you can help me understand why I did not die," he sits back, the sheets twisting across his waist as he turns his gaze over to the jungle canopy shrouding the Hacienda in speckled shadow, "And only I can help you learn why your mother did."

Her heart stutters at the deal laid out before her, at the contract she must sign with her grief, her suffering, her every tear.

Thinking of that cold, unfeeling sea that rages beneath her mother's feet on the cliffs in that same, tear-streaked nightmare, she takes a deep breath at the thought of it ebbing, perhaps even growing to stillness. The image sends a ripple of lightness through her, and perhaps it's hope, perhaps it's naiveté, but all she knows is she'd do anything to be rid of that nightmare, anything to be rid of that storming sea that plagues her every sleepless night. Even if it means giving it all away to him.

Sadie concedes, flinching at what horrors may come next, "Okay. I'll do it. I'll help you. You can... *drink*." The last word leaves her lips in a shiver, silent disbelief filling her veins at her own agreement.

A strong gust of wind washes through the room, stealing away with it all the hope Sadie has that he's nothing but a nightmare. The scent of the jasmine blooms are as real as his hair tousled by the wind, as real as the reflection of the sky in the dark of his eyes, as real as the shadow of her body on the skin of his scarred chest.

"So be it."

She waits for contact, for devastation, for his killing blow—but it simply never comes.

Silas nods once, the tick of the clock strung up against the wall beckoning Sadie back to reality, back to her life, her job, and the island on the edge of the world. But for a reason she can't fathom, she stays a moment longer in his presence. "That's it?"

"Hm?" He raises a brow.

"There's no contract? No handshake? No blood compact?"

Amusement dances over his features, and in a single pulse of her heart, he's captured her hand in his own as he looms over her, a stack of smoke and shadow consuming her vision, her senses, her every thought.

"Is that what you want? My mark?" He tilts his head forward, as if he's studying the flush of blood that rushes through every capillary beneath her cheeks, his fingers tracing across the veins beneath her upturned palm. "Do you want it as a scorch mark on your skin?" his voice grows dark, dripping with smoke, "Or perhaps as an ache inside as I split you in two for my pleasure?" he draws ever closer, phantom fingers trailing across the line of her jaw, a smile forming and faltering on his lips. "Hm," he hums. "I am a demon. But I am no beast."

And he pulls away abruptly, leaving her blood-drunk and breathless.

The phantom scent of his black blood on her skin forces her to rise from her seat, wrapping her arms around herself as that crimson stain resurfaces across her fingers. His scent stings her senses; his smoke, his fire, all of it as inescapable as the deal that's written beneath her skin, etched into the underside of her veins.

But her buzzing phone in her pocket draws a gasp from her lips as she scrambles to pick it up—Maria's name lights up her screen, her voice a frantic jumble as she practically yells into the phone.

"Sadie! Can you come in early? There was some kind of accident up the road and Hector left with Isaiah to go help out. It will just be you and I—I'll make it worth your while!"

Silas rises from the sheets, Sadie's eyes widening at the sight. What remains of his clothes hangs from a long decayed waistband that threatens to destroy any last slivers of decency with every passing moment.

"Uh—no need, Maria." Her eyes are fixed on the demon that passes her by without so much as a second glance, stopping at the sprawling bookshelf at the far side of the room. "I'll help out."

"You are the best." Maria sighs, "When do you think you can get here?"

Silas runs his fingers across the sun-faded spines, the image of a half-dressed demon a distraction Sadie never thought she'd ever have to witness as she forces herself to answer the woman on the other end of the line. "I'll be there as soon as I can *tita*," Sadie assures her before hanging up.

Silas' attention is fully captured by the selection of books laid out before him, and with a deep breath she slips her phone back into her pocket. Stopping arm's length away, she attempts to pull him back to the present, the dried blood clinging to the skin of his chest yet another reminder that this is no ordinary guest—Silas no ordinary man.

"We should get you cleaned up..."

But his mind is elsewhere.

He plucks out a book at random, voice colored with curiosity, "Do those volumes belong to you?"

"They were my—" she stops herself mid-sentence, correcting her course. "Yes. They're mine. You can read them all if you like."

Silas leafs through the hardback's contents, utterly engrossed. Spying the title etched into the spine, Sadie sees *Greek Tragedies*.

"Silas..." she whispers, his name no stranger to say on her tongue than the first time, "I have to go."

He looks up from between the pages.

"But I can't leave you like this," she sighs. "Come with me." Turning on her heel, Sadie digs out a few of her dad's old clothes from the boxes in the closet before making her way out into the hallway and into the guest bathroom where a bathtub that's not quite big enough for a demon sits in against the tiled wall. With no hesitation, she plugs the drain and turns the faucet, allowing the steam of the hot water to fill up the space between them.

Turning over her shoulder, Sadie finds him leaning against the open door frame with the same book still firmly between his fingers. "Water flows freely from this mechanism?"

Sadie nods, "Indoor plumbing." She swallows the lump in her throat, his black eyes watching her with all the curiosity in the world. "It's great."

He says nothing, and Sadie takes the chance to hand him the bundle of her dad's old clothes before dropping her arms limply at her sides. "This should do for now."

Silas' eyes flicker down to the old clothes in his hands, along with the bloodied mess of her robe caught in the same bundle. "I apologize for this... I will find you another."

She almost wants to laugh at the absurdity of it all, but at his sentiment she smiles softly instead. "That's okay. I'll just make a new one."

"Ah. So that is your profession?"

Sadie shakes her head, "I wish it was. Right now it's just a hobby."

"Then what is it you do?"

"I serve drinks." Sadie shrugs her shoulders. "And I have to go do that right now." Shifting her weight, she toys with the sleeves of her cardigan as Silas' eyes search over the planes of her face. Longing for anything to fill the silence, she stutters, "I—I'll pick up some clothes when I'm out. I'm sure I'll find something for you at one of the shops in town."

Silas pushes off the doorframe, standing at full height. Sadie can't help but skim her eyes over the length of his body as he towers over her so easily.

With a quiet breath she whispers under her breath, "At least I hope I do..."

Setting the bundle of clothes and the book down on the stool by the tub, he makes his way towards Sadie with what can only be predator's gaze in his eyes. "There is something changed about you." In two long strides he's closed the distance between them both.

Sadie feels the back of her knees hit the edge of the bathtub, her heart jumping in her chest.

"W—what are you talking about?"

"You look different." He's standing flush close, Sadie craning her neck to meet his searching gaze. "Oh," he tilts his head back, eyes roaming over her body in realization before an amused smile spreads over his features. "Unlike last night... you have decided to dress."

Sadie feels a searing wetness trickling down her legs, and with a gasp she turns to switch off the faucet as hot water overflows from the tub she's backed up against.

Stepping to the side, she wills her heartbeat to still as she fights the heat that's seeped into her skin. *It's just the steam,* she tells herself, it's anything but his eyes, his presence, that wicked smile.

Fighting the blush of her skin, she wraps her arms around herself before turning to leave. "Just... *please* promise me you'll stay here, in the Hacienda. Don't follow me or anything... just stay in your room until I get back. Don't take a single step outside of that door. And don't let anyone see you."

Sadie stops at the threshold, his voice pulling her attention back towards him, back towards the lilt of his voice. "There is a weight in my chest, attached to a chain that lays in your hands," the book is already between his fingers once more, leafing through the pages before he rests his eyes on her one last time, "Break the chain, and you'll be free of me."

She commits his words to memory, the steamy haze of the bathroom threatening to lull her thoughts to nothing but the thought of the demon within.

"But in the meantime—I will make myself at home..." Contentedness colors his voice, "There is so much to catch up on."

With something that resembles relief, Sadie shuts the door behind her, never daring to turn back.

7

WITH A DIRTY RAG IN HAND, Sadie obsessively scrubs at a persistent stain on the bar top of the Taverna, trying her best to ignore Maria's hawk eyes scrutinizing her every move.

Don't mind her. Just clean.

But the sound of her heavy footfall makes it harder and harder to do so.

Just focus and—

"So what brings Odette back home?" Maria's bulging stomach is the first thing Sadie feels as she butts her way into the narrow space behind the counter. Turning to face her heavily pregnant boss, Sadie wipes her hands on the tea towel tucked into her waist apron. "She hasn't forgotten about us, it seems." One hand comes to rest on her hip, the other rubbing circles over her belly. "Even though she didn't bring us any *pasulubong.*"

Internally, Sadie rolls her eyes—the prospect of receiving goodies from Spain of more import than the living, breathing girl here for the first time in years. "It's not exactly a vacation." Sadie lets out a sigh, hyper-focusing on that same stain clinging desperately to the counter top. Maybe it's just the pregnancy hormones, but Sadie swears Maria can see right through her. "It's complicated."

"Come on, Sadie. That can't be all you give me." Maria leans over, snatching the cleaning rag from Sadie's fingers. "This is *Dominic Arias* we're talking about. You have to pay the toll."

"You know how I feel about that..." Sadie crosses her arms against her chest.

The toll, as Maria and her gossip of a sister Louisa affectionately called it, is the price any patron must pay in order to sneak a free drink from the bar. Rumor, heresy, the smallest morsel of anything juicy would be enough to satisfy Maria. And within the confines of a small island town, there's no shortage.

She grins, much to Sadie's dismay. "They say it's bad luck to deny a pregnant woman, you know."

Sadie shifts her weight before conceding. "Fine....They had a disagreement."

"Oh please, disagreement my ass!" She leans one arm against the bar top. "We all know how hot-headed that man can get."

Sadie stiffens at the memory that resurfaces, a memory of her mother turning Dominic out of her dad's wake, denying him entrance into the house he helped restore. Sadie can still remember the feeling of the doorframe pressing against her cheek as she craned her head to hear their argument just outside the front door. Mama never yelled, never screamed—but that was the only time Sadie ever remembered feeling the rage coursing through her veins, her blood. She remembers wondering if that same fury ran through her, too.

"How dare you show your face around here?! Leave or—"

"—Or what? I built this house, Natalia. If it weren't for me, you'd still be living in your shitty little family shack.... You have all this because of me!"

If it was rage running through her mama's blood, it was something else entirely running through Dominic's—something she couldn't name. Something she didn't want to.

But Maria is waiting for more, and the only way she'll lay off is if she has something to sink her teeth into.

"She... she stole his car." Sadie conjures up the first lie she can think of that will satisfy Maria. "And she crashed it."

Maria's mouth opens wide. "No... Not the Porsche? Don't tell me it was the Porsche."

Sadie nods.

"*Ohhhh*. Well, no wonder she's hiding all the way out here."

"Emphasis on *hiding*. If anyone asks for her at the bar—or anywhere—tell them you know nothing."

"Of course." Maria waves her off dismissively, still clearly wrapping her mind around the loss of such wealth. "She always was a careless one, that girl," she tuts, clearly satisfied with this tidbit, her mind already wandering to the next unsuspecting link in her perpetual chain of Chinese whispers.

"Careless is one way to put it." Sadie mutters, taking the cleaning rag back into her possession.

Maria makes her way to the door that leads to the kitchen, hanging back at the doorframe. "I'm gonna take my break now, my feet are killing me. Hector will be back later to help me close up so there's no need for you to stay any later than usual."

Sadie waves her off, "Sure. Go relax."

Maria promptly disappears into the kitchen, doubtlessly making a beeline for her phone.

The rest of Sadie's shift passes with the usual hustle and bustle that comes with the height of tourist season. Returning to that familiar autopilot serving drink after drink—Sadie almost has the chance to forget about the Hacienda, and what awaits her when night falls.

The sun is only just beginning to set, and oftentimes the Taverna would empty out as the amateur photographers would begin to set up capturing that *perfect Port Cante sunset*, leaving her with a lull in service, some space to breathe. The bell above the front doors chimes as Sadie spies the last remaining troupe of backpackers shuffling out of the Taverna with their cameras at the ready. The door clicks shut behind them, leaving Sadie to an empty bar.

Turning on her heel, Sadie leans back against the bar top, relaxing her shoulders at the prospect of a moment's rest—only for the bell's chime to crush the hope out of her.

Slowly, she turns, drawing her eyes across the eerie emptiness of the bar up towards the figure making its way across the hardwood floors, a shadow of a man in spite of the fiery orange glow of the setting sun spilling in from the windows.

It's him.

It was just last night when she felt those same pair of eyes peering deep into her soul.

His brother.

As tall as he stands, he's still a ways shorter than Silas, his dark hair slicked back to resemble those silver screen leading men of old. His clothes are markedly modern, sleek in tones of jewel blue and charcoal black, and unlike his brother, there is no stiffness in the way he moves. He possesses an ease of movement that could only mean that he is here, in his element amongst humans, a wolf in sheep's clothing.

Lorenzo.

It's in the dark beneath their eyes that Sadie can see a resemblance between him and his brother—that hint of reflective film over his pupils concealing the fire that lurks beneath.

Never one to stop and stare, Sadie can't help but make an exception as he makes his way towards his one objective: her.

Transfixed to the floorboards beneath her, the room moves in slow motion as he comes to stop at the other side of the bar, just arm's reach away, resting his hands over the wooden top. He peers around the room, regarding the surroundings the same way a child with a magnifying glass stares down a mound of ants before setting it all ablaze.

"So when you're not playing hostess, this is where you work?"

Whatever seal he places on her tongue breaks the instant he asks the question, and she feels a fire taking root in her throat.

"Why are you here?" she demands, her heartbeat loud in her ears, almost as deafening as his voice echoing inside her skull.

"I'm just another customer. So relax." He raps his knuckles twice against the bar top before speaking, "I want a drink." His eyes are an endless, piercing darkness that Sadie wants nothing more than to turn away from—but she simply can't.

"What do you drink?"

"Tequila."

Sadie whips around to the shelf, snatching the amber colored bottle out from the array of drinks behind her, taking a shot glass out from beneath the counter.

"Ah," he interrupts her, holding up two fingers.

Sadie clenches her jaw, "I don't drink."

He scoffs, "What are you talking about? Of course you do." He tips his chin down, motioning for her to grab another glass in a way that makes her skin crawl. She clenches her fists tight around the one shot glass, an inexplicable pull to draw up another one washing over her. Panic sets into her nerves as her body acts of its own accord—bending to his will. She dips down to retrieve another glass as he drums his fingers over the bar top, languishing in the quick pulse of her heart.

"There we go. Not so hard, is it Sara?"

The way he rolls her name over his tongue sends a ripple of dread through her. *He's just another customer,* his words ring hollow as she begrudgingly sets the two glasses down in front of her, pouring them both to the brim. But when she rakes her eyes back up to his face and his piercing, watching eyes—she knows he is anything but.

"Don't ever call me that."

His eyes flick down to the shot glass before her, motioning for her to drink.

"I'll call you what I need to call you," he smirks. "And as long as you hate the sound of my voice saying that name of yours, then the choice is easy."

The bar is all but empty now, the tables long abandoned for the fiery sunset engulfing the sky, glimpses of the day's final light slowly fading with each passing second. Seconds passing like eternity under this demon's gaze.

"Go on," he commands. "Drink."

With simmering blood, Sadie takes the shot between her fingers, gripping it tight and throwing it down in a hurried rush. As the liquid burns through her throat, he takes the other shot the same as hers without flinching.

Lorenzo drinks the amber liquid down, yet the smile that forms on his lips gives Sadie all the inclination that it's not just the tequila he's savoring on his tongue, but something so much sweeter, wrapped up in all her saccharine suffering.

Silas' hunger for her grief she could deal with, even claim to understand, but Lorenzo she can't forgive. His power lies not in his physical size, nor in sheer strength like his brother, but in the veneer of normalcy, even charm, that he can conjure up with a single wolfish smile. And the fact sends a shiver through her.

Sadie digs her fingers into the flesh of her palms as he takes a seat on the barstool, leaning in closer over the bar, his breath laced with alcohol and nicotine—but overpowering it all is the scent of hellish char. "Listen. I'm not going to waste my time. And I take it you don't want to waste yours."

The sky outside casts his face in an angry glow of color that matches the rush of blood running quick through Sadie's veins, seizing her tongue and willing her to speak, "Then you'll answer my question."

He twirls the empty glass between his fingers, the metal ring wrapped around his pinky finger clinking against it with every rotation. "And you'll answer mine."

Sadie licks her lips, her throat feeling suddenly dry.

"Fine."

He sweeps his fingers through the air, motioning for her to proceed.

Choosing her words carefully, she speaks with gritted teeth, "What do you want with Silas?"

"Is that truly the question you want to answer?" His eyes flash a lighter shade, "What *I* want with my brother? Perhaps you should be asking yourself what it is he truly wants with *you*."

The faintest traces of coal-smoke dance across her senses as she falters momentarily beneath his gaze, "I—I want to know what reason brought you here, to him. You hate each other, yet here you are. After all this time... Why now?"

"Ah." He presses his lips together, "What and why—that's two questions. It's your turn now."

Furrowing her brows, she resists, a mixture of defiance and tequila steadying her rapid-fire heart, "But he said that you—"

Laughter falls from his lips, and Sadie frowns at the interruption.

"Whatever *he* whispers to you is nothing but a fantasy of his own making... empty wishes, empty dreams." He leans in closer, voice dripping velvet dark, "You are nothing more than a vessel upon which he feeds."

Sadie says nothing, forcing the fear crawling at the base of her throat from rising.

Satisfied, he tips his chin downwards, "Silas can turn a dream into a nightmare faster than you have the chance to realize you're even asleep, and you'll never know the difference. All you'll know is you're gone from this world in the blink of an eye. Whatever he promises you, it leads only to one road. Your ruin."

Speechless, her throat runs painfully dry as she allows the weight of his words to press down upon her heart.

"No matter the ecstasy he promises." He narrows his eyes, savoring every twitch of movement, every shiver of fear he strikes inside her soul. "You will become nothing more than a taste of human agony for him to devour. A sliver of a droplet in a sea of suffering he's already consumed... a sea you'll drown in, all the same."

"I—I..." she sputters, fumbling over the words sitting on the tip of her tongue, hating the fact that he has this effect on her.

"Look at that." The dark lull of his words pulls her closer towards him, a wicked smirk on his lips. "It seems you're already in the water."

He and Silas truly look alike in this light, eyes inflamed with a hunger they can't help, a hunger they can never slake. Here Lorenzo stands, his appearance unweathered, his appearance ageless, yet one trait sets him sharply apart from Silas—the lash of cruelty in his eyes that belongs to him and him alone.

"When you reach the depths." He runs his fingers through his ink black hair. "Only then will you see whether you'll sink, or swim." A chuckle escapes his lips, his voice lowering to a near-whisper. "After all, he always did have a weakness for your kind..."

Weakness? Sadie's heart begins to race at the implication. "What do you mean?"

"Ah, ah, ah," he sing songs. "It's my turn." He gives her a smile that doesn't reach his wicked eyes, and Sadie is rendered speechless beneath his gaze. "Since I'm feeling generous, I'll not demand an answer. Not yet, anyway..." He rises from the barstool, wrapping his thumb and forefinger around the rim of the shot glass. "Of all the demons you choose to trust, are you sure you want it to be him?"

The muscle that runs from his wrist up to his forearm protrudes as he presses the rim of the glass hard against the bar top with enough force to make it shatter—but it never does.

Instead, a small ring of blue flame is all Lorenzo leaves behind. Sadie is alone on the floor once more, the sun plunging closer and closer towards the horizon, taking daylight along with it.

Lorenzo's words repeat in her mind as she stands, dumbstruck in the deepening shadows of the bar. But the flame subsides, leaving only a lingering smoke that calls out for her attention. Looking down she sees a scorch mark where the shot glass should have shattered—a blackened ring encasing the mark of something that doesn't belong. Running her fingers over the bumps and grooves, it's undoubtedly the shape of a rose surrounded by swirling thorns burnt into the wood.

If Silas was telling the truth, and it really is her suffering that nourishes him, her suffering that keeps him sane, then just how much agony has Lorenzo devoured to warrant his ageless appearance?

Her thoughts rush, converging upon the realization that it's not the suffering he's seen, but the suffering he's inflicted. Not by his hands, but with his words, his voice, his charming smile. It's all the allure of a rose and its velveteen petals, only for the viperous thorns to strike the moment it's too late.

Espinosa, the name they both share, wrapped up in the scorch mark beneath her fingertips—those jagged, piercing vines not one last attempt at intimidation, but something worse.

A warning.

The overhead lights flicker on as the sound of the backdoor plucks Sadie from her thoughts and back to reality. When she looks at the bar top again, the mark of the rose is gone. Maria reappears and without so much as a second glance, continues on with the night's toil. A toil Sadie plunges herself into gladly, dreading every tick of the clock—dreading what waits for her back at the Hacienda the moment her shift ends.

Hector arrives shortly after Sadie's shift ends, and she doesn't hesitate in snatching up her bag up from behind the counter, yelling out a hurried *bye Maria* over her shoulder as she pushes the back door open, rushing out to meet the fresh air. Stopping beside her bike propped up against the back alley of the Taverna, she takes it all in—the waves, the beach, and the salty air.

All of it washes over her in a tide she wishes would take her out into the dark abyss, but the thought of Silas reigns even over that. He's as much as part of the Hacienda as the narra wood floorboards, his body the brick and the mortar, his eyes the carved panels sprawled out across the ceiling of her bedroom—and the Hacienda is all she has left. It's her home, her past, her everything.

Lorenzo's words dance around the knot of dread pulling taut at her twisted nerves.

"Of all the demons you choose to trust, are you sure you want it to be him?"

And the thought of returning to him, to the place she dares call home, is all too suffocating.

8

GRIPPING THE HANDLEBARS TIGHTER, Sadie takes a turn into the heart of town, the heel of her shoe skidding across the dirt road as she brakes just in front of Port Cante's ever watchful church, where Father Agustin's modest little house sits adjacent, nestled alongside a grove of glossy banana palms.

Craning her neck to see if there's anyone home, she hops off her bike and parks it by the usual bench at the front of the church, the moon shimmering like a pearl, casting dancing shadows over those rustling, split-leaved fronds.

Spotting a movement amidst the well-tended garden that wraps tightly around the front of Agustin's house, it must mean that he's there, and the church is empty. Taking the opportunity, she makes a bee line for the entrance. The sweet relief of incense, candle wax and solitude washes over her as she steps through the threshold and into the dim-lit dark.

What do you think you'll find in here? Sadie scolds herself as she breathes in the comforting scent of sandalwood and candle smoke that beckons her further inside, the answer to her question etched into the black behind her eyelids.

There's not a soul in sight, and Sadie thanks the fact that evening mass has long since ended, the congregation dispersed. Yet in spite of the welcome solitude, the tension in her body remains as her eyes drift over the whitewashed walls, the gilded pulpit, the near-black confessional booth and up to the high arched ceilings. Her nerves only yield when she sees those tear-stained eyes once more. Perched behind the altar and enshrined behind a wall of glass, Sadie's gaze is fixed to those perpetually painted tears staining splintered, wooden cheeks.

It's her—Our Lady of Port Cante.

Port Cante's very own image of the Virgin Mary, *Nuestra Señora de Cante;* a wooden statue standing half the length of Sadie's body, carved in wood that's been weathered, waterlogged and simply withstood the test of time.

Legend boasts of a local girl finding the statue washed up in the shallows of a lagoon not far from here after a monster of a storm. The survival of the image was of course deemed miraculous by the church, her deliverance through the stormy seas to these distant shores all the sign they needed from their God across the sea.

The friars overseeing the mission in Port Cante had nothing to lose and everything to gain in ensuring this unassuming statue become so much more than the weathered piece of wood it is. They knelt at her feet in reverence, venerating her as a symbol of one of the first Marian apparitions in the Philippines, a symbol of their God's reign, His rule, His conquest.

This was back in the 1600s, as Sadie's father always recounted, in the time where apparitions were as real as rain, where saints could converse with Christ and demons whisper into the ears of common man. It was the time where that which could not be explained was attributed either to God or the Devil—and what didn't belong to one, was claimed by the other.

If the statue of Our Lady came to Port Cante as a missive from God; a call to honor sacrifice and suffering, then Silas was sent to reap just that.

Shrugging off her cardigan, she ties it around her waist as she walks onwards down the lonely aisle, feeling so small beneath the splendor, the size, the vastness of the altar peering down at her from the end of the church. Sadie doesn't let herself stop until she's standing at the guarded rail that separates Our Lady's shrine and altar from the pews.

The thought of Silas' presence back at the Hacienda weighs heavy, forcing her to bow under the burden as she presses her eyes closed, breathing in the silence. Parting her lips, she grips the railing tighter, a whisper falling at Our Lady of Cante's feet.

"I don't know what to do anymore, mama." Tears threaten the corner of her eyes, but she fights against them. "Why did you have to go? I... I miss you." A single tear escapes, landing in a droplet over her knuckles as she grips the bannister tighter. "Why did you leave me?"

But the sound of a door creaking open and shut plunges her back to reality. Snapping her eyes over to the side door overlooking the altar of Our Lady, Sadie swipes her tears away, straightening up as she sees Father Agustin making his way over to where she stands, hand raised in greeting.

"Sadie," he chirps, a smile spread across his features.

Slowly, she raises a hand to mirror him. "Hi Father."

That same smile falters as he stops on the opposite side of the guard railing—he can see the wetness of her eyes, and Sadie knows it's too late for her to turn back. "Nice to see you here," he says quietly.

Pulling her hands away from the railing, Sadie folds them over her chest, scrambling to retreat behind her wall of solitude. "I'm just stopping by. I should probably head—"

"—No, no. Stay a moment." He insists, his eyes softening just enough to force her to listen. "I've been meaning to come and visit, but I haven't had the chance. It's been a while since the last time we spoke, no? But I digress. How are you and Isaiah?"

Sadie presses her lips together before offering a feeble answer, hoping it's enough to satisfy him. "We're...we're good. He's been busy with Odette, and I've been busy with the house."

Agustin shifts his weight, tilting his head to the side with watching eyes. He'd always been good at seeing straight through her, and Sadie could never fault him for it. "Sadie, I can see you're troubled. What's wrong, *anak?*"

Only her mother ever called her *anak—my child,* and she had to admit the comfort it brought her, hearing that term of endearment she'll never hear from anyone else. "No," she shakes her head, forcing a smile. "Nothing's wrong. I just thought I'd drop by after work."

"There's someone new at the house isn't there?" he asks, his eyes piercing in that way that never feels like prying—only compassion, always compassion.

Her heart skips a beat, but she stills it with a measured breath. "Yes... there is."

"Hm." He lifts his head, "You know... there is always another path."

Puzzled, she furrows her brows. "What do you mean?"

"The path your parents took does not have to be the path you follow. What your father did, what your mother wanted—a guest house, a destination—that does not have to be what you dedicate your life to. I can see the Hacienda weighing heavily upon your shoulders... just as it did your mother."

Sadie lets out a sigh at this same old tired point of conversation, "Even if I wanted to sell it, between the headache of dealing with the National Historical Commission and the paperwork, I don't know what I'd do without it."

His eyes are soft when she turns her eyes to his, "*Anak,* you are always welcome beneath my roof. The offer still stands, like I told you a year ago. And I know Isaiah would welcome it."

There were always strings attached to that offer, strings that form the expectation of a gold band, strings that feel too much like vines of thorns.

"I appreciate it, Father. I really do. But it's my home..." The sound of those words fumbling from her lips doesn't feel quite right, Sadie knowing it's a lie she only wishes were a truth. "My only home."

Moving in with them was a step she had never committed herself to taking—why should she? Not when there's still the scent of mama's old perfume on the sheets, hints of her father in every preserved detail of the Hacienda. But even that comfort is threatened by the shadow of a demon, a shadow that envelops her mind, her soul, her beating heart.

The silence slips between them like the ocean wind that whistles through the trees outside, and Sadie fills it without thought. "Father...can I ask you a question?"

His gaze softens, never one to stray from a lamb searching for its shepherd's guiding hand. "Of course, *anak*." Unlatching the gate of the guard railing, he crosses the boundary to stand at Sadie's side. "What is it?"

Sadie turns her eyes to the wooden statue of Our Lady, not daring to see his reaction for the question she lets leave her lips.

"What do you know about demons?"

Father Agustin's gait stiffens. "Why do you ask?"

Letting out a breath, she immediately regrets ever mentioning it. "No, it's alright, just forget—"

"—No, no, let me answer," he insists, straightening his posture. "It's a good question."

"I... I've just been having this... nightmare." To say Silas is nothing but a nightmare is an understatement, yet she continues on with the lie, wishing that everything that's unfolded in her life is just that—nothing but a fleeting nightmare.

"Tell me, Sadie."

She doesn't know whether or not its relief that spreads through her as she unburdens herself, but all she knows is she can't hold onto it any longer. "I've been having the same nightmare for a whole year. I'm standing on the cliffs, the day of that same monsoon... I reach out to pull mama back from the edge and it's always too late. But lately, something's changed. I don't dream of mama anymore. All I see is darkness. All I see are shadows. And there's one shadow that follows me everywhere I go. I can't hide from it, I can't escape it, and everywhere I turn I see it—*him*—there in the corner of my eye... Something tells me that shadow is a demon. But I don't know anymore. It just feels all too real."

It all sounds so ridiculous. Ridiculous because it's the truth, ridiculous because she still wants it to be a lie, ridiculous because Father Agustin takes her every word for gospel.

"It is real, Sadie." He presses a pensive finger to his lips, "That shadow, that demon... it's real."

Sadie feels her heart constrict in her chest, yet all she can do is focus on the peering eyes of the wooden statue set up high over them both.

"Evil is tangible. It's what you are seeing in your nightmares, in your dreams. That shadow, that demon that's following you—it's asking to be let in, to enter you, to consume you..." She swears a pained expression passes over his features before he turns away to face Our Lady. "But there's only one way to overcome it."

He turns to face her, eyes boring a hole through her skin as he resumes the role of fervent preacher once more.

"You must suffer."

"Suffer?" she echoes, the word twisting a knot in her belly as she wrings her hands together.

"Your suffering is what will bring you closer to Him, closer to God. It is what He did for us, and it is all we can do, to return the favor... All suffering is a test of his making, to test your faith, your will, your obedience."

His jaw clenches almost imperceptibly, but Sadie catches it before he relaxes his shoulders.

"And you are an obedient girl." He smiles. "You always have been. Your silence has always been your greatest strength... your suffering makes you so much *stronger*."

With a fleeting waft of sandalwood and candlewax, she catches the scent of the words written between the lines, the judgment left unspoken.

Stronger than mama was.

Sadie bites down on the inside of her cheek, heartbeat quickening at the implication, yet Agustin never allows her the chance to verbalize it. "Listen to me, *anak*. There are two facets of humanity. The mortal flesh, and the immortal soul. What the flesh cannot see, the soul will feel."

Sadie needs not turn her eyes to face the statue of Our Lady. In her periphery she sees her tear-streaked cheeks forever glinting beneath the glass of her perpetual tomb.

"What you cannot see in the waking world, your soul will see when you are asleep." He emphasizes, "Dreams often reveal to us what we cannot see in the day to day of our lives. So these dreams of yours are trying to communicate something to you..." He clasps his hands together.

"Then what are they saying?"

"That the greatest test is yet upon you. Will you surrender? Or will you live, and suffer it through?"

She falls quiet, the weight of his words settling upon her shoulders in the shadow of expectation laid out for her, yet all she can feel are those monsoon winds whipping at her skin, and the phantom of her mother standing on the precipice, unable to carry that same burden any longer.

"Are you listening, Sadie?"

She wills herself to face him, to answer, to play the obedient girl. "Yes, Father... I'm listening."

He nods once, satisfied, his eyes becoming unfocused as he looks up towards the altar, voice soft—reverent. "Do you know what they call those that Christ visits in their dreams?"

The wind howls against the banana palm grove surrounding the backside of the church, before Agustin answers his own question. "Saints... they're called saints."

His words catch her off guard, and she stares blankly at the altar and its crucifix. Her eyes run over that broken body, outstretched, nailed and pierced in perpetual agony. But the longer she stares, the more those wounds against that wooden, bloodied cross morph and twist, the wound no longer at his side—but sprawled out across his chest in a gaping, black maw. She casts her gaze up to his eyes, and the face staring back at her in torment looks too much like a demon.

Suffering will bring you closer to Him.

It goes for them both, and Sadie shakes away the thought.

"I need to go—I've taken up too much of your time." Sadie takes a step backwards, ready to make her escape, only for Father Agustin to keep her a moment longer.

"Just remember one thing, Sadie." He peers down at her with solemn eyes, features etched in a seriousness that transcends his priestly calling, entering the realm that only her parents ever reigned. Here, now, Agustin is just a father to a girl desperately in need of one. "Trust in Him."

Him?

Her heart skips a beat, and she almost wants to search his face to make sure of who he's referring to, but she never gives herself the chance as she gives him a curt nod before briskly walking down the aisle and out into the open air. Immediately she's greeted with all the sweet fragrance of the plumeria blooms flanking this hallowed ground from all sides.

The dirt road streets of Port Cante stretch out ahead of her, and peeking through the bowing banana palms is the abyssal black of the ocean just up ahead. A sea breeze beckons her forward, calling out for her to enter the water, to let the waves wash over her and swallow her whole in its endless, rolling tide.

But the ripple of laughter from a cluster of stores ahead breaks the spell, and Sadie makes her way through the plaza, finding her bike exactly where she left it against the same wooden bench.

Tying her hair back into a low ponytail, she lets out a breath as this bottled summer heat envelopes her body, the sea calling out to her once more, a sudden gust bending the palm trees of the shoreline, tousling her hair, willing her to look. She doesn't dare listen to that temptation, to the call of that black abyss as she hops onto the seat of her bike and pushes off the dirt road, the beach becoming nothing but a whisper of a shadow that disappears behind the trees as Agustin's words lap at her ears.

Trust in Him.

It's all she has to do, fall back on faith, fall back on everything she's ever known, everything she's been taught to rely on.

But she's no saint—and Silas is no angel.

9

NIGHT VEILS Port Cante in a starlit shroud by the time Sadie parks her bike at the end of the Hacienda's driveway, averting her eyes from the gaze of the rising moon. She makes her way to the front doors of the Hacienda with a hesitation in her step, her fingers tightly wound around the key to her nightmares.

Pressing her eyes closed as she shoves the key into the lock, the door clicks open. She enters, opening her eyes to find herself standing alone in the empty bowels of the house, greeted only by a note in rushed cursive from Odette that reads:

Gone out with Isaiah. Won't be out too late.

She fights the tinge of envy that runs through her at the thought that surfaces, but she kills it dead before locking the door behind her, her fingers clamping around the keys as the low creak of footfall from the second floor grips her senses.

Dropping the keys into the bowl by the front door as softly as she can, she hangs her bag up on the hook by the door, pulling out the brown paper bag brimming with the only clothes she could get her hands on at this hour, carrying it against her hip before throwing herself into the darkness of the Hacienda, making her way up the stairs two at a time. Coming to a stop before the guest room that was once her father's study, she takes a deep breath with her fingers tight around the handle.

Twisting the brass, she enters, and she's met with a room bathed in moonlight, the night breeze blowing in from the open window like waves crashing upon a shore of books—paperbacks, magazines, hardcover volumes scattered in tall piles all around her.

Silas is a dark shadow seated on the bedside chair, angled so that the moonlight halos him in her light.

"I was wondering when you would return." His voice calls out from behind the pages of a book, his eyes never once leaving the page as she enters what's now well and truly *his* domain. Casting her eyes across the room, she spies the breakfast tray she left for him this morning picked clean apart, not a trace nor a morsel of food left behind. It feels like a small victory that she never has the chance to celebrate as she spies a familiar box sitting beside Silas.

It's a banana box perched atop the windowsill, and the mere sight sinks Sadie's heart. Instinctively she rushes over to the box's edge, peering into the bundle of old blankets until she spies a flutter of movement, and she relaxes her shoulders.

"You neglected to feed him," Silas says calmly.

The starling's single crimson eye pokes out from his nest of blankets, peering back at her as if to say, *did you expect him to tear me apart?*

But the sight before her is far from it. A fig sliced into quarters sits just within the bird's reach, along with a porcelain saucer brimming with fresh water. Sadie feels a tinge of guilt well up deep within her as she strokes the starling's glossy plumage, chiding herself for feeding a demon but not the innocent starling under her roof.

She answers softly, "I... It slipped my mind." She turns to face him, never deigning to think she would say what comes next. "Thank you."

She doesn't dare turn to see his reaction as she focuses on the starling, his steady heartbeat beneath her fingers is all she needs to calm her nerves, and she straightens herself up, adjusting the brown paper bag she's carrying against her hip.

"Here. These are for you." She tucks her hair behind her ear as she makes her way over to the edge of the bed, promptly spilling the contents out across the sheets. A pile of navy, ash gray and charcoal shirts, pants and all the other essentials she could get her hands on at the late-night general store. "They should fit."

He rises from where he sits, resting the book page-down on the windowsill beside the boxed starling as he comes to join her side, dwarfing her in utter shadow.

"I hope."

He's stark tall, broad-shouldered, and bare chested save for his scar, his skin now scrubbed clean of blood to reveal the clear strength in his hands to rend skin and crush bone—yet here he is, surrounded by paperbacks and clothbound volumes. Baudelaire, Byron, Shelley to Austen and then Tolstoy and Nabokov, he's playing catch up on centuries-worth of literature, centuries-worth of change, of woe, of human suffering.

Sadie pulls out a gray marle Henley shirt, holding it up before his chest in an attempt to measure it out, but he takes it from her hands without a word, along with a pair of charcoal jeans from the pile.

Tearing away the remaining tatters from his body, she lets out an inaudible gasp as he strips down, forcing her to whip away and face the sprawling bookshelf in the opposite direction. Cheeks courting scarlet, she wills herself to focus on the sun-faded spines staring back at her as the rustle of Silas undressing fights hard to pull at her attention.

Red, black, ivory white... she names each spine's color as she twists her fingers together. *Mahogany brown, duck-egg blue...* The floorboards creak behind her, and she finds the tip of her nose edging closer and closer towards the shadow over her shoulder.

"Hm," he remarks, prompting her to turn. "A strange fit."

She casts her eyes over the gray Henley shirt stretched taut over his chest, the sleeves already rolled up to his elbows, and down to the black jeans that are in need of letting out at the hem. Aside from that, the clothes are somehow as befitting as they are fitted.

"You'll get used to it."

He stretches his arms out, getting a feel for the fabric as if he's slipped into a second skin, before turning his eyes back to hers.

"This is all?"

She nods once. "Welcome to the twenty-first century."

Satisfied, he turns back towards the windowsill, restless fingers still only when he has the book he set down back in his hands.

Quiet blankets them both, and Sadie twiddles her thumbs for but a moment before catching the pool of tattered fabric at the base of the bed. It's what he stripped off, and she reaches over to bundle the rags up in her arms, debating between throwing them in the trash or leaving them where they lay.

Wind rattles the capiz shell windows, and she thinks of something better.

Stopping at the box beside Silas, she adds to the starling's nest with the tattered fabric. The starling stirs as she wraps him up in black brocade, yet he remains peacefully slumbering as Sadie picks out a single ribbon of withered brocade, winding it around her finger, and examining the dirt-stained fabric, ravaged by the centuries in a way its owner was not.

Silk, she thinks to herself, *this is silk.* She thumbs the stiffened scrap, its luster long gone. But there's still some gold left in its threaded veins, a glimmer that's almost as captivating as the sound of his voice awakening her from her thoughts.

"Come here."

She turns to face him, a cool wind blowing in from over the moonlit jungle canopy beyond the window, rustling the treetops and the space between them like a star kissed sea. She presses her lips together, a tinge of self-consciousness creeping up on her cheeks that she brushes away as she inches closer towards him, where he's leaning into the night as if he's reading to the darkness itself. The stars are brilliant, her eyes following a stray bat flitting across the sky before it disappears into the thicket.

"You have quite the collection." He takes his eyes off his book for the first time, turning his attention solely to her as he leans his elbow on the windowsill beside her.

"Mm," she answers. "I've read them all inside and out—but they don't feel like they're mine. They belonged to my parents. It's how they met..." she trails off, caught in the scent of the faded paperback between his fingers. "My mom owned the only bookstore in Port Cante, but then she couldn't afford to pay the lease and—" she stops herself, realizing she's baring her memories to an indifferent audience, an inhuman audience.

But to her surprise, he wants more. "And?"

"What?"

"What happened?"

"Oh." Twisting her fingers together, she continues, "She met my dad. He wandered in as a tourist and offered to pay for everything." She turns her eyes away from the stars, the twinkling lights still lingering across her vision as she rests her gaze on Silas. "She refused him of course, but he bought the entire stock when she closed up shop as an apology. A few months later, they got married. In secret."

"A strange courtship," he remarks.

A smile threatens to pull up at her lips at the thought. "I guess so."

Looking out at the stars, he turns his gaze back to the book in his hands, reading by moonlight. "And now these are all yours."

Sadie nods, the lightness of the memory slipping away into that all too familiar melancholy. "All mine... But it doesn't feel like it."

A silence nestles itself into the air between them, and as she stares up at the night sky, she dangles her arm out the window, thinking how easy it would be to reach out and touch a star, to feel it beneath her fingers—but his voice pulls her back to the confines of the Hacienda.

"Your father is not from here?"

She turns to face him, not recalling the last time she'd spoken about her parents. "He's half. His dad was Spanish, from Barcelona, and his mom from San Vicente."

He tips his head down in understanding, "And what became of him?"

"He passed away," she blurts out, almost surprised at how casually she does. "One minute he was here... and next he was gone."

"He died in this room, didn't he?"

Sadie presses her lips together, the phantom birdsong taunting her senses. "Yes. He did."

Silas looks away, retreating back into the depths of the book in his hands, leaving Sadie to her own thoughts. He's standing so close, the room dark, the door shut behind them—yet there's nothing about this moment that feels claustrophobic.

"You know everything about this house, don't you?" she asks into the night.

"So do you." He flips a page. "Yet you bury it deep inside you."

Shutting her eyes, she lets her thoughts fade into the cicada song beyond, running her fingers along the windowsill in an attempt to soak up this old Hacienda's memories through the pads of her fingertips and retreat back into her own childhood. *If only it were that easy.*

But Silas pulls her back to the present with his voice barely a whisper. "*You are a woman marked for sorrow,*" he murmurs, the words sinking into the depths of her mind.

"What did you say?" She turns to face him, his gaze fixed upon the moonlit page.

"Sophokles' writing. A new translation."

The meaning seeps into her blood like venom, and before she has the chance to taste it, she lets out what she's been holding in, "Your brother came by work today."

Silas flicks his eyes up from the page, ever as still as a statue. "And what did he say?"

"Nothing that made sense." She casts her eyes away, hoping he won't see through her. Yet she can still feel the steeliness written in the sharpness of his eyes. "Nothing I don't already know..."

"What do you mean?"

"You feed on human suffering. *My* suffering. What are you going to do when you've bled me dry of my tears? Move onto the next one? Whoever inherits this house after me?"

He frowns. "You think I have a choice in the matter?"

"Choice has nothing to do with it. It's what you are." Sadie lets her tongue loose, testing the waters swirling between them. "And you're nothing more than a demon."

He lowers his gaze to the jungle canopy before drawing them back over her, shutting the book and setting it on the window sill. "Hm."

"Hm?" She narrows her eyes. "That's all you're going to say?" Shaking her head, Sadie turns her body completely, standing parallel to his as she lets the inkling of doubt speak for her, "Are you really going to help me find out what happened to my mom? Or is all of this just for your benefit?"

"What do you think? Truly?" He turns to face her.

She casts her eyes away, his gaze too penetrating. "I... I don't even know if you're real. You could just be that part of me that wants to make sure that I'll never forget how lonely I am. Made into skin and bone... Made into my own personal demon." She lifts her eyes to meet his gaze, the tidal swell in her chest that follows quick becoming one she wants to drown in.

"You say choice has no part in this, but you are wrong." He takes a step closer, lidded eyes as unreadable as shadow. "It is the core of the matter... Is it really me who reminds you of your loneliness?" There's hardly a sliver of distance between them, and he savors every pulse of dread that rushes through her veins. "Or is it you who hangs onto it?"

She says nothing in response.

He continues, "I have been asleep for centuries, but I am no stranger to the dreams and memories that whisper between these walls... behind your eyes."

She softens her gait. "What have you seen?"

Silas takes a step backwards, leaving her in the starlight with nothing but his eyes in the darkness. The shadows of the room begin to stir, threatening to consume him, the Hacienda; all of it.

"Just watch."

And with her next pulse, she finds herself blinded by a light. Night has faded, replaced instead by the soft blue of dawn, the breath of the wind knocking against the front doors—she's standing in the foyer of the Hacienda. Sadie snaps her eyes up towards the shuttered windows by the front door, and with a gasp she realizes where she is—*when* she is.

It's that morning, that day, that moment in time before the loneliness took hold. The door handle jingles desperately, and through the low howl of the winds, Sadie can hear a voice.

"*Sara!*" It's him, Father Agustin, his hair tangled with leaves, clothes soaked to the knees with flood water.

Sadie makes her way to the bottom of the stairs, and in a haze she opens the door, ready to face him and the news that he carries. But the moment she pries the door open, he bolts forwards, phasing through her like a phantom in a dream of the past.

That's exactly what this is.

"Sara! Where are you?" Agustin cries out, darting his eyes along the walls of the Hacienda, desperately searching for any sign of life within it.

A dream.

The sound of sobbing fills the air, and Agustin's shoulders stiffens as he locates its source—the bathroom up ahead.

Sadie trails behind him like a shadow as he wraps his hand around the brass handle, inhaling sharply before peeling the door away from its frame.

"Sara..." Her name is a quiet gasp from his lips as he lays his eyes on the scene before him.

She almost wants to look away, to run and hide from the trembling girl huddled up in the bathtub ahead—but how can she when it's her own eyes staring back at her? Her own eyes pleading for shelter in the wake of a storm, a shelter Sadie wishes she could give her.

She knows what comes next, Father Agustin scooping her up into his arms, cradling her head to his chest.

"Sara... Your mom—we lost her in the storm."

The next breath she takes is like ice water to her lungs, the shock, the sting of those words bringing her down to her knees as the dream begins to fade away like waves retreating farther and farther from shore until a voice calls her back.

"Sara," that voice calls out, the sound of it a knife that shatters the dream—yet as Sadie comes to, it sounds less like Agustin and more like a demon. It's behind her, and she pries her eyes away from this fever memory only to be met with the demon who conjured it up from the depths of her heart.

He knows more than just your name.

Silas stands tall above her, ever the shadow of black he is—skin like marble, hair a tangle of smoke. His eyes like two stars peering back at her, a universe of night to a dreamer on a speck of dust.

You shouldn't be here, she should say to him, not in this dream, not in this memory. Yet even amidst the pain bound up in this place, his presence doesn't feel like an intrusion. He holds his hand out for her to take, and she feels compelled to take it.

A way out... That's what his presence feels like.

Softly, he wraps his fingers around hers, lifting her to her feet.

But he turns away before she can witness a reaction, and he begins to walk onwards, only for the ground beneath him to tremor with every step. Sadie follows as the dream bows to his path, the stairs twisting under them, the hardwood floors tainted with ash.

"How can you do this?" she asks, voice quiet.

He glances briefly over his shoulder. "A demon must learn all the ways to reap what nourishes us—be it through passive nightmares or the carnage of war. Even before I was cast under the ground, I had two centuries to learn all the ways through which a demon could harvest woe from the very best of my kind."

She continues following him, his words sinking into the recesses of her mind. *He can only be telling the truth,* she thinks to herself, *he's done this longer than I've been alive, longer than I'll ever be remembered.* All the confirmation she needs is in the near surgical precision of his dissecting her heartache, slicing the tear-stained memories out for her to see with her own two eyes.

He stops when the memory has completely faded away behind them, the outline of a door materializing before them—the door she recognizes as her bedroom.

"Where are you taking me now?" she asks, her voice a soft murmur in the dark.

Stretching out his hands, the shadows that cling to his being fall from his arms like velveteen bat's wings.

"Wherever you want to go."

And the ground gives beneath her, and she's falling through the sky.

"*Ah!*" Shooting out of bed, she pants; breathless, yearning for air. Searching the room with a desperate tremor, she lets out a sigh when all she finds is stillness. Sinking into the cool of her sheets, she breathes in and out, the moonlight streaming in from outside casting her bedroom in a nightglow that's far from the reassurance she seeks.

He knows everything about you.

Every agony. Every tear. Every moment of grief.

Devouring my suffering, she tells herself. That's all this is, that's all he's doing. It would be so easy to accuse him of prying her open, of splitting her heart in two the way that knife did his—but she knows it's a lie.

It's all her doing. It's her own hands tearing apart her armor of flesh, ripping through the brick and mortar she's been hiding behind all this time, her nails clawing against every brick she set, fighting against the barriers she built when she walled her grief up alive.

Sadie screws her eyes shut at the thought of his presence in her darkest memories, forcing the feeling of his fingers around hers away as she sits upright against the headboard. The box housing the injured starling is back on her nightstand, not a coo or a murmur coming from his makeshift nest of towels and fabric scraps. Reaching out for her phone beside the box, she allows the harsh light to blind her, welcoming the distraction. Instinctively she opens Isaiah's messages, expecting a slew of texts, a slew of half-apologies, of half-plans for a *next time*.

But there's nothing from him.

And a pang of loneliness shoots through her.

She types, the glow of her screen a painful brightness that she wants to get away from the moment she hits send.

Sadie: Are you on the way back?

Pressing herself up and out of bed, she wraps her arms around her sides, swaying as she paces around the room in an attempt to rid herself of the heat crawling under her skin.

It's sometime after ten o'clock when the lights of Isaiah's pick-up illuminate the dark of her bedroom, and Sadie doesn't move an inch until she hears the front door open. Odette's melodic laughter creeps in from beneath the slit of her bedroom door, Isaiah's voice following soon after.

Smoothing out her hair and her dress, she makes her way out to the upstairs living room when she hears Odette pad off to her room. With only the light of the moon shining through each pearlescent square of the capiz shell windows to guide her way through the dark, every raw nerve beneath Sadie's skin is illuminated as she lays eyes on Isaiah standing by the couch.

"Hey." Is all Sadie can say in greeting, and all Isaiah can do is shoot her a questioning glance that says *what's wrong?*

But Sadie looks away, and he doesn't push. Instead he does what he does best—he wraps his arm around her, planting a kiss on her cheek as he pulls her down onto the couch, the closest thing to a quiet relief soothing her nerves as he laces his fingers through hers. Despite the lack of texts, the late hour, despite the booze lacing his breath and Odette's perfume clinging to his shirt.

Trust in Him, Father Agustin's words echo in her ears, a dull refrain to rally faith that does nothing but lose more and more of its meaning with each passing moment beneath Isaiah's gaze. How can she have faith in Isaiah when there's nothing left inside her to bestow it?

She shakes her thoughts away, sinking into the depths of Isaiah's arms, drowning her thoughts in his comforting, reassuring, easy touch.

You should be thankful, she chides herself. *Always be grateful for him.*

10

"HOW WAS WORK?" Sadie asks, feigning a smile.

"Busy. As usual. There was an accident up the road that we had to go help clear up, and I am exhausted—which means we better make the most of my downtime tonight." His lips pull up into a smirk as he snakes his arm around her waist, pinching her side.

He leans in to kiss her, but his beer soaked breath forces her to turn away sharply.

She braces herself as she waits for him to protest, to guilt her, to force her into the pliant girl he so wants her to remain, but a buzzing on the coffee table captures his attention, a welcome distraction to whatever it is he was going to say.

"Is it yours?" he asks, pulling away to grab the phone on the table.

Sadie shakes her head, recognizing the sunflower yellow phone case as Odette's. But there's no ringtone, it's on silent. Two words flash bold across the screen: *The Devil*.

Sadie's heart stops at the name, thinking for a second it's some twisted joke meant for her—but rational thought prevails, and she realizes it must be Odette's pet name for her father. The ringing eventually stops after what feels like an eternity, and when Sadie's eyes land on her notification screen, she sees this call isn't the first.

The Devil (12) missed calls.

A text appears on the screen.

Answer me Odette.

Then another.

There are consequences for your actions.

And a final:

You will repent, one way or another.

Sadie pries her eyes away from the screen just as Odette returns with a tired smile sprawled out across her lips. A prickle of guilt stabs at her stomach as she realizes perhaps it's not been all sunshine and roses for Odette all these years—not with a dad like Dominic Arias.

"I'm exhausted..." Odette yawns, before curling up on the loveseat, traces of sand still clinging to her toes. "Nothing beats the beaches here on Cante."

Isaiah chimes in, "Nothing like home, right Sadie?"

"Right." Sadie smiles softly, trying hard to disguise the discomfort settling deep into her nerves.

"You know there's only one place left we haven't been back to..." Odette sits up, a mischievous glint lighting up her eyes. "The one place that was practically our hideaway."

Isaiah catches on, rubbing his hands together as the memories come flitting back.

"Is it still there, Sadie?" Odette leans forward, hope brimming her eyes, "Corazon beach?"

The thought of that secluded little grove of palm trees and white sand sends the sting of nostalgia through her veins.

"Of course," Sadie answers, and it's all Odette needs to rise to her feet and make her way down the staircase two at a time, leaving the two behind with nothing but a giggle of child-like excitement trailing in her wake.

Sadie and Isaiah share a brief glance before following her to the ground floor, knowing there's no stopping Odette when she has her mind set on what she wants.

Stopping at the front door, Odette reaches out for Sadie's hand. "Say," Odette's voice lowers, "Where is *he*? Shall we ask if he wants to join?"

"No!" Sadie blurts out before taking a breath, feeling Isaiah's eyes watch her carefully, "He's asleep." She turns her eyes away with a whisper, "Let's just go."

"Follow me." Isaiah gestures as they step out into the cool night air, Odette following close behind. It's not soon after before their two silhouettes are swallowed up by the long overgrown jungle path.

Sadie follows a ways behind, memories of the past beginning to lap at the shore of her mind as she follows, crossing the threshold between the estate and the dark thicket that surrounds it.

Snaking her way through the overgrown gumamela trees and unchecked growth flanking the loamy path, Sadie remembers the way to the cove of palm trees her mother dubbed Corazon Beach as if it's imprinted against the back of her hand. It's almost frightening how quickly the jungle takes over with only a year's notice, how quickly a path, a memory can be erased given enough time. The thought would be frightening to Sadie if it hadn't been such a comfort, perhaps it would even be horrifying if it hadn't been everything she'd been counting on all these sleepless nights.

The moon is almost completely full yet the thick vines and glossy banana leaves high overhead strangle the light, diffusing the stars and the sky light until it's nothing but an echo over Sadie's skin.

Feeling her way in the dim, only the sound of Odette and Isaiah's voices beckon her onwards, the lilt of hers and the depth of his twining together to become one indistinguishable call that pulls her towards it.

By the time Sadie hears the ocean lapping softly at the shore, the light of the moon against the water overtakes her vision, and she squints to adjust. Beneath a tree that hangs over the water's edge, Isaiah and Odette sit side by side, the two of them huddled close together, perhaps a little too close.

Sadie steps on a twig to make her presence known.

For a second Sadie swears she sees them both scramble to sit upright—but she shakes it off, along with those persisting envy-dipped doubts.

"You made it." Odette calls out, brushing her fingers through her hair, Isaiah leaning back against the trunk of the tree.

"I haven't been here in a long time." Sadie murmurs, more to herself than anyone else as she casts her eyes across the length of the bay stretched out before her, the moonlight a mesmerizing dance across the water's surface.

Corazon Beach is a miniscule, secluded strip of sand more than anything else, where a dense line of palm trees stop dead at the water's edge. It's the perfect place to get away, the perfect place to escape—yet Sadie can't help but feel like it's anything but.

"How can anyone get stressed in a place like this?" Odette sings out, soaking her legs in the water.

"I don't think anyone could get stressed being around you, party girl," Isaiah remarks, Odette splashing water up in his direction in response.

"If you spend more than a week with me, then you'll know that's not true," she laughs. "We used to go here all the time... I remember now. Corazon beach—didn't you name it that, Sadie?"

Sadie bites the inside of her cheek, leaning against the low hanging branch of the tree separating her from the other two, focusing on its sway against the water's surface before answering.

"My mom did."

A silence befalls the two, and Odette casts her eyes away.

"She called it Corazon beach because between these palm trees, the water, the canopy—it's dead quiet. Quiet enough to hear the beating of your own heart."

Isaiah whispers under his breath, "Well, she was right."

Sensing the heaviness in the air, Odette shifts topic as she kicks at the water, the sound of the splashing waves at her ankles breaking the silence. "You know, Barcelona is great. But Port Cante beaches can't be beat."

"I always wanted to go to Barcelona," Isaiah comments, stretching out against the fine sand. "But you've probably been to more places than we ever will."

Sadie sinks down into the sand, sitting just out of reach from the water's edge, Isaiah shooting her a glance in the dark.

Just play nice is without a doubt what Isaiah is insisting with his dark eyes, yet Sadie focuses hard on the clouds moving fast across the sky, never turning to face him, never allowing those words to sink into her thoughts.

"Tell us about your favorite." Isaiah prompts Odette, allowing her to take the reins of the conversation.

Unsurprisingly, Odette's eyes light up at the topic, as she answers with a smirk, "Well, which place *isn't* my favorite is the question to ask." With an eager giggle, she begins hurling the names of cities she's been too into the air. Starting with capitals, to their major landmarks, then to the small towns, the country sides, and the stories that come with it all. They go on and on until Sadie feels as if she's been set on a globe, Isaiah and Odette perched on either side, spinning it round and round at a dizzying pace.

"If you haven't travelled the world by your mid-twenties... and I mean pack out of your small town and *see* the world beyond—then you just haven't lived. Some people spend their whole lives never knowing what's beyond the garden fence... and they're happy with it."

Her vision begins to spin faster and faster, the sound of their two voices growing louder and louder with each passing moment.

"The Grand Canyon under the starlight..."

"Looking up at the Notre Dame from below."

"The bustle of Tokyo!"

"Majorca's crystalline waters."

"No place like Santorini in the summer."

Every place, every scene, every vivid image floods Sadie's mind like jeering visions that dance over grave soil—grave soil marked with a tombstone engraved with her initials.

Her pulse beats wildly in her chest, the spinning so intense that she just can't take it anymore. Shooting upright, Sadie rises to her feet.

"Sadie..." Isaiah lands his eyes on Sadie, "You okay?"

"Can we talk for a second?" Sadie clenches her jaw.

"Oh... sure." He rises to his feet, brushing the sand off his skin as they make their way into the privacy of a cluster of palm trees, away from Odette.

"What's the deal with you two?" Sadie narrows her eyes.

"What are you talking about?" Isaiah tilts his head.

"You and Odette haven't left each other's side since she came. It seems an awful lot like—"

"—like what?" Isaiah's lips press into a thin line, and Sadie can't stop herself from wincing at the glare he shoots her. He's searching for a way in, a fracture in her resolve that he's become so attuned to finding no matter the topic, no matter the time of day.

"I..." Sadie never has the chance to finish her sentence as Isaiah wraps his fingers around her shoulders with that surefire confidence he mastered long ago, his touch just enough pressure to enter through the cracks and melt away whatever she's thinking, just enough force to crush the doubt out of her heart. "I... I don't know. I'm sorry, Sai. I just feel so..."

"Hey. I know what you're doing is a lot of work. She's a lot of work—but don't worry, alright?" He flicks his eyes up to the stars, before pulling her into his chest. "One day we'll get out of this place. I'm bound to get my own auto shop one day, and we can move to the big city before you know it," he brushes her hair behind her ear in a motion that sends a tinge of anxiety over her. "And you'll never have to worry again."

"Sai, that's not—" Sadie begins to pull away, only to be interrupted by Odette.

"Guys look! Did you see that shooting star?"

Isaiah squeezes Sadie's shoulders, peering deep into her eyes, "Hear that? Must be a sign that something good's coming. Why don't you head back to the Hacienda? Go and rest. I'll take Odette home." He smiles, leaving her with a kiss on the forehead and a slew of words on her tongue left unspoken, a voice unheard.

Isaiah and Odette's voices intertwine with the sound of the sea and the stars, and Sadie can't help but feel like an outsider looking in. Turning on her heel, she lets out a breath as she turns towards the loamy path back to the Hacienda—but before she disappears into the darkness behind the palm trees, the sound of laughter calls her to turn over her shoulder.

Hidden behind the width of a palm frond, Sadie peers out from between the jagged edges to see Odette and Isaiah sitting flush close on the sand; moonlit and star-gazing. Her heart skips a beat as she realizes it wasn't Odette's laughter she heard, but Isaiah's.

The wind rustles the palm fronds she's hidden behind, and for a moment Sadie feels the cold rush through her, the scent of salt water suddenly nauseating as it washes over her in the breeze.

When was the last time you made him laugh?

Balling her fists at her side, she fights back this feeling with all she has left, turning whip fast on her heel to rid herself of the fact that she'll never be Odette; she'll never be that happy, carefree girl sitting on the beach under the starlight.

And she heads back to the only thing she knows.

Her home, her life, her Hacienda.

Making her way back through the dense line of palm trees, Sadie doesn't stop until she sees the outline of the Hacienda's front doors unfolding before her. Sadie takes in a deep breath, the nausea in the pit of her stomach dissipating the minute she crosses the threshold.

This is where you belong, she thinks to herself as she makes the ascent to the second floor, the warm lamplight of the hallway light casting a candle-like glow over each door that stands solemnly shut before her. Secrets seep from beneath each door, countless memories, centuries of history—and tears prick at her vision at the thought of her becoming just another ghost in this hallway, another demon buried under the ground.

She hears the creaking of a floorboard, and she whips around in the dark, for a brief moment believing Isaiah has followed her back to the Hacienda. Only he can make this house go away with a kiss in the dark; but even she knows the taste of him is nothing but a band-aid over a wound that's never going to heal.

She holds her breath for a moment, lingering.

He's not coming for you, she tells herself.

And she swallows her tears.

Making her way further down the hallway, she stops when a door creaks slowly open before her, and she stares into the darkness with hazy eyes.

It's *his* room—he's beckoning her inside.

Music plays softly from within, and her heart beats faster at the melody. It's too familiar; too comforting; too reassuring.

And like an echo to the song that summons it, she enters.

11

THERE'S no doubt Sadie knows this song, and judging by the way the hairs on the back of her neck stand on end, she knows it must be from one her dad's old records. The melody envelops her as she comes to a stop at the record player tucked away by the bookshelf, spying an empty vinyl sleeve that reads *Natalie Cole* across the top laying neatly beside the spinning table.

The music is a soothing lull as she sways beneath the jazz, her heart swept up in the nostalgia of her mother's favorite song —'*Unforgettable*'—the ache as sharp, as strong, as clear as the duet song that wraps tight around her senses.

It can only mean Silas has already started leafing through her parents' collection of vinyls, and like everything else in this house, he won't stop until he's devoured it all. Of course, she can't blame him. All he's had is an infinite amount of time, and the hunger for life that comes with all those centuries of silence must simply be insatiable. Yet Sadie on the other hand, has an appetite that's as lacking as the time allotted to her mortal clock as it *tick, tick, ticks* away.

She presses her eyes closed, wrapping her arms around herself in the darkness of what used to be her father's office, where he drew his last breath, where the line between *before* and *after* is forged in the shape of his unconscious body sprawled out over the floorboards.

But the record skips and the door clicks shut behind her, breaking the spell she's caught under.

"Have you had enough of your companions?" Silas asks, his voice a dark echo in the sudden quiet of the room that forces her to open her eyes. She turns to see him sitting on the edge of the bed, a different book in his lap, his eyes fixed to the page, reading beneath shadowy light.

Immediately she's drawn back to that earlier dream, her nightmare—that wound she tried to forget now ripped red raw, her skin sliced open, anguish dripping from the gash to his delight.

Fire dances on the tip of her tongue, and she makes no effort to extinguish it. "Haven't *you* had enough of a fill from me?"

"A strange question," he replies, drawing his eyes upwards to meet hers. The sight of that midnight black gaze and the even tone of his voice forces her to fumble. "For one who entered of her own accord."

His eyes are that same impenetrable stillness that peered back at her from the depths of his shallow grave, yet it's not like that first night they met. This time is different. For a moment she thinks perhaps it's his clothes, the mark of modernity imprinted in the textiles, the labor, the make—but even that is still nothing more than illusion.

He's still a man out of time, and she's a girl without a question to his answer.

"As much as you wish to pretend you prefer solitude, it is clear that's the furthest thing you desire."

She crosses her arms over her chest, the skirt of her sundress swaying with her movement. If there's one thing she's sick and tired of, it's playing psych patient to a demon. "And what makes you say that?"

He's silent—and irritation drives her closer to where he sits, not thinking of what it is she'll do when she reaches her destination. She doesn't know what it is she expects when he motions for her to sit beside him, and she doesn't know what it is that washes over her the moment she does.

He places the book in her hands without a word, his fingers wrapping around the base of her wrist with a lightness that feels like nothingness as he takes her hand in his and places it over a particular paragraph, her finger resting over a particular line.

Sadie lets out a breath at his closeness, his forwardness, the sound of his command, "Read."

And she does. Slowly, she focuses on the words he's laid out in front of her. *"Loneliness, like fever, thrives on the night..."* she reads aloud, scanning her eyes over to the top of the page, "Truman Capote." Her voice is a near whisper as she scrambles away the meaning of the words chasing her; desperately trying to get away from the demon who set them in motion.

"And after all," he encloses his hands over hers, shutting the book and setting it down on the bed. "You waited for him to follow you."

Her shoulders drop almost instantly. *Is it that obvious?*

"Is it not true?" he persists.

Rendered silent, she simply tries her hardest not to focus on the feeling of his eyes on hers. A task that's easier said than done.

"In a congregation, a crowded room, even with a smile on your lips... you are alone."

She turns to face him, craning her head to meet his dark gaze. His hand lingers on hers, burning away the last remaining slivers of hesitation from her skin. It would only take a single gust of wind to push her forward, into him—into the void she's been so close to falling into.

A silence fills the space between them, his hooded eyes searching until the deep baritone of his voice finds the answer.

"Eres Solita."

She feels his eyes roam over the planes of her face, yet there's no turning away. Not here. Not now. Not anymore.

"Solita..." she echoes, its taste on her tongue like the coming of dawn. "*Alone,*" she whispers. "It means alone."

He pulls his hand away, leaving Sadie to the mercy of its meaning.

The name sits between them for a moment, Sadie committing it to her memory, breathing it into her lungs, tasting it on her tongue. This is the mark she asked for, his brand upon her skin, her soul, and all her sorrow—and it's here, now, with this name she realizes her life lays not in his hands, but in the palm of her own.

He's close, closer still when he continues, "There is no shame in loneliness. I know it well."

She blinks back at him, her voice soft as she thinks of the time he spent beneath the house, buried to be forgotten, to rot away into dust. "You would know better than anyone. Better than me."

"You give yourself no credit."

"Credit for what?"

"For *being*. You are alive, aren't you?"

The question hangs in the air between them like smoke, and even she can't dare to lie to a demon.

"I am."

"You remind me of myself... before this wound, before this curse." He peers back at her, a flicker of surprise for her curiosity written in his eyes like pinpricks of starlight. "We are alike."

The desire to know, to see, to understand him takes hold of her pulse as she asks, "How?"

"I wanted to die, too," he answers. A cold wind blows across the treetops, rattling the window panes in a hard gust of wind. "My life in Seville was ruled by my father's shadow. I was subject completely to his plans, his command, his merciless will."

"What did he want from you?"

"One thing," Silas answers, voice quiet. "My obedience. He wished for nothing more than for him to be the judgment, and for

I to be his hand. What the eyes of the face seek out, the hand acts on its behalf."

"And that's what you did," she whispers, sitting on the edge of the mattress, so close to the enigma that he is. "You took what he wanted." She needs not ask what it is he took, the answer written plain in the bitter red reflection of his eyes.

Tension ripples across the line of his jaw. "Yet if one hand disobeys, the other pays the price..."

"Your brother?" Sadie asks, "He paid the price?"

Silas says nothing, his eyes brimming over with a shade of darkness that threatens to consume him whole—but Sadie calls him back to the present.

"You lived your whole life for his will... that's why you wanted to die—because you never saw a point, did you?"

He casts his eyes away briefly before breaking the quiet. "Just as you do."

It renders Sadie speechless, and she has no choice but to endure the tide of his words as they engulf her utterly. "I've seen it in your dreams. The thought of following your mother's footsteps... the thought of following her over the edge and drowning in that same sea. It comforts you, doesn't it?"

There's something in his voice that wrings the truth out of her, and she slices through the silence. "It does," she answers, twisting the fabric of her dress between her fingers, letting out the breath she's been holding. "It's the only comfort I have in that nightmare. The fact that there's an out... that there's an escape, that when I die I'll see her again."

"You are willing to gamble away the brief life you have, in the hopes of reaching another that may not even exist?"

Sadie nods.

"How foolish."

A melancholy smile pulls up at her lips, knowing it's nothing but the truth. "It is..." Sadie admits. "But that hope is all I have left. It's the only thing that keeps me going."

His eyes land on hers. "Death is not what you think it is. To sink into the grave is nothing like the dream-filled sleep you envision."

She shakes her head, wishing for once he won't shatter this one illusion, this last comfort. "Then what is it?"

"Nothingness," he answers plain and true. "An eternity of nothingness. You return to the time before you were born, laying amidst the cinder and ash of what came before. Yet there is no waiting, no hoping for the chance at rebirth... there is only nothingness."

Sadie presses her lips together, feeling her heart constrict at the thought of all those times she stood at the precipice of her nightmares, merely waiting for a gust to blow her into the sea.

"Is that so bad?" she lets the question out without a thought, casting her eyes across the planes of his face, searching endlessly for an answer she wants to hear, for the answer that will send her over the edge. "Could it be any worse than the pain of living?"

Yet she never would have thought that it would have been a demon's voice that pulls her back from the precipice.

"Yes," he answers. "It is. For I've lived that death. A death of nothingness, centuries of sleep that had led to an awakening that's no rebirth, no second chance, no redemption."

Her heart wrenches in her chest beneath the sting of his words, the lash of his sorrow.

"*Solita*," he calls her by her new name, christened in loneliness and written in shadow. "Keep your grief," he asserts, the murmur of an unfamiliar feeling echoing through her bones. "It is the only thing that keeps you alive."

She breathes in the night wind before replying, "And it's the only thing keeping you sane."

Only the cicada song and the silence whispers the *yes* both need to hear, both need to know, both need to drown in.

Sadie breaks the silence first, turning to face him. "Silas," his name from her lips is a wisp of smoke that wraps around her, underlined with the scent of something darker, something bitter still. "Why do you feed from me when you can starve and forget it all? Your past, your father—everything you did for him?"

"To forget my past is to forget what I am." His eyes brim with some distant emotion, the breath from his lips so close to her own, his voice laced with an unbreakable resolve. "And I must never forget."

Smoke.

She places the scent, *it's smoke.*

Whether it's his own blood that lingers, or someone else's, Sadie never has the chance to ponder as he breaks her gaze, his eyes set on the shadows spilling lengthwise across the floorboards, this midnight hour stretching out endlessly before them. "You wish to see? See what I must never forget?"

Her eyes are fixed to the line of starlight illuminating his profile, a flicker of fire pooling in the dark of his eyes as she nods. "Yes... I do. Dredge up your past the same way you do with mine..." She leans in closer, her nerves alight with the thought of his past so close to her present. "This time it's my turn to taste."

He clenches his jaw at the mention of that last word, before pulling a mask of resolve over his features. "Then come with me."

She narrows her eyes, instinctively drawing back when she sees there's fire dancing beneath the dark film of his eyes. *How,* she wants to ask, but the time for that question has well and truly passed, whatever remains of it going up in smoke the moment he upturns his hand, all for her to take.

Without a thought, she places her palm face down in his, the flame dancing behind his eyes flickering brighter in the darkness as the air around them begins to shift.

The humid summer air is swept away in a gust of wind that batters the sides of the Hacienda, giving Sadie half the chance to blink as she feels the bed beneath her begin to give way.

The floorboards creak, the bedframe bows, the woodgrain deteriorating in a plume of smoke as the sheets beneath her twist around her body in serpentine motion. The frame beneath her begins to crumble, the wood and sheets melting into a salty, bitter tide.

And she falls.

Through the darkness, and into a dream of the past—not hers, but *his*.

A cacophony washes over her through the void as she plummets through the past, a din of men's cries, the clang of metal on metal, and the sharp sting of waves crashing upon a distant, foreign shore.

Sadie falls forward, making contact with what can only be the crunch of sand and the swish of water beneath her. On her hands and knees, she's soaked through to the skin, waves lapping at her thighs, sea spray kissing her elbows. The water is a cool relief as she regains her senses in the dark, the pace of her pulse returning to her breath by steady breath.

Silas' voice calls for her, both from everywhere and nowhere at once.

"Open your eyes."

She obeys, looking down at the foamy shallows, the pull of the tide forcing her to dig her fingers into the sand, only for her arms to tremble the moment she sees what's staring back at her.

The water, the sea—it's stained red.

Horror seeps in through her skin as she forces herself upright, the tide receding to reveal she's alone with countless bodies strewn across the shallows. Fragments of bone splinters gleam darkly in the dusk amidst the broken seashells as Sadie crawls her way out of the shallows, coming face to face with a disemboweled torso that rises up from the bloodied sand like a dune of flesh, the ribs jutting out from the gored wound like fingers reaching out for her soul.

Her lips part, a whimper of terror escaping as she finds a pair of lifeless hollows staring back at her through the dim, the sheen of this corpse's blood-soaked helmet lying beside him a cruel crescent of a reflection in the black of his eyes.

Propping herself up onto her knees, she stares wide-eyed at the scene before her.

The stench of death and saltwater clings to her every pore as she sets her eyes across what must be a battlefield. The wastes of this beach lap at the foot of a lush cliffside, with a fortress set in stone rising just above the greenery, its battlements scraping the dusk painted sky. A commotion of voices resounds from up ahead, followed by something dark flying across the evening sky that ends with a deafening roar of crumbling stone.

It's a siege, she realizes, *and the city is splitting in two.*

She's centuries back in the past, spirited away to a distant shore, the pale sky yawning out above her a stranger, the sea crashing over the shore a foreign sight. Yet as Sadie casts her eyes across the bodies littering the sand, there's no trace of a scavenger's mark, no seabirds nor wild dogs that have come to feast upon the spoils.

This death is new, she realizes, wrapping her arms tightly around herself. *This bloodshed fresh.*

Surrounded by corpses of fallen soldiers, Sadie darts her eyes across the carnage, upon the gambesons slashed open, revealing the pierced flesh beneath, plate armor punctured, turbans unraveled, chain mail dyed through with the stain of blood. She'd only ever imagined scenes like this from between the pages of Spanish history books, yet here she stands at the shore before a sea of corpses adorned in their own entrails and discarded weaponry.

Facts her father insisted she learn stir through her memory, Sadie recognizing their contrasting armor as belonging distinctly to the era of the Reconquista.

Two opposing forces lay slaughtered before her—the Catholics bearing the sigil of the Crown of Castile, and those bearing the trappings of the Emirate of Granada. Yet no matter their allegiance in life, death unites them all beneath the same, singular fate.

The longer she stands amidst this miasma of death, the faster Sadie realizes these men did not meet their fates at each other's hand. This was no simple battle, no two-sided fight. There's a fury exacted upon these bodies akin to a predator feasting upon unsuspecting prey.

This is a massacre, terror coils in the pit of her belly as a deafening crackle of stone ripples through the air—the city's walls are splitting in two, the groan of what must be a trebuchet being readied for another round signaling that this siege is near its end. Save for the din of the siege up ahead, there is nothing but silence.

The silence that comes with the presence of danger, the dread quiet that comes with the hidden threat that lays waiting beneath the shadow of night.

But the crunch of bone and sand forces her to draw her gaze back towards the wastes, over the battered bodies and up towards a lone soldier that bursts forth from a pile of hollowed corpses beside her. A gasp escapes her lips, drawing back onto her elbows until she's backed up against the ebony hide of a fallen horse.

The soldier struggles for air, blood oozing from his lips, his breath fervent, his lungs coated in his ichor as his own chainmail acts the anchor that keeps him from surfacing for freedom.

He must be the last of his men, the sole survivor—yet there is another presence that encroaches fast upon the battlefield, arriving with the veil of night that blankets the beach as the sun plunges deep over the horizon.

Through fleeting light, the sound of her heartbeat is loud in her skull as the trapped soldier yearns for escape. Pity wells in the depths of her stomach, yet she forces herself to remember this is nothing but a memory of a demon, this man's fate long sealed.

From the spilt blood rises a cloud of impenetrable black, Sadie's flesh prickling as the smoke stack whittles away, revealing the figures of two men. One remains cloaked in utter shadow, revealing only his hard, aged features while the younger of the two steps forward, crouching down beside the soldier and his useless, futile attempts at prayer.

Both their eyes gleam incarnadine red, but Sadie's heart catches as she lays her eyes upon the younger of the two, recognizing the features she's come to know so well.

Silas.

Here she sees him as he was—a man sculpted by carnage, a demon in the thick of where he belongs. His world, his Hell, his Paradise.

Donning light armor steeped in gore, Silas rests his fingers over a longsword sheathed at his side, its blade soaked through with the souls of these dead men. His sharp features seem deadlier in this dusk light, the adornments of war and blood casting him in an immaculate glow that can't possibly be anything other than divine. For it's only divinity that can be so callous, so indifferent, so utterly *inhuman.*

"Silas..." she whispers his name, hoping somehow it will act the anchor back to the lonely being she's come to know, yet it's nothing but a fruitless attempt as a clumsy fumble of Spanish falls from the fearful soldier's lips.

"Ten piedad," the soldier pleads, his voice a gurgle of agony that only elicits an amused murmur from the older man. *Have mercy,* is what he's pleading, yet his prayers have fallen upon the wrong ears.

"There is no mercy here," the older man commands in Spanish, his eyes flaming pools of ruby. "This is a place of war."

Silas is expressionless, regarding the writhing soldier with all the indifference of an executioner to another pound of flesh, his God, his judgment beside him, withholding the warrant.

"And where men war, demons feast." The older man murmurs, a wicked grin pulling up at his lips as he turns his head towards the besieged city. "Though how it saddens me to see this feast coming to an end... yet there will be more. There will always be more." Contentment laces his words, driving a chill through Sadie's heart. "As long as there are faithful men like you." He turns to face this weary soldier, his smile fading into solemnity as the soldier begins to whisper the Lord's Prayer under his breath.

"How I savor the taste of the faithful," The older man muses.

"Your devotion to the hope of finding salvation beyond the valley of death is admirable." His voice is worn well on his tongue in recitation of a dying man's last rites—it's a refrain embedded into his soul, wrapped up in something resembling pride. "Yet the moment you see that hope is nothing but folly—that is your true salvation. A salvation sweeter than the promise of Paradise itself..." He nods his head once in Silas' direction, "A salvation that lays in the hands of my son."

That man... Sadie watches him disappear into the night, *it's his father.*

The warrant is signed, and Silas becomes his father's hand.

Rising to his feet, Silas towers tall over even his father, carnage simmering through his veins as he unsheathes his longsword, his one hand wrapped taut around the hilt, the other over the crossguard as he positions the sword's tip over the soldier's exposed face.

The soldier's eyes are screwed shut tight, his prayer an incomprehensible jumble as he awaits his end.

"Your fear is our blood," Silas' father calls out his final command, "And how we must drink."

And with that, Silas pushes down against the crossguard, the tip of his longsword plunging into the soldier's skull with all the ease of knife piercing silk. A bloodied gurgle rises from his lips as his life is snuffed out, his anguish devoured, his pain consumed.

Twisting away, Sadie screws her eyes shut tight. Fear tremors through her very marrow as the stone of the besieged city cracks under the weight of another blow, ribbons of blood erupting from the grotesque wound as Silas pulls his sword out from the caved in skull of this ill-fated soldier.

Sadie's lips part in terror as a warm spatter lands across her cheek, a droplet of hot blood smeared against the tip of her tongue. It sinks into her taste buds, filling her senses with the tang of a feeling that burns clean through the pink tissue.

Rage.

Silas' rage—it tastes of spilled blood.

At the heart of the city up ahead is a vicious siege, but this bloodied beach hosts a darker night. Not simply a massacre, but a demon's feast. All these bodies, ribs cracked open, insides hollowed out; every man who lays dead on this beach died the same way.

At *his* hand, beneath his father's gaze.

Opening her eyes, she's met with Silas' eyes. For a moment she swears it's her she's looking at, the velvet night wrapping him up in all her shadows, amplifying the reflective film of his crimson eyes.

She meets him where he stands, ever the demon he is, only for the spit and crackle of a distant flame to call out to her in the dark, his figure fading away into the night.

A cold wind blows over her, bringing with it the cries of the besieged city up ahead. Clamping her hands over her ears, she steels herself against the cacophony closing in on her, her senses alight with a fire that burns closer and closer with each passing second.

Open your eyes, she hears the same whisper of Silas' voice nestled against the shell of her ear—but how can she be sure it's *her* Silas and not the blood wrought demon standing over her? She shakes her head thrice to be rid of the deafening fire, only for the heat and the smoke to wrap around her in a suffocating embrace. It's all too much, this heat, that fire, his past—her eyes shoot open, her mind bending beneath the weight of this inferno of a memory as she comes face to face with a pyre violently ablaze.

"Kill them, Silas!" A voice echoes out through the dark of this memory, the voice of his father.

The besieged city and that bloodied night sky are all but gone, leaving Sadie with nothing but the company of the fire before her. Squinting into the near-blinding firelight, she sees blackened shapes concealed beneath the flame—unmoving, perfectly still.

"Kill them!" His father's voice is a crack of a whip.

The smoke creeps into her lungs as she sucks in a breath, spotting the curve of a jaw, the maw of a mouth, the faintest traces of a feminine face twisted by the heat. There's not a body tied to the pyre; but three. Three slender figures, all of them women.

Their faces are melted, almost unrecognizable if it weren't for Sadie's proximity to the flame. With their skin dripping like wax from the charred muscle beneath, there's nothing much more to hold the shape of their faces upright, the fire pulling down at their mandibles so that it looks as if each woman is letting out one final, silent plea of agony.

"If you will not light the fire, my son..." His father's voice comes with a hard rattle of wind, bending the flame for but a moment before fanning it into a towering inferno. *"Then I will do it myself."*

All those hollow eyes, those twisted, sunken faces stare back at her, their heads turned on their bone-splintered necks. Yet it's not her they stare at, but a figure standing behind her.

Before she has the chance to turn, she feels a heavy hand wrap around her shoulder, fingers digging into her skin.

It's him, she thinks to herself, she knows it in her heart—the demon she knows. The threat of those same incarnadine eyes seeps fear into her nerves, yet she sinks into his touch all the same as he pulls her to his side.

With a firm hand he keeps her where she stands, entranced by the flaming pyre. She watches him as fire light dances over the dark contours of his profile, his eyes red only in reflection, not from within.

A low, eerie whistle blows through them both—coming from the pyre itself. The three sunken faces contort, their gaping voids for mouths moving to speak, to sing a song of accusation.

"You killed us."

His jaw hardens as the three women begin their ominous refrain, the smoke billowing from their pyre reeking of burnt flesh, of an agony Sadie can taste in the air. It's not cruelty that wraps around her tongue, nor the plain carnage of the beachside massacre, but something else entirely. The song the three burned women sing offers another note to Silas' suffering, and it's tinged black like a strip of char on a piece of meat. Sadie stares wide-eyed into the flames, her mind racing with a thousand thoughts that converge upon a single realization.

Regret.

He feels regret.

"You let us burn."

The smoke winds its way past her lips, over her tongue, into her throat. The heat of the fire combined with the bitter black smoke rends the breath from her lungs, and instinctively, she reaches out for the first solid mass she can lay her hands upon. "Silas..." With limp fingers she touches his arm, her heart tremoring as the eerie siren song rattles her very bones. "I—I can't take it." Her lids grow heavy, their melodious accusations thick in the air.

"You let us die."

She presses her eyes closed, arms wrapped around herself in an attempt to still the tremble in her fingers, the metallic tang of blood still clinging to the tip of her tongue.

"All of it for you."

The taste is too much, too strong, too *bitter*.

But a harder wind blows, extinguishing the flame and the smoke in a single gust that sways Sadie where she stands.

Silence reigns—and it's a relief.

"*Solita*." Silas' voice is soft, coaxing her to open her eyes.

Blinking back against the dark, she sees his hand at his side, palm facing upwards in an offer of touch that never before seemed as inviting as it does in this moment.

She holds back what can only be a whimper as she winds her fingers through his, the flats of their palms meeting like two open, bleeding wounds. The contact stings for but a moment before she surrenders to the feeling of his blood on hers. His rage, his dark regret, entwining with her sinful sorrow—and how she holds onto it with all that she has left.

"Come," he urges her forward into the darkness, the pyre and those charred women all but swept away, back into the recesses of his memory.

"Where to?"

Sadie swears it's melancholy lacing his voice when he answers, "Someplace sweeter."

And the dark swallows them both.

❧ 12 ❧

SILAS' fingers wound around hers in the darkness is her only guiding light through the abyss of his memory. A light she knows comes from a fire stoked deep within him, an inferno that hungers eternally for human suffering, her suffering—no matter how placid the exterior, no matter how gentle his touch.

They walk through the darkness for what seems like forever in a blink of an eye, the only indication they've reached their destination is when he stops in his tracks, a distant wind blowing in from a plane unseen.

Suppressing her fear as he relinquishes her hand, he leaves her with nothing but the phantom of his warmth. "Silas?" she asks, her voice an echo of confusion in this abyss, a moment of fear in his absence. The horrors of his past, the blood wrought from his hands swirl around her thoughts with all the bitterness of that blood-stained sea. An ocean of sin drips from his fingertips, yet if a monster is what he truly is—then why does she miss his absence at her side?

"Close your eyes." His voice is near, yet the shadows billow over his figure, concealing all but for his face.

The voice of reason deep within urges her to search his eyes for any trace of ill-intent, but her heart answers for her, surrendering to his command.

Her gaze meets his one more time before she obeys, closing her eyes, welcoming the cool breeze that tousles her hair and kisses her skin. Silas' presence is swept away by the wind, leaving Sadie to her own devices as the gust overtakes her, swaying her where she stands—but the wind dies down and her senses awaken with the murmur of rushing water.

Pinpricks of strange familiarity ripple over her skin, and this time she opens her eyes without needing his voice to coax her. Her heart rises as she lifts her gaze upwards, staring wide-eyed at the sight before her as she realizes: *this isn't his past.*

It's a dream—*my dream.*

Rising tall in columns of stone stands the Trevi Fountain stretching out before her in all its ornate splendor. She's in Italy, in Rome, standing in a dream she's held close to her chest for countless years before the death of her father, obliterated completely the day her mother abandoned her. Yet here it is, a dream raised from the dead.

But it's not the Italy she's seen in photos, not quite the Rome she's seen in films. The Trevi's elegant stone sculptures twist and writhe in unnatural shapes. The soft glow of the fountain lights are dominated instead by a crimson haze, the teal blue waters cast in a blood-dark hue. The faces of the Tritons and the horses stare back at her in demonic jest; as if they know they exist only as a cruel inversion of something that simply cannot be.

"This isn't right..." She stares at the mesmeric nightmare before her, letting herself walk over to the fountain's edge, the rush of falling water filling her ears. Peering over the edge, Sadie is faced with the reflection of a lonely girl, arms clasped desperately around herself. "This can't be real."

"It is." Silas' voice calls out from behind her, a black silhouette materializing in the reflection of the water. "It's as real as your tears... as real as the pulse of your heart."

She turns to face him, fire igniting from deep within her. "Why are you showing me this? After everything I've seen... after everything you are?!" Her eyes run over this expanse of a dream, a patch-work imagining of modern day Rome, of all its cobblestone streets and terracotta streaked buildings. It's all from his making, his piecing together of a place that he's only seen between the pages of books, through photos, through the potent want of her dreams. She drops her shoulders, sitting back against the lip of the fountain, her voice a sigh of surrender. "*Why?*"

He says nothing, only stopping where she sits, holding out his hand. She draws her gaze down to his palm, where the dull gleam of something metallic peers up at her.

She lets out a breath the moment she realizes what it is—it's a coin.

And it's nothing more than a cruel reminder of the past that once was, of a future that will never be.

"It is what you wanted, is it not? Like your companions—they have grasped what they wanted, leaving you with nothing but a house on the edge of the world... here, take it." He holds his hand out, and she plucks the coin from between his fingers, pressing it hard against the flesh of her palm until she can feel the indentation she knows so well. Sadie dares not look back to the creeping shadows sitting on the shoulders of those stone sculptures, nor up towards the ink-black sky and the blood-stained waters below. Her gaze is fixed solely to the dull shine of the coin between her fingers.

"They were right..." she inhales. "They'll get the real thing, and all I'll ever have is *this.*"

With a sigh she allows herself to draw her eyes up to the smoke-stained sky, and to the statues towering tall above her; remarking in their grandeur, the beauty—how far she is from home. Again and again the threat of what he is thrums beneath her skin, but she doesn't hear it anymore. Not when his touch lingers across her skin, that phantom warmth slicing through her skin and upturning everything she thought she buried deep inside her. Everything she swore would never see the light of day.

She sits back against the edge of the fountain, only for Silas to join her side, the proximity sending her over the edge of restraint as she lets her fear, her anger, her doubt dissipate in the wind, leaving nothing left but her sorrow.

"I... I'm not afraid to live, if that's what you're thinking. It's just, I've never set foot out of this island, let alone Port Cante. I was born in that house, home-schooled in that house..." She drops her gaze to her hands and the coin between her fingers, her voice a quiet admission. "My whole life has been the Hacienda—it's my mother and father's life work, their gift, their dream. I've never seen what's beyond the horizon, what's beyond the line of the sea... and sometimes I think it's not because I can't..." She lets out a breath, "It's because I don't want to." She lifts her gaze to meet Silas' watching eyes. "The thought that it's better out there, that there's a life outside of these walls, just waiting for me... that's what scares me. I can't help but think that everything that's happened to me, everything I'm left with—it's all I deserve. Including the Hacienda that's nothing but a cage. My only cage... my only home."

"Hm," Silas replies, some realization dawning upon him. "It's simpler than you think, *Solita.*"

She feels her heart pulse faster at the sight of the water's reflection dancing over the shadows of his face.

"You are as free as the starling you've taken into your care. Nothing more, nothing less."

Sadie turns to face her reflection in the water, brushing her fingertips just against the water's surface as she fights the meaning of his words, ripples forming beneath her touch until her image disappears into nothingness. Keeping her gaze on the water, her mind's eye drifts to that distant sea stained red with the blood spilled at Silas' hand. All those bodies, all that death, and the haunting voices of those three, charred corpses strung up against that burning pyre claw at her thoughts, severing what remains of her hesitation.

"Those... those women that burned. They said you let them die..." she pauses, testing the waters. He's markedly silent, and she turns to face him, his eyes obscured by the velvet night. Yet at the mention of those charred three, she can see his suffering in plain. "Who were they, Silas?"

He's silent within himself, fighting against her question the same way she did his words just moments ago. Yet one side reigns —which one, she doesn't know. Silas leans his elbows over his knees, jaw clenching as he lets the answer loose, "Estefania... Eufemia... Aldaura." Every name is a lick of fire against his tongue as he dredges up the past in a ritual of invocation, a summoning spell to call forth those three charred corpses—but they never come back. "My sisters. They were my sisters."

Sadie feels her heart fold, the thought of his family beyond Lorenzo sending a ripple of sadness through her. But she continues on, "What happened to them?"

He says nothing, the silence yawning out before them like the black-dark abyss of the sky overhead. "My father—he killed them. He lit their pyre and forced me to watch, and I did nothing to stop him, for it was my punishment..." He forces the words out in an expulsion of a memory that's as searing as it was the day it occurred. "Punishment for a past sin."

For a moment she can feel the phantom lattice screen of a confessional booth separating them both—she the confessor, he the penitent at her mercy. "What was your sin?"

"I killed."

Sadie twists the fabric of her dress in her lap, tongue moving of its own accord, hungry for his penance, ravenous for his suffering.

"It can't just be that..."

"I killed someone who was not mine to kill."

She balls her fists, "Who?"

"A human..." his voice is soft, a near whisper. "A woman."

Why sits on the very tip of her tongue, but it never takes the leap into the silence that settles between them. *Why* is too piercing —too intimate—and instead Sadie settles for the next best thing. "What was her name?"

Silas' face is carved in tension, "I... I don't remember."

And she believes him.

The woman he killed, a human like her—it's all the confirmation of everything Lorenzo warned her of, manifest in Silas' own words. *A weakness for humans* is what Lorenzo said, a taunting reminder of the line drawn between prey and predator. A silence lulls between them, and she feels him begin to ebb away in his attempt to remember, her nerves tangling at the thought of his hands around her neck.

But he brushes those thoughts away with a single word.

"*Solita,*" he pulls her back to the present; to his side, to this dream beneath the twisted Trevi. "Do you think me a monster?"

Sadie toys with the coin between her fingers, her tongue moving before her thoughts, "No. I don't."

He's quiet, and for the first time it's Sadie who's rendered him speechless. "Why do you say that?"

Silence fills the space between them, yet Sadie feels an unfamiliar lightness spread through her veins as she answers, "Because you took me here, didn't you?" In spite of it all, his rage, his past, that ocean of blood—she smiles, the coin between her fingers lighter than air. As nightmarish as this conjuration of the Trevi is, it's the Trevi all the same.

Shaking her head, she wraps her arms around herself as the gravity of it all dawns upon her. "It's just my luck." She can't help but let a laugh fall from her lips as she sits in a nightmarish realm beside the demon who brought her here.

"Luck?" he asks.

"Just my luck the only way I'd ever see Italy is here. With you— with a demon's deal hanging over my head."

"If it's luck you believe in, then do what you came here to do. What you've always wanted to do." He flicks his eyes down to the coin in her palm, watching her with waiting eyes.

"Mm," she murmurs. "You're right."

She shuts her eyes, holding the coin up to her chin. Faintly, the melody of music finds its way into her psyche—that same song playing from the record player on the other side of the veil. She attempts to focus her mind, but she's restless. She could wish for an endless stream of tourists to come to the Hacienda, for its former glory to return, for it to stand another hundred years—yet she can't bring herself to commit to any one of them.

"I..." She opens her eyes, met with the same curious gaze. "I think I'll wait."

He peers down at her, perplexed. "Why is that?"

"I don't know..." She pulls her eyes away from his. "I don't know what I want any more."

"Then hold on to it until you do," he replies, a rush of wind billowing through the square, quickly becoming a gust, and Sadie blinks at the incoming debris the gale carries with it—and when she opens her eyes she finds herself laying on the bed in Silas' bedroom, only the sound of the record player humming the same song reminding her she's back in the real world. The waking world.

Silas is nowhere to be found, but the sight of the Trevi lingers in her mind, the wetness on her fingertips telling of the fact that she dipped her hand in the font's waters, that she was truly there. In another place, in another realm, but there all the same—the scent of him lingering on her all the confirmation she needs.

Making sure the darkness conceals her, she returns to her bedroom with the coin close to her skin as she slips in beneath the covers, the cool linens a soothing lull to her summer soaked skin. She lays in a state of half dreaming for what seems like hours until she hears that familiar soft knock on her door.

She barely moves a muscle when Isaiah enters the room to say goodbye. Yet she doesn't raise her voice or put up a fight as she realizes he's back so much later than he should have been. When he leans over the side of her bed, she doesn't quite know why she feigns sleep when he kisses her cheek and whispers a hushed *goodnight*.

Because perhaps for once, it is.

13

FOR THE FIRST time in a year Sadie dreams not of the cliffs, nor the raging tide, nor her mother.

Tonight, she dreams of Silas.

He's a mass of shadow at the edge of her bed, a shade of night the same hue as that smoke smeared sky, eyes a crimson the same as that blood-stained sea. Yet in the shore of her bedroom, there are no hollowed corpses strewn across the shallows—there is only her, paralyzed against the tide of her sheets, pierced by those incarnadine eyes.

This is what Lorenzo meant.

He moves closer, the reflection of an inferno staring back at her. She can feel those flames begin to lick at her skin, the crackle and hiss of some dark fire growing into a cacophonous roar.

He can turn a dream into a nightmare faster than you can realize.

She struggles to move, but her body is nothing but a dead weight as she attempts to escape the flames clawing at her skin—but he's flush close now, all around her and nowhere at once, one hand hovering above her body with a hellscape behind his eyes. Sadie's limbs fill with lead as the dark radiates from his body in waves, and in the blink of an eye she feels his fingers at her throat, his index finger coming to rest at her pulse, tangling with the chain at her neck.

She gasps—his touch burns her.

There's not a trace of the demon she's come to know.

"Silas..." Her plea is a drop of water in the heat, yet it doesn't go up in steam.

He stops as if he hears her, yet the pain he leaves in his wake ripples through her. Blinding, searing, unbearable fire.

She awakens with a gasp, shooting up out of bed with a mist of sweat clinging to her forehead, limbs wrapped up in the sheets, heart racing. A distant rooster crows, and Sadie scrambles to her feet, the room cast in the pale light of dawn. Clutching the mattress' edge, she wills her pulse to steady, her attention captured by the starling at her bedside.

A crimson eye pokes up at her from the depths of his cardboard box, and Sadie lets out a sigh at the sight. Leaning over the bedside table, she brushes her fingers against his jet-black plumage, lifting his wing to check on his stitches, only to be met with some resistance.

"You're looking better..." she smiles, before rising to replace his water, moving the half-eaten figs closer to where he's nestled. "But you have to eat more."

The bird coos in response, before shutting its eyes as if to ignore her request.

"Hm." Sadie presses her lips together. "Stubborn thing."

Leaving the bird to slumber, Sadie runs through the shower, raking her fingernails against her skin, desperate to be rid of this oppressive summer heat. Even the cold water proves to be futile the moment the sun wraps around the Hacienda, filling every room with the unforgiving glow of morning light.

Sadie slips on a fresh blue sundress that buttons up from the hem to the neckline before stopping to stand in front of her reflection. Brushing the tangles from her hair, she smooths the fabric over her hips, toying with the pearl pendant resting between her collarbones.

Although it was nothing more than a nightmare, Sadie forces herself not to linger on the feeling of Silas' fingers tangled around this same chain, nor the lick of a phantom burn he left in his wake.

But the waking world comes calling, and Sadie thanks the short, sharp knock against her door as it lifts her from this spell, carrying her towards her bedroom door. She rests her fingers on the handle, furrowing her brows as the smell of something burning wafts up from the floor below.

"Before you say anything Sadie, I was just trying to do something nice."

It's Odette. Sadie pulls the door open to reveal an apologetic face hovering close to hers.

"What did you do?" Sadie asks, steeling herself for the worst.

A grin pulls up at Odette's lips. "I made eggs... kind of."

Letting out a deep sigh, Sadie rubs her temples, "If you can call whatever that smell is eggs, then thank you."

"Hey, I tried." Odette winks. "I disabled the fire alarms so it wouldn't wake you up in a panic, but you can thank me later." She turns on her heel, not giving Sadie the chance to reply as she makes her way back into the hallway, calling over her shoulder, "Tomorrow is the Festival so *we* are going into town today. I need to buy a dress to wear—and so do you."

"But I—"

"—You said we would go. No excuses!" Odette lingers at the bathroom door, shooting Sadie a determined glance.

Knowing there's no winning this battle, Sadie lets out a sigh before conceding. "Okay, okay... I'm coming."

Odette nods once, triumphant. "Great. Be ready in twenty... I already called the cab."

And with that, Odette shuts the bathroom door behind her, the sudden quiet followed by the sound of the showerhead.

Leaning against her doorframe, Sadie fends off the heaviness of her bones as a wave of tiredness washes over her, but the wave is swept away the moment she hears movement from the hallway beyond, and her heart catches in her chest, knowing who it is.

With careful steps she makes her way out into the hallway, casting her eyes in both directions. The door to the bathroom is shut, the sound of Odette's shower karaoke the only other sign of life in the house, yet Sadie can't help but look to the last door at the end of the hall. Holding her breath, she lingers, waiting for him to emerge from the shadows with those same mesmeric crimson eyes.

The urge to knock on his door and enter his domain thrums through her fingertips, her mind stirring at what she'll see. Will it be a rage rapt demon behind the door? Or the shape, the illusion of a man called Silas?

The groaning of pipes from the bathroom captures Sadie's attention, and she lets it carry her away from Silas' room and back into the depths of the house, only to be met with the sound of a low, distinct creak. Stopping dead in her tracks, she stares dumbly at Odette's bedroom door. It's ajar, just enough for her to see the mess of clothes strewn across the bed, her open suitcase, the array of used tissues littering the nightstand. With no sign of Odette's shower singing letting up, she lingers, swayed by curiosity.

With a deep breath, Sadie slips into her room.

The air carries the scent of some expensive, foreign perfume, the sting of it against her nostrils potent. But the vibration of Odette's phone against the dresser pulls her towards her phone— where it sits open and unlocked.

Sadie catches a glimpse of the latest message, the name at the top of the screen written in bold:

Isaiah.

Curiosity melts into want, and then into need as the phone buzzes yet again, the urge to read her messages mounting. Sadie glances over her shoulder, the sound of Odette's singing faint under the sound of the shower running—she's alone.

With another step forward, Sadie picks up Odette's phone, their messages as clear as daylight.

Isaiah: Maybe if you spend some more time with her, you'll see she's just the same as you left... Underneath it all, at least

Sadie furrows her brows, pressing her finger to the screen and scrolling up to see the previous messages.

Odette: She's not the same girl any more. Did you see how she just zoned out and stormed off last night? She's a shell of the girl I grew up with. It's like she's... dead inside.

A heat forms under Sadie's cheeks, and she drops her arms to her side, until she catches a glimpse of their last set of messages.

Isaiah: About last night...

Sadie's heart constricts, mind racing as she devours every word.

Isaiah: We really shouldn't do that again.

Odette: It's not a big deal. It's not like you guys are official, right?

Of course.

It's all her fears manifest in a few simple words, all the justification of her solitude she ever needed. The sting of loneliness, the ache of death, and the numbness that comes with an empty house... none of it hurts quite as much as the voice that tells her it's all she'll ever get—it's all she deserves.

The pipes squeak as the shower stops. Sadie almost drops the phone back on the dresser, quickly making her way to the door to escape Odette's suffocating perfume. With fevered breath, she finds her way back to her own bedroom. Standing at the foot of her bed, she watches the wind tousle the bed curtains; the only movement in a room full of stillness.

For a moment she screws her eyes shut tight, wishing this was nothing but a bad dream, a continuation of that fiery inferno she felt last night. But it's nothing like the feeling of fire at her skin—*it's so much worse.*

Odette's footsteps outside her door breaks the stillness, and Sadie opens her eyes to see her leaning against the door frame. Her hair drips remnants of water, the sunflower yellow of her camisole tracking droplets as she peers over at her with a raised brow.

"You done dreaming?" Odette asks, a half smile on her lips.

Sadie reaches for her handbag, slinging it over her shoulder. "Yeah," Sadie answers, a numbness pulsing through her every vein, her every nerve. "I'm done."

✤✤✤✤✤

THE SCENT of fresh fabric and the droning hum of the sewing machine fills Sadie's senses as they reach the second floor of Louisa's tailor shop. Sister to Maria, and one of the only purveyors of *haute couture* in this small slice of the Philippines, Louisa is as stern as she is short. Standing at 4"9, she commands the attention of an army the way she holds the measuring tape across Sadie's shoulders, forcing her to stand stiffly upright—as if it's armor she's measuring her for, anything to protect her in the heat of battle.

"If only you came earlier, I would have made you a more beautiful gown!" Louisa barks, and all Sadie can muster is an apology as she stares at her reflection in the full length mirror strung up against the wall.

"I'm sorry, *tita*. I just haven't had the time." The lie is a weak one, but the frantic energy of working a last minute deadline prevents Lousia from sniffing it out.

Louisa tuts in response, peering back at Sadie from behind her thick glasses, her tongue faster than her fingers. "I don't understand what occupies your time, Sadie." She stops for a moment, meeting Sadie's gaze directly. "It's not like the Hacienda is full, is it?"

Sadie bites down on her tongue, irritation filling her mouth. "You're right. It's not," is all she answers, thanking the fact that Louisa is too absorbed in her measurements to notice her clenched jaw.

Odette doesn't hesitate to fill the silence, pulling out her phone to show Louisa a slew of saved images—each one a modelesque, put together, fair-skinned Filipina more beautiful than the last; all wearing modernized, sleek cut Maria Clara dresses. Sadie turns away from the sight, focusing instead on her reflection. From the tired lines beneath her eyes, her frazzled hair, her sun-soaked skin—she's all the imperfection, the sorrow, the loneliness that Odette simply *isn't*.

Louisa coos over Odette's choices, and she doesn't hesitate to start her alterations. It's late afternoon by the time the two step out of the stuffy little tailor shop, Odette carrying the brown paper bag containing the two Maria Clara dresses she requested. Both are as tight fitting and contemporary as Louisa could alter in the given time, both of them stamped with Odette's seal of approval; the only seal that mattered.

"Come on. Let's get these home." Sadie sighs as they make their way back into the heart of town. Odette follows as Sadie leads them through the winding stalls of imitation brands and knock-off luxuries that grace the beach side of Port Cante's sprawling market, now closing up for the day.

A silence settles between them, and Sadie turns to Odette with a soft smile. She shouldn't say it—shouldn't suggest it.

But quiet vindication stirs inside her, and she simply has to act upon it.

"I'm going to visit my mom." Sadie commands, "Come with me."

Of all the things Odette expected, judging by the wide-eyed look on her face, this is the very last on the list.

What are you doing, Sadie? She scolds herself, expecting the worst, but it never comes.

All Odette does is nod. "Sure. I'll come."

"It's not far." Sadie assures her, as they walk side by side through the heat-soaked streets of Port Cante until they reach the churchyard. In silence they make their way down the dirt path lying between the two twisted palm trees that serve as the guardians to Port Cante General Cemetery.

The earth beneath is bone dry, yearning for the reprieve of a downpour. *Looking at those darkening clouds, it seems like it's not too far off*, Sadie thinks to herself, as they make their way through the winding path and the jungle's overgrown greenery.

The winds rattle the trees overhead, the two casting their eyes across the crumbling concrete crosses and sun-faded markers jutting out of the earth like rotting splinters of teeth. Countless graves sit tightly stacked, with only faded names and forgotten dates to commemorate whomever lay beneath. Amidst a spray of overgrown hibiscus, Sadie comes to a stop before two headstones that lay side by side.

Odette toys with the handle of the brown paper bag as they reach their destination, a clear nervousness woven into her movements.

"Here we are." Sadie leans forward and runs her eyes over the names of her parents etched in cold, unfeeling stone.

Enrique Pasiona

Running her fingers over the silver plated letters, Sadie feels a twinge of guilt as she looks around at the other graves lovingly tended to with flowers, candles, and the occasional framed photograph.

Natalia Pasiona

"One day I hope she can lay beside you, dad." Sadie whispers, letting her fingers slip from the letters of his name, only for Odette's voice to pull her back to the present.

"She's not... she's not buried here?" Odette asks, voice quiet.

"There was never a body." Sadie stands upright, "There was no closure. No sense of peace... Her real grave is there." She turns towards the sound of the crashing waves up ahead, letting the lapping ocean fill the air between them before the words fall from her lips, "She jumped from the cliffs of Infanta Bay."

An uncomfortable silence sits between them, and Sadie relishes in it.

"I...I never knew."

Of course you didn't.

"There's a lot that you don't know, Odette. There's a lot that happened when you were gone." Her eyes land on Odette, pinning her to where she stands in spite of the winds that begin to pick up. "My dad died... and mom killed herself." She takes a step closer, Odette shifting her weight in response. "Isaiah and I... we didn't have anyone else."

"Sadie, I'm so—"

"—You're not sorry." An unfamiliar taste lines her tongue as Sadie doubles down. *Bitterness,* she recognizes the flavor as she doubles down, "Why should *you* be sorry?"

Odette crosses her arms over her chest, the darkening skies above casting a shadow over her bright yellow camisole.

"What's the deal, Sadie? Why did you take me here? To lecture me?"

Tension thicker than the summer heat winds around them both like a dwindling thread reaching its end in the bobbin of a sewing machine. Every revolution, every spin of the bobbin is one moment closer to the inevitable end, an end Sadie has no fear in reaching. Not anymore.

"You chose to come here, remember? You chose *this place* as your little hide out from your dad—it's nothing but an escape for you. Just a beach you can pack up and fly out to whenever you feel like it. Just because you *can.*"

Odette casts her eyes downward for a moment, and Sadie can see the sting of her own words on the other girl's face, if not guilt, then regret—pain, loss, hurt.

"But you never came back for us. Not once in all those years did you ever reach out or try to see if we were okay." Hurt laces Sadie's words as she shrugs, "I guess you just didn't feel like it."

"I..." Odette parts her lips, at a loss for words. "It's not because

I didn't feel like it," she answers, drawing her eyes up to Sadie, features hardened, no longer playful. "It's my—

"—It's not just your dad," Sadie accuses, fists balled at her sides. "It's *you*. Because what could possibly be so horrible in your perfect little life that you'd have to come here?"

The resolve in Odette's eyes melts away with each passing word, but Sadie feels no pity. Not when all that dominates her thoughts is the image of Odette and Isaiah together, together like they should be, together like they always wanted before Dominic whisked her away.

"And by the way..." Sadie's voice is quiet as she drops her shoulders, echoing the text message she sent to Isaiah earlier, "We are official, Odette. We are."

The words are stuck in Odette's throat, and the look Sadie shoots her keeps them there. Odette inhales sharply, "I can't do this... *You* can't do this, Sadie."

"Do what, exactly?"

"Take your misery out on everyone else! Just because you're miserable doesn't mean everyone else has to be, too!" Odette's words battle against the growing winds, her fingers threatening to pierce the brown paper bag she clutches to her chest, as she readies to storm off. But she lingers for a moment longer, softening her voice, "Sadie... You can't hide behind death forever."

And the thread runs out.

A dozen curses dance on the tip of Sadie's tongue, but Odette turns on her heel, storming off and disappearing down the broken path as countless graves watch with lifeless eyes.

Sadie is alone once again.

Time stretches out before her like the crystalline blue that stretches endlessly out around the coast of Infanta Bay. With Odette gone, Sadie feels a weight lift from her shoulders, only to see a shadow at the corner of her periphery. Sadie turns, a part of her hoping that she'll see the shape of Silas take form in the shadows, his eyes resting on hers, his voice drowning out the silence of the cemetery.

But he's not here.

She doesn't dare think of what could happen if she lets herself drown in the fantasy she's created—so she breaks the spell, turning her back on the sea and the silence, heading back to the only place she has left, the only place that will take her.

THE REPRIEVE SADIE searches for is nowhere to be found the moment she steps through the Hacienda's front doors. Making her way up the staircase two steps at a time, she breathes a sigh of relief when she sees Odette's door open, the room devoid of its owner.

Dropping her shoulders, she continues through the eerie quiet of the house only to be met with an open door—the door to her bedroom. Candle smoke wafts in from beyond, and immediately Sadie knows something is wrong.

Pressing her lips together, she pushes her door open wider, greeted by a specter of a dress.

Hanging from her bed canopy is the crepe de chine Maria Clara from the tailor shop staring back at Sadie with an ink black stain splashed across the length of the bodice in what can only be retaliation from Odette.

Sadie clenches her fists at her side, watching the ink-marred skirt rustle in the breeze from the open windows. Shutting door behind her, Sadie strides across the room to shut the windows, choking the wind and forcing the room into utter stillness.

Yet the shadows still dance, twisting lights urging Sadie to turn and set her eyes upon Odette's last laugh. Turning, she sees her room beset with dozens of lit tea candles strewn across every flat surface—her room turned into a memorial mass.

All these candles, the cruel ghost of a dress strung up at the altar of her bed—it's all Odette's cruel trick, a cruel mockery. Sadie can still hear Odette's voice against the shell of her ear.

You can't hide behind death forever.

Yet here it is, a twisted joke staring back at her in plain.

Gnashing her teeth together, Sadie storms forward to rip the dress off the hanger, her cheeks red hot, heart pacing out of control.

Snatching up a pair of embroidery scissors from her vanity, she begins hacking away at the ink-stained fabric in a violent fury, not stopping until she's hunched over the foot of her bed with nothing in her hands but ribbons of embellished lace and crepe.

Odette's voice rings in her ears.

Stop hiding, stop hiding, stop hiding.

It grows louder and louder until she can't take another second of it. Bundling up the fabric remnants and the scissors along with it, she hurls the mass of ruined fabric across the room, burying her face deep in her hands.

Odette was right, she thinks to herself, *I shouldn't take my misery out on her. Not on anyone else.*

Fighting back tears, she lifts her head from her hands, wrapping her arms around her waist.

It belongs to me. Only to me.

But the scent of smoke catches her attention, and through the haze of bleary eyes she sees the spark of a fire growing before her. It's the dress—it knocked over a candle; the fabric burning up in tendrils of smoke. The flame moves all too quickly, devouring the Maria Clara, jumping from the rug to the lace curtains to the muslin bed drapery—ready to consume the rest of the room encasing Sadie. Scrambling for the cardboard box on the bedside table, Sadie scoops the bird up in her arms, his little heart beating frantically against his ribcage.

Fumbling for the door, she's stopped in her tracks as a lick of fire consumes a polyester robe strung up behind the door, forcing her backwards from the sudden flame. Heart beating rapidly, she wills herself to wrap her fingers around the handle, only for the flame to scorch her fingertips, sending her backwards.

Clutching the starling to her chest, she backs away from the flaming door until she's dead in the center of her bedroom, the tea candles blinking back at her in mockery amidst the crackling fire— but it's less the flame he has to worry about, and more of the smoke that rises from it.

Directly in the path of the fire glow, Sadie can't even stare her own death in the face as the thickening cloud of smoke obscures her vision. She crawls onto the floor as low as she can, ambling backwards until she's backed up against the foot of her bed, the searing heat of the fire surrounding her on all sides. The starling flutters its wings in desperate motion, feeling the agonizing heat quicker through his paper-skin. Sadie curls her arms tightly around him a futile attempt to protect him from the fumes, yet even she knows the bird is dying in her arms; she'll feel his last breath long before her own, all she can do is to stave it off for as long as she can.

Each passing second leaves her with less air in her lungs, and more of a desire to slip away into the dark haze beckoning her towards it. There's no escape; no way through, no way out.

With a sharp sting of an inhalation, the starling's heartbeat sputters; the organ consumed by smoke, devoured by the dark. His frail body stiffens in her arms, yet she holds onto him with all she has left as her vision grows dim, limbs turning to lead as a haze begins to lull her to a sleep that's never felt quite so enticing.

But there's a wisp of a movement up ahead, and she parts her lips as a darkness emerges from the fire before her. Inadvertently, she sucks in more smoke as she draws her stinging eyes upwards to the silhouette standing in billowing black before her.

Time has all but slipped away as she stares into a pair of eyes aglow with hellish red, reflective in the dark.

The fire around her has grown into a cacophonous roar, the

heat clambering up her fingers; through her veins and seeping into the blood beneath. Yet she's transfixed to the bird in her care and those incarnadine eyes peering down at her from the flame.

This is where he comes from, she tells herself—the fire, the smoke, the endless inferno.

He's exactly the demon from her nightmare, unfazed by the heat as his eyes flare a brighter shade of ruby. He's moving closer and closer towards her through the smoky haze, the veins of his hands aglow with the same shade of flame that encases him from all sides.

Sadie waits.

She waits for his command over the fire to reclaim her body into dust and ash, she waits for the searing, burning brand of his touch against her skin, but it simply never comes.

Silas crouches down before her, the Hacienda bending beneath the weight of a wind that rattles the windowpanes, a gust that throws open the windows she shut, a force that opens her bedroom door and allows the smoke a means to escape.

Cold air wraps tight around her body as the wind howls hard against her senses, forcing her to shut her eyes. Her hair whips violently against her skin, threatening to take the starling from her arms, and the breath from her lungs. But the wind dies down, and silence reigns free.

The crackle and spit of the flame is gone, extinguished by the force of the wind, coaxed away by Silas' shadow. The silence is deafening, engulfing Sadie in a tide as cold as it is all-consuming, leaving only lingering smoke before it dissipates into nothingness.

Opening her eyes, Sadie's vision blackens at the edges, her limbs filling with lead just as it did in her nightmare of that red-eyed demon. With an aching pulse, she feels herself begin to slump forward, only for a pair of arms to wrap around her waist, pulling her upright. The smoke has weakened her, yet her grip around the starling is unyielding as Silas hoists her up into his arms, her fingers finding purchase around the fabric of his shirt, dreading his touch yet needing it all the same.

She can feel his breath against her cheek, his voice colored with some distant emotion as he tilts her chin upwards to meet his dark gaze.

"*Solita...*" he says her name—and it sears her bones in a way a fire never could. This is the brand upon her immortal soul, not a scorch mark nor a tremor of agony, but sweetly, simply, a name.

She wants to say his name in return, to taste it on her tongue, but the smoke in her lungs strangles her breath, and all goes dark.

14

SOLITA, the name that isn't quite hers dances in her mind, a tenuous tether to a world that's slipping farther away with each passing second. But soon enough, Sadie is too far gone, floating in an ocean she does not recognize, cast adrift in a place she cannot name, cannot make sense of.

Pressing her eyes closed, she focuses on the feeling of the pearl necklace across her collarbones, and by the time she opens her eyes, she feels solid ground beneath her.

Blinking back against the bright light, it fades away faster than her heart has the chance to still. She looks up, left with a scene before her that's all too familiar.

She's standing in the foyer of the Hacienda—but it's not *her* Hacienda.

It's dawn; the sky a blue pale enough just to fill the foyer with soft light as she makes her way over to the bottom of the wooden staircase. Running her one hand over the railing, she takes a deep breath in awe of the fact that suddenly her surroundings seems so *new*.

Rich tapestries woven in shades of bottle greens, saffron

yellows and fiery reds adorn the mulawin wood walls that Sadie had grown so accustomed to seeing bare. Scenes depicting men at the hunt, women amidst lush, lavish gardens and animalia of all kinds peer back at Sadie through the pale morning light—yet one scene rises tall above the rest, a vibrant tapestry stretching out across the length of the wall above the staircase, looming over her in a scene that can only be from the Book of Revelation.

A skeletal figure rides atop a pale white horse, sword drawn and gleaming in gilded thread in the wake of crimson, cutting flames devouring a sea of bodies—all sinners claimed by the inferno. It's a warning more than anything else, a warning against the inescapability of a man named Death.

That drawn sword, sure-fire posture, the corpses in his wake—Sadie can't help herself from recognizing a shadow of familiarity between this figure and the demon that stood on that beachside massacre. It's only here, standing beneath the gaze of Death upon his pale white horse, does Sadie realize where she is. *When she is.*

The starling song is loud from the plumeria tree beyond the front door, but a marked silence blankets the estate.

A breeze blows through the open windows, and Sadie hugs herself to fend off the chill, the air growing thicker with each passing second. She narrows her eyes as the wind carries a bitter stench into the Hacienda—like smoke, mixed with something foul. Something inhuman.

And then there's that thud.

Again and again that loud, discordant thud resounds throughout the Hacienda, followed by silence and the creak of a door. Faintly she can hear the murmur of voices, prompting Sadie's feet to react faster than she has the chance to think as she slips into the narrow hallway that leads to the kitchen. Shrouded in darkness, Sadie presses herself against the open arch way, spying the vague shapes of two figures at the end of the hall—one belonging to a man, the other a young girl.

Their conversation is hushed for a moment before the man takes his leave, Sadie hiding away in waiting as his footsteps pass over the kitchen. Making sure he's gone, Sadie lets out a breath before peeking out into the dim, catching the rustle of a friar's robe for a brief moment before he disappears into the Hacienda.

Turning to the other side of the hall, the shape of a girl slips into the room at the end of the hall, Sadie furrowing her brows as she leaves the door ajar behind her.

With her heart hammering in her chest, Sadie follows, plunging herself into the dim of this vast room that's otherwise eerily empty save for the same girl clutching something tightly to her chest, staring at the center of the hardwood floors with a vacant gaze.

A lengthy mahogany table sits pressed up against one side of the room, with all its matching chairs pushed to one side, leaving nothing but a vast space that yawns out before them both. Sadie steps closer, noticing the paler colored floorboards, and she realizes —they're freshly set. Crouching down to her knees, she runs her fingers across the handiwork, seeing the nails driven deep into each board, heart beating quick at the thought of the demon hidden beneath.

But the sound of the girl's voice beside her captures her attention.

"You will never awaken..."

Sadie rises to her feet, stepping closer to the girl dressed in maid's garb, her voice a steely refrain, the language she speaks— some old form of Tagalog—transcending the barrier of time that separates them both.

"As long as my blood runs. As long as my heart beats."

There's a familiarity Sadie senses between them, written in the girl's features, etched into the color of her eyes, the ochre brown of her skin, the curve of her lips, the silken black of her hair—it's as if she's seen this face before, in her grandmother, in her mother, and in herself. It's a familiarity that becomes all too overwhelming the moment she spies what it is the maid has clutched between her fingers; an iridescent pearl.

"You will not stir. You will not wake."

Sadie furrows her brows, knowing it can't possibly be the same pearl around her neck now, it can't possibly—

"Your dawn will never come."

Her heart sinks. The familiarity of those words rushes over her in a tide of shadow, the same darkness that crawled up and out of the grave she unearthed, the same darkness that claimed simply:

My dawn has come.

Sadie swallows her fear, reaching her hand out to touch her, but she phases through her shoulder like a knife slicing through air. The room begins to sway; this dream beginning to ebb as the sound of waves fill her senses. An icy cold laps at her ankles, and Sadie sees water at her feet.

Searching for anything to hold onto in this dream of a memory, Sadie finds nothing—the low creak of the door resounding as that smoke black haze begins to fill in the edges of her vision once more.

The shape of another figure arises from the dark, bringing with it a soft voice, a soft murmur. This voice speaks in Spanish— Spanish wrapped up in a sorrow, a quiet desperation Sadie can't help herself from feeling drawn to.

She reaches out towards the figure, only for the water lapping at her ankles to tighten around her skin in a vice-tight grip. Without the chance to scream, the water pulls her into its depths, and she's plunged back into the same swelling ocean of her nightmares before a firm hand around hers brings her back— breaking the surface.

With a gasp she awakens.

The sheets beneath her aren't her own; neither this bed, nor this room. Immediately, she withdraws into herself, clutching at her throat as the sting of smoke still clings to her insides. Casting her eyes around the dim, she sees she's lying in Silas' bed. The soft light of dawn streams in from beyond the window which can only mean she must have slept through the night.

"There you are." Silas' voice greets her, his figure a dark shadow in her peripheral vision. "You're awake."

Her heart catches at the sound of his voice, and as her vision adjusts, so does the image of him standing so close to the edge of the bed. The sheets smell so much of him—of clean linen, of saffron flowers, of rich earth. She curls her legs up against her chest in an attempt to draw a line around her thoughts.

"I was there..." she flounders, voice a breathless whisper. "I saw it..." Sadie clutches the necklace around her neck, a cold sweat clinging to her skin. "I saw the past."

Sadie chews the inside of her lip, the maid's words dancing in circles around her scattered thoughts. *You will never awaken,* is what she said. The steeliness in her voice far from a plea, and more of a promise.

Her thoughts consume her senses until he breaks the spell she's under.

"What did you see?" he asks, his voice wrapped up in the same smoke that clings to her tongue.

Looking up to face him, the words fail to budge from her lips, but she forces them out, one by one. "I was here. At the Hacienda. I could smell burning. I could smell death."

"Salbador..." Silas casts his eyes away, his memories stirring. "My father. He was burned by the friars after they discovered who —*what*—he was."

Sadie feels a wave of nausea wash over her at the thought, and she wraps her arms around herself in an attempt to coax the stench away.

"Tell me," his voice is colored with the need to know more as he leans in ever closer, "What else did you see?"

Sadie twists the pearl at her neck with nervous fingers,

intoxicated by the foreign scent of him, of his past, and of that horrible, hideous smoke. The pearl is at the heart of what's kept him asleep; it's a part of his curse, the tether that binds them together. She can't bring herself to tell him—not when she still feels the heat of the inferno inside him, the feeling of his fingers against her skin, against the chain around her neck.

With a hoarse voice, she answers, "I... I don't remember."

He leans back against the chair, his eyes growing distant for a brief moment, until she pulls him back to the present with a sharp gasp.

"The starling!" She shoots upright, "Where is he?"

Silas turns towards the box on the bedside, thoroughly charred.

Sadie's heart sinks into the depths of her soul, only for the sound of a soft chirp to lift her gaze to Silas' shoulder, where a glossy black starling peers up at her with its crimson eye, outstretching his wings as if to say *here I am*.

"He's alive!" She chokes out, "he's... he's here." A grin spreads across her lips at the sight of him, and immediately she stretches out her arms, her heart welling the moment the starling perches on her index finger. "You made it," she smiles, stroking the bird's jet black plumage as a strange affinity for this creature fills her every vein. "You're here."

The starling tilts his head in response, peering back at Sadie with a brilliant crimson eye before flittering away back to Silas' shoulder, where he sets the bird to rest atop a bundled up towel.

With a choke of a sob Sadie presses her hands to her face in an attempt to force the tears she can no longer control back inside her, the fear of loss spilling quick from the corner of her eyes in a downpour she's ashamed he has to see. "I felt his heart stop beating," she cries, voice soaked through with all her mortal terror. "I felt him die in my hands." Dropping her hands from her face, she folds them across her collarbones, where a deep pain erupts. Her throat is unbearably dry, raw from crying, the insides of her lungs stained black with lingering smoke.

"Silas..." she chokes out his name, coughing at the scent of smoke that still clings tightly to the walls of her lungs. She hacks until tears of pain form at her eyes, and she viciously wipes them away until she has nothing left but her red-rimmed eyes as she faces the demon at her bedside.

"Such tears for a little life," he murmurs. "And here I thought you found death a comfort." Sadie swears she sees the shadow of softness splayed out across his features, but he rises from his seat before she has the chance to take it in. "Give me your hand," he commands as he looms over her bedside, her heart skipping a beat at his sudden closeness. It's not the first time he's said it; and it's no less of a stranger the second time.

Whatever she wants to say is strangled by the sting of breath; choked by the burn of the smoke as she concedes, and she gives him her hand.

Gently, too gently, he wraps his hand around her wrist, his touch the anchor that keeps her tethered as he leans in ever closer. She can feel his breath against hers, his eyes inches away from hers —close enough to see the tears, close enough to see through her white lie. He raises his other hand up to her throat, hovering a hair's width from her skin and the necklace around her collarbones.

She parts her lips at the feeling of his fingertips at her chest, whatever apprehension that lays sleeping beneath her skin crushed out of her as Silas moves the pearl necklace over without a second thought. Lightly, he trails his fingers downwards, unbuttoning the first two buttons of her dress until he has access to her heart, where it beats unbearably fast.

Pressing her eyes closed, she feels a lightness spread out from where he touches her; seeping through her skin and into her lungs —rising higher and higher until it passes through her lips in a breath that's free of pain.

She lets out a gasp, taking in clear air as the smoke coating the inside of her lungs dissipates.

Yet there's a warmth inside her that stays exactly where it is as he withdraws his touch, rising to pace towards the open windows. In the silence that blankets them both, she hopes he won't hear her hammering heart. In an attempt to conceal it, she draws her legs closer against her chest, wrapping her one arm around her shins, the other reaching over to pet the starling on the nightstand.

Did he do the same to you? She thinks to herself, stroking the green-black iridescence of his neck. *Did he take back the smoke from your lungs?* Softly, the bird trills. *Did he put the pulse back in your heart?*

She turns from the starling to the demon silhouetted at the window, a whisper of wind rushing through the treetops, carrying with it the faint scent of those midnight-sweet jasmine blooms— yet the wind never cools the heat beneath her cheeks.

"Silas..." she calls out for him.

He turns towards her, eyes reflective in the dark.

"Why did you save me?" The question rises from her lips like a plume of smoke, her fingers lingering at the base of her throat, "Why didn't you let me burn? Why didn't you let me die?"

The ghost of his fingers across the flesh of her neck lays sleeping under her veins as she twists her necklace aimlessly.

"The fire..." His voice is soft, "It does not belong to you."

She furrows her brows, twisting her legs over the side of the bed in an attempt to close in on his meaning. "What do you mean? It belongs to *you?*"

He turns fully to face her, eyes brimming with some distant emotion as he answers, "Yes... Fire cannot destroy a demon. Not truly. It can't burn what it belongs to."

"And that's what you did?" Her voice falters beneath the thought, "Take back what belongs to you?"

He took her smoke-tainted breath through touch alone, an action that she realizes is simply a demon taking back what belongs to him.

The fire, the smoke, the burning inferno—it's all his.

He's silent, and it's all the confirmation she needs.

He took the fire back from my body, the smoke from my lungs... he saved me. Her mind is a haze, the stench of charred flesh playing upon her senses along with the feeling of his hand at her heart.

Forcing herself from the looming abyss, she digs her nails into the edge of the mattress as she leans forward, hungry for understanding. "But your father, he burned... and so did your sisters. I saw their bodies, I saw their death."

"You did." His jaw clenches. "So burned their mortal flesh, ending their life in this world, giving them life everlasting in another."

"Where are they now?" she asks, the prospect of *where* sending a shiver through her, "Hell?"

Silas shakes his head. "No... Someplace worse." He turns his eyes to the treetops, his voice spilling out into the jungle thicket. "Hell is no pit of fire, *Solita.* Hell is the canvas of your grief, painted in all the hues of your sin, your sorrow, your everlasting suffering." He drinks in the sight of the jungle dark before the sun's rays come out to pierce through her shadowy heart.

Of course he's right, she chides herself. Hell is nothing like the pit of fire Father Agustin preached of during countless sermons, nothing like brimstone and flayed flesh. Hell isn't torture, not flagellation, nor eternal fire. It's something familiar, something Sadie has known every sweat-soaked night since that fateful monsoon.

Silas' voice comes with the sound of distant, phantom waves, "And your Hell... yours is stained the color of the sea."

Sadie's Hell tastes of suicide. Her Hell tastes of saltwater.

Focusing on stilling her rapid-fire heart, she digs her fingers into her skin, eyes cast down at the wrinkled sheets pooling around her, as Silas makes his way over to where she sits, the floorboards creaking under his weight. He comes to sit beside her, sitting impossibly close. Yet she refuses to face him, not wanting his words to sink in.

"Your Hell is your solitude."

She presses her lips together, speechless as the sky begins to lighten—morning light fast approaching.

"Every night you dream of your mother, don't you?" Silas asks, "You dream of saving her from her demise. Every night you reach out to pull her back from the edge of death."

Sadie shakes her head, his voice the knife to her opened wound. "And? Why are you telling me this?!" The last word comes wrapped in hurt, but Silas never wavers.

"You asked why I saved you..." He lifts his fingers up towards her cheek, brushing against the flesh the way he would a wilted flower—gently, gently, gently. "The dead do not need saving, *Solita*. Only the living do. And to which do you belong?"

A breath escapes her lips at the warmth of his fingertips and whatever response that sits on her tongue dissipates into naught but steam.

Her eyelids grow heavy at a touch that can only be profane. He knows every inch of her suffering, her grief, her innermost fears in a way that only a demon can. Yet the softness in his eyes is anything but violation. Her heartbeat thrums, as she peers back at him through the quickly fading dark, his body so close, his scent intoxicating.

His thumb sweeps across her bottom lip, the capillaries beneath her skin entwining with the veins beneath his palm, twin pulses beating in tandem, a lullaby, a song that can't possibly be anything other than sacred.

But the wrinkled petals fall, and he pulls away, a line of an incision left across her bottom lip where his fingers trailed, bleeding out with every heartbeat. Sadie brings her fingers to her lips, expecting to see crimson staining her skin, but when she turns her gaze away from Silas she sees not a trace of blood. There's no cut, no wound wrought from his fingers—but the sting of him prying her apart is there all the same.

When she looks up from her fingers, she sees he's gone. Sadie leans back against the pillows, his voice against the shell of her ear the only tangible reminder he's here, beside her, buried deep under her skin.

"Go back to sleep," he whispers, voice soft, his body a faint shadow at her bedside. "There is still some darkness left in the sky."

She obliges, falling back into his sheets, sinking into sweet surrender.

15

Sadie awakens to a sickly heat. It's the type of heat that presses down against you from all sides and angles with no reprieve. Not when it's entwined in the very air, in the dry breath of the earth as it yearns out for the day the rains wash away the stain of another year. Twisting onto her side, she's met with Silas' empty room.

She listens to the birdsong beyond the window, the Hacienda deathly still in response. She hears no traces of Odette in the house, meaning she and Silas are its only occupants—the last owner and the very first; bound together by a pearl-tipped chain that glitters gold around her neck.

Swinging her legs off the side of the bed, she rubs her sides in an attempt to coax away the nightmare of yesterday's fire. An attempt that proves useless when smoke still stains her skin, char woven into the fabric of her blackened dress. Worse still, she breathes in the scent of him lingering on the sheets, her hair, her skin.

Cradling her head in her hands, she fights against the near-deafening cry of the birds beyond the window, the light of day too blinding, leaving her simply too *bare*.

But there's no trace of the wounded starling at her bedside table, and immediately she rises from the sheets in search of him. Thankfully, she doesn't have to search too long, for the sound of pecking captures her attention, and she casts her eyes to the stack of boxes pushed up against the far side of the room.

Remnants of her father's belongings that her mother packed away years ago sit collecting dust—save for a box tipped over, its contents spilling out across the floor in entrails cast in ivory.

A trill slices through the air, and she whips her eyes upwards to see the offending starling triumphantly perched atop the box, his glossy black wings outstretched. *He acts every bit the phoenix risen from the ashes,* she thinks to herself, smiling at the sight of the stitches at his breast—the wound no longer inflamed, the little starling well and truly on the mend. She reaches out to stroke his feathers only for him to retreat behind the tower of boxes.

Drawing her eyes back to the mess on the floor, Sadie drops to her knees to sweep it all up, only to stop in her tracks the moment she realizes what it is staring back at her.

Parting her lips, she reaches out for the familiar fabric spilled out across the floor. It's a vision of white; a fitted bodice edged with lace, sleeves set in the finest *nipis* fabric she'd ever seen, the skirt a near iridescent ivory that matches the pearl around her neck.

It's her mother's Maria Clara. She runs her fingers over the soft skirt before bundling it up in her arms, breathing in what remains of her mother's perfume. The last time she saw this dress in proper light was when it was on her living, breathing body two festivals ago.

Sadie screws her eyes shut tight, fighting hard against the tears she's been battling for so long. Burying her face into the soft fabric of her mother's dress, she forces herself to hold it all back, hating the fact that the tears shed yesterday did nothing to empty the well inside her. She realizes instead that it was nothing more than a leak in the wall of the dam holding back her grief, the fracture set, only a matter of time before the fault unleashes the flood of her suffering.

Sadie forces herself to focus on her breathing in one last attempt to keep her tears from brimming over, turning her attention to the ash staining the hem of her dress—a stinging reminder of last night's fire, last night's shame.

Smoke clings to every strand of her hair, and she rises to her feet, needing to be rid of it. Taking the Maria Clara with her, she makes her way to the bathroom.

Stripping off what feels like a burnt layer of skin, Sadie lets the cold water rush over her, scrubbing at her flesh until her senses are smothered in the fragrance of soap. Toweling herself off, she doesn't give herself the chance to linger at the mirror as she runs a comb through the thick of her hair. The scent of smoke is all but gone with the façade of shampoo, yet she can smell it all the same, lingering deep beneath her skin and her collarbones where she can still feel the warmth of Silas' fingers wrapped taut around her pulse.

Letting out a breath, she steels herself as she peels off the towel, slipping into the ivory Maria Clara. The *camisa* blouse is sheer and lighter than air as she pulls it on over her simple silk slip, the delicate lace sleeves fanning across her forearms. Carefully, Sadie steps into the ivory skirt, tying the waist tie closures with deft fingers before pinning the embroidered *pañuleo* across her shoulders, twisting her pearl necklace to sit just atop the lacy neckline.

Peering into the mirror, she smiles at the familiarity, at this fleeting nostalgia, yet it fades faster than she has the chance to savor it. The image of the girl before her is but a mere echo of her mother, a whisper of her blood, a murmur of a memory.

There's no bringing her back, Sadie tells herself, fists balling around the delicate fabric of her mother's dress. *There's no turning back the clock.*

Smoothing the fabric down over her hips, she tucks her loose hair behind one ear as she exits the bathroom and steps back out into the Hacienda's dark hallway, trailing the ivory skirt behind her.

Twisting her fingers together in the dead quiet beneath the endlessly high ceiling, Sadie comes to a stop at the threshold of her own bedroom, heart aching as she pushes the door open, greeted only by the aftermath of yesterday's rage. Standing beneath the doorway, she draws her eyes across the fire damage. The antique bedframe stands irreparably burnt, the linens and the fabric of the bed curtains nothing but blackened ribbons, the rug charred, and a thick stroke of ash sitting like a streak of paint across the length of the ceiling above. The damage is bad, but not quite devastating— and it's all thanks to Silas.

All thanks to a demon reclaiming the fire that belongs simply to him.

From the depths of her handbag strung up over her vanity, her phone buzzes. In a single swift motion, she snatches it up in her hands, grateful she didn't throw it onto her now ruined bed in the heat of the other night. She opens the message that lights up her screen.

Isaiah: Odette's with me.

A moment passes, and Sadie bites down hard on the inside of her cheek—*of course she is.*

Isaiah: Whatever happened between you two, she feels bad about it.

Swallowing the lump in her throat, she wants to type, should type, *I do too*—but here amidst the ashes of yesterday, her resolve has only strengthened, and she slips her phone back into the bag, leaving him on read.

"You're upset..." A voice emerges from the ruins, Sadie's heart jolting forward as she turns to face its source.

Silas leans against the doorframe, his figure filling it out with ease. The starling is perched on his shoulder, his crimson eye gleaming as he remarks, "I can taste it."

Sadie stiffens, his eyes roaming over her face and the length of her body and the dress that adorns it. Embarrassment creeps up on her cheeks at the feeling of being caught in a dress that isn't hers; in a dress she shouldn't be wearing.

"It's... it's this," she lies, knowing that all she's doing is biding time from his watching eyes. He knows her suffering like he knows the inside of his sealed casket, but it doesn't stop her from trying to regain even the smallest semblance of control over what he turns his attentions to. "It belongs—*belonged*—to my mother. What do you think?" she asks, hoping he'll take the bait as she smooths the fabric down over her hips, the ankle-length skirt swaying gently with her movement.

"As becoming as it is," he lingers on her dress before adding quickly, "That is not why you are upset." He lifts his hand up towards the starling, who promptly hops onto the crook of his finger. "It's something else."

Warmth forms beneath her cheeks at the compliment, but she chides herself for even acknowledging it as he gestures to the smoke streaked ceiling.

"Is it the damage?" he asks.

Sadie casts her eyes downwards. "It's not that."

"Then why do you feel this way?"

"*Why?*" Sadie frowns, facing her ash wrought bedroom. "As long as I'm suffering, that's all you should care about... The *why* means nothing to you."

He's already seen so much of her, and every attempt to resist is just another line Sadie draws in the sand between them, only for the shore to wash it all away again, taking with it all illusion of a divide. She holds his gaze in a measure of silence that sends a tremble through her very bones, the realization dawning upon her that there is no line, only the sand and the sea beating endlessly upon it. Tide after tide, after tide.

Silas says nothing as she strides over to where he leans, his attention fixed on the cooing starling as she slips easily past him and into the hallway. Retrieving a broom and a bucket of cleaning supplies from the closet, she returns with resolve written in the tension of her shoulders, only to be stopped at her bedroom's entrance.

The width of his body is blocking her way, and when he shows no signs of moving, she curses her height for it.

"Is this how you plan to ease your burden?" he asks, stroking the starling's emerald tinged neck.

She stares straight ahead, willing him to disappear. "I don't plan to *ease* anything but this mess. Now move," she commands.

"You think by sweeping the ash away, the scent of smoke will disappear?"

"Silas, *move.*"

The starling flitters away from his fingertips, coming to rest on the edge of the charred bed, leaving Silas' attention entirely on Sadie as he doubles down, "Is it the fire that burdens you?"

Sadie clenches her fingers taut around the broom's wooden handle.

"Or your starting of it?" His voice is a softness that sparks the embers of her irritation.

Her shoulders tense, pulse flaring. "Why does it matter to *you*?!" She cranes her neck to meet his dark gaze, unleashing her anger. "Why do you care about my suffering when all you need to do is feed from it?!"

He's expectantly silent, as if this is the reaction he wanted to draw from her lips, the taste of her anger just another flavor on the tip of his tongue—but it can't be all. Not when there's a shadow of softness etched into the black behind his eyes.

Sadie casts her eyes downwards as her voice lowers to a near whisper, "I know you need my tears, Silas. I've given them to you all this time... but asking me to explain them is just cruelty."

Her words sink through the air between them for but a moment before Silas concedes, and he allows her through.

"Thank you," she murmurs as she slips by him and into the ash of her bedroom. Tucking in the hem of her skirt to her waistband,

Sadie gives herself no time to linger as she plunges herself into the routine of deep cleaning.

Sweeping away the charred fragments of fabric littering the floor, she clears away the debris scattered across the hardwood floors with a violence she never thought she had in her. Silence reigns for what feels like an eternity, as Sadie pushes her weight into sweeping away the ash, the stillness broken only by the chirp of the starling as he flits from perch to perch. She doesn't once look up to search for Silas amidst the debris, yet her hold on the broom handle tightens instinctively as she feels his shadow pass her by.

The tension lasts for only a second as she senses no pull from him; no more demanding, no more prying. When she looks up, she sees him standing by the foot of the bed with something between his fingers.

Peering into his hand, she sees ribbons of fabric, curled up in waves of melted fibers over the flat of his palm.

"This is where it started." Silas says to himself, and Sadie feels pinpricks of shame breaking through her resolve.

"It was one of the dresses Odette and I bought just yesterday," she replies under her breath before aggressively sweeping at an ash stain that just won't seem to budge. "All that effort just for her to ruin it the way she did—I mean really? Ink? You couldn't be any pettier even if you tried." Sadie looks up from the broom's handle, the sight of Silas examining the remains of that ink-stained Maria Clara softening something deep inside her. "But ink didn't cause *this*," she admits, casting her eyes across the damage. "I did."

Sadie turns away, yet she can feel his eyes on hers, following her every movement as she throws the broom back against the wall before coming to sit at her vanity with a frustrated sigh. Untucking her skirt from her waistband, she lets the hem pool at her ankles as she attempts in vain to braid her hair.

Sadie presses her eyes closed as she wishes desperately for just one thing—for her mom to appear behind her, poised and ready to braid her hair the same way she did every morning on the day of the festival.

But when she opens her eyes, all she has is the demon standing beside her reflection in the mirror. Sadie's shoulders tense at his sudden closeness, dropping the braid between her fingers into a cascade of black across her shoulders.

"May I?" he asks, the question catching her off guard.

She peers back at him through the reflection, knowing exactly what it is he means to do. Unhallowed it may be wherever he walks, wherever he draws fiery breath—but unhallowed is anything but the touch he promises, the touch she needs as she answers, "Yes."

He knows her every dream like the veins that run through his own body, her every nightmare like the pulse of his own, scarred heart.

What makes you think he doesn't know what you really mean?

He raises his hands to the base of her neck, the motion of his fingers brushing against her spine sending a ripple of electricity through her every nerve.

What you want?

Her breath hitches in her throat as his fingers wind through the ends of her hair, smoothing down the loose strands until he separates her hair into three neat strands.

What you need?

And he begins to braid. Her heart beats impossibly fast, thoughts a disarray. The question forms and dies on her tongue, the simple, easy motion of his hands twisting through her hair all the answer she needs. *His sisters,* she realizes, *his sisters taught him.* The same three sisters who were burned by their father all in retribution against his first son. They died so he could live, so he could become the monster his father wanted he be, the monster he's anything but as he twists the finished braid into a loose bun at the base of her head, reaching a hand over her shoulder for the pins to secure it in place. Instinctively, she bows her head as he slips the pins in place, watching his deft movements through the reflection of the mirror—an unfamiliar feeling creeping up within her heart. But she shakes it away, forcing her thoughts back to the day that stretches out ahead of her.

Twisting the pearl around her neck, she breaks the silence, "Tonight is the Festival of Our Lady."

"Our Lady?" he asks.

Turning back to face him, she sees a curiosity written in his eyes, and she satiates it. "Legend is that a woman found a wooden statue of the Virgin Mary floating in the shallows of a lagoon not far from here. No one knows where she came from, nor who she belonged to, but she was everything the friars wanted. Everything they needed... their miracle."

"Hm," Silas replies. "Of course."

"But she's more than just a statue, according to legend. After that same girl took the statue back to the church, she said the statue would speak to her."

With an unreadable expression he prompts her further, "And what would she say?"

"I don't know." Sadie shrugs. "I wasn't there."

His marked silence captures Sadie's attention, and she turns around in her seat to face him, watching his eyes grow distant the way they did whenever he retreated back into the past. *His* past.

"Don't tell me you were there." She smiles incredulously, only for it to falter when he remains silent, "Were you?"

Oh.

"Of course..." she scoffs, reminded once more of the cavernous divide of history that stands between them both, "Of course you were." She lets her curiosity take hold, "Do you believe the statue really spoke to her?"

"I do."

Sadie crosses her arms as a cold wind blows in from the windows.

"But I don't believe it was the Virgin speaking... It was something else."

Sadie feels her heart skip a beat, twisting the pearl between her fingers as the desire to know surfaces on the tip of her tongue only for the sound of an engine rumbling outside to stop it from ever materializing.

The noise captures her attention, and she rises to her feet, making her way over to the window to see Isaiah's pick-up in the driveway. Her stomach sinks as she sees his car door open, cursing the fact that he owns a spare key.

Landing her eyes back on Silas, she sees he hasn't moved from his spot, nor his gaze moved from her. He motions to speak, but Sadie silences him with a single word, "Stay."

And he does.

It doesn't take long for Isaiah to let himself inside, the sound of footsteps from the foyer echoing in the silence between them. "Sadie!" Isaiah calls out, and he's fast approaching the base of the stairs.

Sadie drops her shoulders, inhaling a deep breath, her nerves a tangled mess at the thought of what comes next.

"Sadie! Where are you?" he calls out again, louder now.

Steeling herself, she fixes her hair as she moves to meet him at the threshold of her bedroom as she calls out, "I'm in here."

The footsteps are dead close now, and Sadie flicks her eyes to Silas standing by her charred bed, his eyes as unreadable as ever.

"There you are." Isaiah's voice pulls her to the door, where he stops at the threshold. It's foolish to expect his gaze to linger on her—it's the first time she's allowed herself to look *nice* in years, but Sadie expects nothing more from Isaiah as his gait immediately tenses as he sets eyes on the figure standing behind her—that, and her ash streaked room. "And you."

The inkling of guilt and shame lay splayed out across the ash streaks littering her bedroom. *Let him see the mess you made,* a voice inside her commands, *let him see the mess that you are.*

But Silas steps forward, as if sensing her thoughts, the room around them twisting in shadows beneath his presence as he makes himself known.

"What the hell happened here?" Isaiah closes the distance between he and Sadie, taking no time to hesitate in wrapping his fingers a little too tightly around her wrist. His eyes come to land on hers for the first time. "Did he...?"

But Silas finishes his question for him, "Did I what?"

The air in the room is getting thicker—and it's not the summer heat anymore.

"I knocked over a candle, Sai. It was an accident." Sadie presses her hand to Isaiah's chest in an attempt to cool him off, but there's a fire under his skin that's burning not for her; but for him and his damaged pride.

"I wasn't talking to you." Isaiah's grits his teeth.

Silas steps closer, trailing in his wake a shadow growing in size with each passing moment. "And I was. So answer—what is it you think I did?"

Sadie presses hard against Isaiah's chest, but he pushes her to the side as he steps forward to meet Silas at the center of her room.

"I think you're not just here for a getaway." Isaiah steps closer. "I think you're here to cause trouble. You think you can just come to this country and do as you please? Nothing here belongs to you."

"Hm." Silas answers, Sadie's eyes nervously flickering between the two as she spies tendrils of shadow moving across the floor, encircling Isaiah in a serpentine motion he doesn't see, doesn't notice. Why would he, when he's only human? "I would say the same for you."

Isaiah clenches his fists, and Sadie motions to pull him back, only to be pushed away once more. "Isaiah, please—"

"—Stay out of it, Sadie," he hisses, his eyes never moving once from Silas. "What did you do here? What did you do to her?"

Sadie's heartbeat quickens, anticipating the tail end sting of his reproach. "Isaiah!" She grips his arm, watching in dread as Silas' shadows creep up over his body, intertwining with the ivory lacework of his *barong* shirt, moving closer and closer towards his throat.

But Silas answers as coolly as the wind that blows in from over the jungle canopy. "Nothing she hasn't done to herself."

And the heat grows all too much.

It's no longer a matter of calming Isaiah; but stopping Silas.

The shadows are dancing around the skin of his throat now, a deadly circle just waiting to tighten—and only Sadie can stop it.

"*Silas!*"

His eyes come to land on hers, and it's almost searing the moment she feels it—but in a heartbeat the shadows dissipate, the room returning to its natural state.

"It's okay, Isaiah... He's telling the truth." Sadie pulls Isaiah away, his knuckles white hot at his sides. "Come on—let's go." She wills him to face her, and when he does, she motions for them to leave. "*Let's go.*"

And he obliges.

Taking her hand in his, Sadie almost winces at his grip as he pulls her out of her bedroom. Turning over her shoulder she sees the shape of a demon retreating deep into the shadows of her room; his eyes flickering a shade of red that imprints itself into the back of her eyelids as they make their way out of the silence of the Hacienda.

Slamming his car door shut, Isaiah grips the steering wheel hard enough for the veins in his hands to rush to the surface. Sadie climbs in beside him in silence, the air between them almost suffocating.

"You know why I came here?" he asks, voice low as he sets his eyes on Sadie. The hairs on her arms bristle, and she keeps her eyes focused on the Hacienda standing tall before them; watching, straining to listen to every word between them. "Because I wanted to do something with you. I wanted to take you out for the first time in forever because I care, Sadie. *I care.* Can you believe it?"

Frowning, she meets his gaze, "What's so hard to believe?"

"That you care half as much as I do."

"You make it hard to believe it when you treat me like that..." she whispers, twisting her fingers in her lap.

"Like what?" he narrows his eyes, twisting the key in the ignition, the rumble of the engine drowning out any hope of her voice being heard.

Like this.

The Hacienda watches intently, its capiz shell eyes boring a hole into her flesh—yet for the life of her she can't say the words. She can't bring herself to make the accusation.

With a shake of her head the conversation is dismissed, and Isaiah drives them away from the Hacienda, as fast and as far as he can.

It's all she can do to sit in silence, dreading the Festival and the inevitable flood of pilgrims already awash across the streets of Port Cante. The sun's rays are unrelenting on her skin, and Sadie can't recall the last time she couldn't wait for the darkness to wash away the stain of daylight.

16

WITH EVERY CARPARK full to the brim in preparation for the Festival, Isaiah parks by a grove of banana palms adjacent to Infanta Bay beach, with only the steeple of Port Cante's church piercing the clear blue sky overhead. Wiping the sweat from her brow, Sadie fans herself with her hand, not recalling a day as hot, as unbearable, as suffocating as this in years.

By the time she shuts the car door behind her, the morning sun is shedding into its midday skin, the clamor of voices from the gathering crowd at the church up ahead rising over the trees.

"Come on," his voice is closer to a command than anything else as he leads her through the flush of the crowd filling the plaza, Sadie stopping to watch as the statue of Our Lady of Sorrows is hoisted up on the processional barge crafted specially for this occasion, bedecked with sampaguita garlands and countless candles, still unlit.

Through the din of the picture-taking tourists, Sadie looks up at the wooden statue, the world around her growing quiet for but a moment.

It's the only day of the year Our Lady is not locked up within the confines of the church, and as they pass beneath her gaze, Sadie can't help but wonder what she thinks of her veneration.

She must hate the spectacle, she thinks to herself, as it's a reminder of everything she can't have, a reminder of the living she has no place amongst.

The procession begins at dusk, with a river of tourists and pilgrims alike carrying the statue of Our Lady towards the same lagoon she emerged from centuries ago in a re-enactment of a miracle the faithful so desperately need to be true. But between now and that moment, Isaiah insists on spending the day soaking up the sun, the heat, this summer daze.

The main street of Port Cante is filled to the brim with stalls of every kind, selling anything and everything to appeal to all walks of life in what's undoubtedly the town's biggest tourist draw. Isaiah stops at almost every stall to charm every local vendor, from his friends to distant relations to every gossip willing to listen to his idle chatter.

Stopping at a stall selling pastilla candies in their cacophonously loud cellophane wrappings, Isaiah leans over to greet one of his twice-removed aunts, flashing her a smile as he slips his arm around Sadie's waist. "Isn't she beautiful, *tita?*" he asks, a grin on his lips that prompts Sadie to bite down on her tongue.

"Mm," his aunt agrees, giving Sadie a onceover that makes her feel as if she's the one up for sale, wrapped up in the plastic cellophane of a Maria Clara that isn't hers, suffocated in the trappings of something that she simply isn't. "You two make such a cute couple..." she remarks, the smile that's plastered on her lips lingering for a little too long before she nods at Isaiah with a knowing glance that sends a wave of dread through Sadie.

Politely, all Sadie can do is smile in response before pulling away from Isaiah's grasp, stopping to stand at a stall selling mangoes in all the extremes; from sugar sweet dried strips to the fresh-cut, unripe and puckeringly sour slices sold with a pinch of salt. The day has waned along with Sadie's patience, the looming dusk drawing the tourists towards the church, where the procession will begin with the lighting of those endless waxen candles.

Toying with the lace of her sleeves, Sadie longs for a reprieve from the crowd—anything for solitude, anything to be away from all these watching, piercing eyes. Her thoughts wander to the Hacienda and Silas beneath its roof, the feeling of his fingers brushing against the base of her neck, weaving through the thick of her hair. Heat warms her cheeks at his phantom touch, but Isaiah's hand wrapping around hers plunges her back into the present.

"Sadie?" Isaiah turns her around to face him. "You okay?"

Nodding, she feigns a smile she hopes he doesn't see through as the sun begins its descent beyond the horizon, casting all of Port Cante in a warm, golden glow.

"Good," he replies. It's clear that in parading her around through town, she's back in his good graces—yet there's something that dances behind his eyes, a seriousness, a sincerity that strangles the calm inside her. A calm that goes up in smoke the moment he begins to move, urging her along with him. "Come on. I'm taking you to a surprise."

Sadie has no choice but to follow, dread forming at the thought of his last surprise—a girl named Odette. She doesn't dare say her name or give fuel to the doubts set deep in her soul. *Endure it,* she tells herself, *just until the Festival is over.*

Leading her through the throngs of people pouring into Port Cante's church for evening mass before the procession, Sadie hardly has the time to catch her breath as he takes them both out onto a narrow dirt road that stirs up the depths of Sadie's memory.

"Quick," Isaiah urges, the thicket of the jungle fast approaching. "Before it gets dark."

Glancing a final time over her shoulder to see dense ribbons of life winding into the church, Sadie follows, allowing herself to disappear into the dense line of greenery beyond.

"Where are we going?" she asks.

"You wouldn't follow if I told you."

He's right—and knowing what's coming, she'd rather have whatever words they'll exchange as far away from the prying eyes and listening ears of Port Cante as possible.

Taking her silence as a yes, he walks up ahead, pushing aside overgrown vines and branches. Sadie doesn't dare dwell on the last time they took this path, the last time he led her here—despite all the years, it all seems too fresh, still too soon. When the canopy of palm trees break above their heads, she's temporarily blinded as they step out from beneath the shady undergrowth and into the sunlight.

The shallow, secluded lagoon that was once the background to Isaiah, Odette and Sadie's childhood stretches out before them— limestone cliffs jutting out from the water tower tall above the trees, mangroves clinging to their feet, branches bowing over the shallows to cast a protective circle around the water's edge, making whatever that goes on in this little sanctuary virtually impossible to see unless you're standing directly on the sandy bank yourself. It was for this reason the three of them would steal away to escape their elders and their stern, watchful eyes.

With the water a shade of blue that matches the dusk sky, Sadie walks over to the edge of the water, peering down into the mirror-like reflection, where the crystal clarity of the water creates a dangerous illusion that makes the bottom appear closer than it seems. The looming cliffs scrape against the evening sky, stretching out mercilessly along the side of the island that Sadie refused to visit ever since that fateful monsoon—the day her mother went to these same cliffs and never returned.

Sadie wraps her arms around herself as she takes a step back from the water, afraid she'll see her mother's face peering back up at her.

Isaiah walks ahead, motioning for her to follow. She joins him beside the old banyan tree that hangs bent over the lagoon, its cascading branches brushing just against the water's edge.

He stands with one foot on the hull of a long abandoned *banca*

—their favorite hideaway, nestled between thick arms of snaking banyan roots. Sadie takes his outstretched hand, sweeping her trailing dress up beneath her as she joins him in watching the water, the two of them side by side atop the upturned boat. The sunshine dances over the surface of the water with a cool summer breeze, but as soon as it dies, the lagoon turns to glass.

"Remember when we used to catch fireflies here?"

The question comes out of nowhere, but the memory doesn't. When she blinks, she can still see the glow of the fireflies dancing over the surface of the water in the dark behind her eyelids.

"I remember."

He speaks softer, his voice a low hum in the shade of the banyan tree, "The day before every Festival... we'd sit right here."

Sadie pries her eyes away from the roots beneath them, afraid to see a glimpse of the two of them, phantoms of the past he conjures up with every memory.

"After your dad's funeral—we came here. It was here we admitted to ourselves we needed each other. Where we realized we should be together."

Sadie shuts her eyes, feeling his eyes intently on hers, despising the feeling of his voice dredging up these grief-soaked memories. "Sai... Don't," she warns him, digging her nails into the skin of her palms.

"It's where you first told me you loved me... remember?"

Sadie shakes her head, pressing her eyes shut.

"Sometimes I wonder if you really meant it," he accuses, and with those simple words the fire sleeping in Sadie's veins awakens.

Her eyes shoot open, and she turns to face him with blazing eyes. "Of course I meant it, Sai." Biting down on her tongue, the rest of the sentence slips past her lips, "Did *you*?"

"Hey. Look at me." He inches closer, his voice returning to that softness he abandoned just moments ago, Sadie instinctively drawing back at the sudden change. "I meant every word I told you."

Heat creeps up beneath her cheeks, but it's not the warmth Isaiah usually brings out of her—this one licks at her insides like burning coals.

He twists his fingers around hers, pulling her close, ensuring she endure every word he has to say. "Sadie..." he whispers, willing her to face him. "Who else do we have but each other?"

It's on the very tip of her tongue, the urge to tell him she knows what Odette said—their messages, their past—all of it. *Is that really proof, Sadie?* The voice eats away at her resolve, only the sound of her fast beating heart filling the silence between them as he unleashes the sum of all these years between them, every heartache, every moment of vulnerability.

"Who else can you turn to when things get tough? Who else do you have to wipe the tears away if it isn't me, hm?"

She has no choice but to listen as he plays on her emotions the only way he knows how—by offering the promise of comfort, familiarity, of unbearable *safety*. It's a sweetness she doesn't deny as he leans in closer, his eyes lidded, brimming with the confidence that she's nothing but pliant under his gaze, nothing but the same scared, lonely girl afraid of the dark that's closing in fast over Port Cante. He brushes a stray strand of hair behind her ear as he continues, "I'm the only one who understands you... and you're the only one who can keep me in check." The last word leaves his lips in a smile that fills her with an unfamiliar feeling, her nerves untangling the moment she sees her own reflection in his eyes—the image of a girl she no longer knows, of a girl that doesn't exist. Not anymore.

"Odette," Sadie murmurs. "What about Odette?"

Quiet reigns for but a moment before Isaiah pulls away completely, the softness behind his eyes melting away into nothing but steel, his face shrouded in shadow.

"I don't know what the hell you're talking about," he replies, voice hard.

"What are you doing, Sai? Why are you telling me all this?" Sadie frowns, twisting her fingers together, exasperated.

Isaiah rises to his feet, pacing across the sand with a nervousness that she can't ignore, and he can't defend.

"What are *you* doing? Back at the house... You said his name. Like there was something else going on between you two."

It takes the envy in his eyes for Sadie to realize the taste of his words, once sweet, is poison on her tongue. Nothing else, nothing more.

"I—I can't do this right now." Sadie doesn't look him in the eye as she rises from the overturned boat, her skirt trailing sand as she meets him in the middle. "I can't do this with you. Not again."

Pressing his palms to his sides, he keeps his voice even, cool— suppressing the fire Sadie knows he has within him. "Why don't we just get this over with... stop everyone's talk and just show them that we're not kids anymore?" He runs his hand through his hair, "You know it's all my uncle wants... it's all he ever talks about."

Sadie casts her eyes to the surface of the lagoon, where a hard wind stirs it up—she dreads what comes next, not wanting to turn, not wanting to acknowledge where he wants to take her.

Isaiah lets out a deep sigh, and when Sadie turns to face him there's a black velvet box between his fingers.

Her heart stops at the sight.

"He even gave me this." Isaiah flicks the box open to reveal a simple silver ring, a princess cut diamond set in its center. "It's the same one my dad used on my mom."

Used; not gave, not gifted—but used. Like a coin in a slot machine, pumped full of a reward that doesn't exist, that isn't real.

"Isaiah," Sadie shakes her head, fixed to where she stands, "You don't know what you're doing." Her throat runs dry as he pulls the ring out and twirls it irreverently between his fingers.

"Come on—this is the answer to all our problems. It'd make things so much easier. For both of us. We can start fresh—you can sell the Hacienda and we can use the money from that to buy a house somewhere closer to the city; you can do whatever you want, and I can open up my own shop, like I've always dreamed of."

He takes a step closer, but she pushes him away with a twisting panic rising in her chest, "Sai..."

"We can have everything you've ever wanted. We can leave this town, we can travel. I can take you wherever you want!"

"Sai." She frowns, the sound of his voice a droning lull.

"Better yet, we can go to France, see the Eiffel Tower like you always wanted, see everything you want to there and—"

"—*Isaiah!*" Sadie's voice echoes across the lagoon before the wind snatches it away, allowing silence to fall as the sun sinks deeper and deeper into the horizon.

"Italy," she says quietly, her heart brimming with an emptiness that can only be regret—regret that she ever believed he truly cared for her. "My dream was Italy. I always wanted to throw a coin into the Trevi Fountain. The Eiffel Tower was Odette's dream..." Sadie shakes her head, before facing him beneath the final rays of daylight. "It's not going to happen, Isaiah."

"But it's what everyone expects, Sadie! It's what they're all waiting for—so why shouldn't we?"

A spark lights the embers in her belly, the heat rising from her lips in a wave of rage. "Why the hell should I care what anyone on this island thinks? What any of them want *me* to do? I'm all I have left, Sai. And I'm fine with that." Her voice softens as the words leave her lips, as the realization settles into the recesses of her mind. Her heart begins to race, the fire inside her clawing at her insides until she simply can't take it anymore. "I need to go," she mutters, pulling away from his gaze.

"Jesus, Sadie. Where are you going?" Isaiah darts forward, reaching out to grip her forearm.

"It doesn't matter to you." Sadie hisses, "After all, it's not like you'll be alone, right?"

Isaiah furrows his brows, her words rendering him speechless as she forces her way out of his grip and back down the overgrown path. The dark clouds are rushing in quick from over the sea—night veiling the ocean and the jungle canopy, blanketing the procession that must be well under way by now to the very same lagoon.

Come rain or come shine, Our Lady makes her way through Port Cante, suspended high above the pilgrims that carry her in a river of candlelight towards the other side of the lagoon that Sadie wants nothing more than to escape from.

"Sadie!" Isaiah calls out after her, but the sound of the winds are louder, carrying his voice towards the sea where it drowns.

Plunging herself into the thicket of the jungle, Sadie forges forward, anger boiling through her veins. She's quick on her feet, pushing back overgrown branches and protruding vines—yet the deeper she winds through the dense line of palm trees, a smear of light up ahead tells her she's too late in avoiding the incoming procession.

Our Lady has already arrived.

The dirt road that leads to the lagoon is streaked with candle light, Our Lady of Sorrow rising tall above the rest, perched beneath a gilded canopy, carried by the bowed heads and bent backs of countless pilgrims. Floating on a cloud of fragrant jasmine, garlands of sampaguita hang from every nook of her canopy, releasing their potent perfume into the air, marking the night with the light of her tears.

Hearing the faint call of Isaiah's voice from the quick growing dim, he can't be far behind. Sadie acts fast, knowing there's only one way to lose him. Slipping into the crowd, there's no turning back against the tide of the procession, and so she follows alongside the statue of Our Lady, swearing the statue greets her with a glance of those splintered eyes.

She's in the thick of it now, maneuvering between a tide of people and their whispering prayers. There's not a soul in sight without a candle in one hand and a hymn paper in the other, and when the front of the procession begins to slow she spots a break in the crowd, rushing towards a quiet spot beneath the shade of an old, overgrown mangrove tree.

Glancing over her shoulder, she sees the crowd has stilled. The processional barge is lowered, and the statue disappears into the crowd.

Letting out a breath when she sees no trace of Isaiah through the crowd, Sadie pushes aside the spindly mangrove branches, finally finding a moment's reprieve from the solemnity in the quiet of her own thoughts.

The re-enactment of the statue's discovery is about to begin, and Sadie leans back against the mangrove trunk, pressing her eyes closed as Port Cante is plunged into the shadows of night. Here at the lagoon they will anoint her in the brine waters from which she was born, pull her out from the womb of the earth in the same fashion that first girl who found her did. Only this time, it's anything but natural, anything but sincere. This festival is nothing more than an attempt to keep this echo of the past alive. It's all that it's ever been—a desperate attempt at holding onto a world that no longer exists, a world that's nothing but a distant dream.

The sound of footfall across the loamy earth captures her attention and immediately, she's on her guard.

"Sadie?"

Her eyes shoot open, and she's met with a haze of candlelight, blinding at first as she adjusts her vision before the silhouette becomes clear. It's Father Agustin, clad in a gold chasuble, a warm smile on his face. "Taking a break from the crowd, I see."

"Hi, Father." Sadie sighs in relief, thankful it's him that discovered her, and no one else on this tiny island town.

"I hope you don't mind if I join you for a moment." His hands are clasped together, striding over to where Sadie leans against the mangrove trunk without need for confirmation.

Agustin stands beside her in silence, letting the hum of prayer from the procession ahead fill the space between them. "Just look at you," he remarks, glancing over the length of Sadie's Maria Clara.

"Not that little girl I always remembered. You're so... grown up."
His voice is soft, almost sad. "You look just like your mother."

The weight of his words press down on her shoulders in a vice
of guilt. Guilt that her faith has turned into nothing but cynicism
over the course of a year, guilt that her nightmares have become
the only reminder she's alive, guilt that she feels no obligation to
pray to a God she knows isn't listening. Sadie wills herself to smile,
focusing on the candle light up ahead as night well and truly
envelops the lagoon. "Thank you, Father."

Father Agustin thankfully breaks the silence, his voice taking
on a more serious tone as he asks, "How is he treating you?"

He. Either God, Isaiah, or the demon she's bound to.

She swallows the lump in her throat, before forcing the answer
out in a sigh, "He's been like he always is..."

Agustin nods, the lines in his forehead deepening as he unclasps
his hands. "He doesn't show it, you know.... He really cares."

Sadie says nothing, letting her thoughts wander to Isaiah and
their argument, his words still thrumming through her bones.

"He has a different way of showing it, but it's the truth." Father
Agustin continues, yet all Sadie can feel is the twisting knot in the
pit of her belly, the tangle of Isaiah's every word, his every insult
seeping into her skin in a haze of shame that rises to her cheeks.
Shame at all she's let him do to her over the years, shame that it
takes meeting a demon for her to wake up to the fact.

"Have faith, Sadie."

She presses her eyes closed, digging her fingers into her palm.
"It's not about faith, Father... it can't be, when it doesn't exist."

Up ahead, the crowd parts as the procession lifts the statue of
Our Lady up from the waters of the lagoon, a salty brine dripping
from her pores, giving truth to the perpetual tears carved into her
wooden cheeks.

"I know how it feels to have a lapse in faith, *anak*." Father
Agustin's voice is soft—personal. It's nothing like the lecture she
expected, and she turns to face him. "I know how it feels to be

helpless, to be without hope, to feel like there is no one listening to your prayers... to feel like there is no God above."

His words ripple through her like a jolt of ice, and she can't help herself from the guilt that threatens to claw its way into her nerves at the thought of Father Agustin bearing the weight of grief, just like she.

"I'm... I'm sorry, Father."

He shifts where he stands, the gold thread of his chasuble catching in the candlelight.

"It was the day of my brother's memorial mass... it was a long time ago, as you can see." His eyes wrinkle as he dredges up the past, the grief of losing his brother—Isaiah's father—faded over by time, leaving only the scar of loss and the phantom pain that never subsides. "Isaiah came into my sole care, and I felt truly alone. Being the young boy he was, he retreated into his own grief, and so did I. I had no one to turn to, no one to help me. So I stood before the statue of Our Lady, and did the only thing I knew how to..."

The procession whispers a prayer as they wrap the statue up in linen cloth, drying away the saltwater, drying away her tears.

"I prayed," Agustin whispers.

Sadie turns her eyes away from the statue, sensing Agustin's eyes on hers.

"I prayed... and she answered."

Sadie furrows her brows. "She... she spoke to you?"

"I was alone before her altar. And I heard a voice. A beautiful, miraculous voice."

Sadie feels her skin prickle as he recalls this divine message, a shadow clinging to the belly of his revelation that she can't help herself from thinking is anything but sacred.

"I was terrified, of course. Speechless. What would I have to say to her? I didn't know. I still don't."

"What did she say?" Sadie asks.

He shakes his head, casting his eyes towards the endless line of pilgrims praying at Our Lady's feet before turning back to Sadie with a solemnity written on his lips that's as good as stitches sewing his mouth closed.

"It does not matter what she said to me, *anak*. All that matters is that even in the most hopeless of times, in the darkest of hours —God is listening."

Sadie tenses as the softness in his voice hardens into the same sermon-like tone she'd come to know so well from years of Sunday Mass—she knows what's coming next.

"Even in this darkness, He is listening... all you have to do is call out for Him. Pray, and He will answer." His hand comes to rest on her shoulder, and she twists her fingers together, wishing time would sweep her away beneath its current, hoping for the tide to drag her out and away from this moment, away from the sentimentality she knows is coming. "How proud your mother would be of you, *anak*. How proud she would be to see you today. A beautiful girl. Smart, responsible... obedient."

Sadie turns her head, not allowing him to see her wince at the last word.

"You know, Sadie... you've always been like a daughter to me."

Her lips part to say something—but he's already moved on, refusing her the chance to resist.

"And that's why I want you to be happy."

"How can I be happy, Father?" Her cheeks are hot, regretting the words as soon as they leave her lips—but there's no stopping now. "How can I be happy when she left me the way she did? Without a word, a letter, not a single trace of explanation." Sadie lets the words roll off her tongue, in what feels like an expulsion of everything she buried deep inside her the day her mother died. "All she left me is that monster of a house... *The Hacienda Espinosa*," she scoffs. "What kind of goodbye is that?" Her voice falters as a glassy film forms over her eyes, all her scattered emotions turned loose. She whips her gaze towards Agustin. "Why did she kill herself, Father? Why did she think that the only option left for her was to abandon me?! To leave me like this —*alone?*" The last word comes out in a whimper, but he doesn't allow her the chance to unravel as he wraps his arms tight around her in an embrace that can only be the love of a father to a daughter that isn't his.

Sandalwood, saltwater, and candlewax engulfs her senses as she swallows her tears in Father Agustin's arms. The low hum of prayer from the pilgrims throwing themselves at Our Lady's feet is nothing more than background to the whistle of a cold wind through the trees, colder still when he unburdens himself with his next words, his voice low.

"Your mother could no longer bear her burdens, Sadie—that is why she took her life. She broke under the weight of what lay on her shoulders. It was never about abandoning you... she told me everything she did, it was for you."

A sharp pain slices straight through her heart, forcing her to pull away completely. "What do you mean she told you?" She searches his eyes for an answer, only for her racing thoughts to come to the conclusion. "The confessional... of course. She took confessional, didn't she? What did she say, Father?"

"*Anak,* you know I can't tell you. What is said in the confessional is between me and the penitent..." Agustin shifts his weight where he stands. "It is of the utmost confidence—"

"—She's dead, Father! She won't object." Fire courses through Sadie's veins, the need to know more rushing quick through her blood. "To know what was going through her head those last few days would mean everything to me... you of all people should know that."

Father Agustin is caught beneath her fiery gaze, and she doesn't let up until he breaks. He swallows whatever it is in his throat before releasing his shoulders, conceding; for how could he deny a girl with nothing left in the world?

"I... you're right," he sighs, an unfamiliar expression crossing Father Agustin's features, and she swears it almost looks like guilt as he lowers his voice to a near whisper. "She... she came to me one evening, long after service, for confessional."

She frowns, pulse quickening. "What did she say, Father?"

He turns his eyes to the candlelit statue up ahead, the sea of pilgrims dwindling down. "It was the week before the typhoon, before she passed. She was not herself... she was incoherent."

So much truth can pass through that lattice of the confessional, so much said in the dark that only Father Agustin knows, that only he can tell her. Hungry to know the unspoken words, she turns whip-fast to face him. "You knew why she did it and you never told me?!"

"Instead of the bright woman I had known all my life, she was withdrawn and—"

"—Suicidal." Sadie wraps her fingers around her sides, fingers digging into the fabric of her mother's dress as the sting of helplessness courses through her veins. "She was suicidal. She needed help, and you didn't give it to her. You're telling me about this burden of grief she carried—yet no one ever helped her carry that weight!"

"It wasn't *just* grief, Sadie!" His voice is raised, but the sound of the wind conceals it from the rest of the procession. Shaking his head, he drops his shoulders, composing himself in a softer tone. "It was not just grief on her shoulders. She was..." he trails off, searching for the right word, "...rambling."

"Rambling? About what?"

Father Agustin swallows the lump in his throat before answering, "Demons."

Sadie feels her heart seize up in the embrace of the twisting, thorned vines of the name Espinosa. *Demons—of course.* She turns away from Agustin, pacing away as her mind rushes with the tide of a thousand thoughts.

"She was devastated by your father's passing. It didn't surprise me that she would think an evil force was the cause of her pain, especially with how suddenly your father died."

"W—what did she say about demons?" Sadie turns to face him,

balling the fabric of her skirt between her fingers. "Please, Father... I want to know."

"She believed there were demons after her. Plaguing her existence, tormenting her with nightmares."

Sadie takes a deep breath, careful not to let the tremble in her voice show. "More than one?"

He raises an eyebrow, "I... I don't know."

"How many?!"

"Sadie," he frowns. "It doesn't matter anymore."

"It matters when it's all I have left." Sadie watches him with piercing eyes, the truth so close—just arm's width away.

Agustin keeps his gaze fixed on the statue of Our Lady, the last pilgrim prostrated at her feet, one last plea, one last wish. "In her rambling state she told me of her latest nightmare, a dream she believed was a warning."

"Her nightmare—what was it?"

"She didn't go into great detail," he shifts uncomfortably, tension written in the line of his jaw.

Sadie presses harder for the truth, "What was it?!"

"A man," he answers simply. "She dreamt of a man with red eyes."

Sadie unclenches her fists at her side, her pulse ringing loud in her ears, only broken by the sound of the crowd up ahead beckoning Father Agustin over to head the procession back to the church.

"Red eyes...?" she whispers, the question falling on deaf ears as Agustin merely squeezes her shoulder, the candlelight calling him back towards Port Cante. Yet he lingers a moment, wrapping his arms around her shoulders, forcing her to listen.

"That is why I told you what I did at the church. If you are having that same dream, that same nightmare—then all I can do is tell you to suffer it through. Listen to me, Sadie. Don't let it break you the way it did your mother," his voice takes on a desperate tone. "Her grief made her weak—but *you*—not you. You can be so much stronger if you just have *faith.*" With his last word he pulls her into a hug that she can't seem to get away from, no matter how much her thoughts scream for solitude.

"I'm sorry, Sadie..." he whispers. An apology; that's all he can offer. "I'm so sorry." He pulls away, holding her at arm's width. "Isaiah... you should go to him. I trust that he will take care of you. Spend the rest of the Festival together. Watch the fireworks, enjoy tonight..." He smiles a smile that doesn't reach his eyes. "Sadie?" Father Agustin asks, concern lacing his voice.

Sadie is frozen where she stands, the thought of her mother's final nightmare reigning over her thoughts. That final nightmare was that of a red-eyed man—a warning—a demon. Her blood runs hot at the thought of a demon tormenting her mother, driving her further into her grief, her suffering, her suicide. Yet her thoughts wrap tightly around the core of the question burning a hole in the pit of her belly: *Which demon?*

She presses her eyes shut, the feeling of Silas' open, pulsing scar beneath her fingertips rippling through her every nerve, the promise of starlight and a world beyond the walls of her grief beckoning out for her in his velvet black eyes.

If her mother's nightmare truly was a warning, then for Sadie, it's already too late.

"*Sadie,*" Agustin repeats himself, forcing her back to the present. "I'm telling you now what I told her after that confessional... keep your faith, and you will be set free. Do you hear me?"

Father Agustin is right. Faith is all she needs—yet be it to a demon's heart or her own, she no longer knows.

With a quiet breath, she breathes out her response, "Yes, Father. I hear you."

✤ 17 ✤

SADIE'S RAGE has all but dissipated, leaving a hollow wound where her anger once took root. Father Agustin is haloed in candlelight as he leaves Sadie alone in the darkness, returning to shepherd his devoted flock, where he must tend to his other children and all the other lost souls.

A cold wind wakes her from her reverie, Sadie awakening from the haze of her thoughts to see the revered statue being hoisted back up upon her processional barge where she's protected by her gilded canopy bedecked in swaying sampaguita garlands and unceasing candle flame.

From here the procession will wind its way back towards the church, and deciding she doesn't want to be left alone with the phantoms of this lagoon, Sadie decides to follow alongside the river of light. Turning into the undergrowth, Sadie finds her way along a narrow foot path that runs parallel to the dirt road, the sea of candlelight smeared against the writhing, wicked trunks of the night's jungle.

She ambles in and out of the light glow, following alongside Our Lady of Sorrows and the river of pilgrims that carry her back to her prison until the silhouette of the church comes into view. Sadie stops at a crumbling concrete wall that marks the edge of the jungle from the dirt road, waiting for the crowd and Our Lady to forge on without her, taking with them their prayers and hymns, leaving Sadie with nothing but the bat calls and cicada song entwined with the undergrowth.

Here, she's wrapped up in the velvet night and the jungle that worships it as she crosses the boundary and makes her way down the center of the unlit dirt road, far behind the procession, where their prayers are nothing more than a faint hum in the distance. An ocean wind blows over the tree tops, rustling the banana palms and plumeria trees surrounding her on either side of the road, nothing but dark shadows to keep her company until what must be the only street light for miles rises up from the dry earth.

It's an old beam of metal, the flickering light illuminating a dilapidated sign that reads *Port Cante Lagoon: Home of Our Lady of Sorrows*. Sadie casts her gaze up ahead, focusing on writhing flurry of moths swarming around the flickering bulb, a memory stirring deep within her.

"Look Sadie," her mother whispers, a smile pulling at her full lips as a moth flutters at the lamp hanging over the Hacienda's front doors. "It's your dad. He's come to say hello."

It's an old superstition the elders hang onto, that moths are the visiting dead, a moment of contact between the living and the long gone in the form of a moth's fleeting, ashen wings. It's a superstition Sadie can't bring herself to believe in, not when that swarm of spirits crowding around that half-broken bulb will all burn in a flicker of a flame if they dare get too close.

Sadie stops at the light's edge, looking away. She can't bear to face the sight of another death, even if it's just a spirit, even if it's just a moth.

A hard wind tousles loose strands of her hair against her cheeks, swaying the fabric of her dress, stirring it up until the ivory fabric is a specter at her hips, a specter that dies the moment Sadie feels a pair of eyes boring into her skin.

There—up ahead, beneath the street light is a black silhouette, crimson-eyed and solemn. He's a familiar silence in the middle of this lonely road, and he calls her towards him with the whistle of the wind through the trees.

Sadie squints into the dark, the suggestion of a demon's shadow all it takes to make her pulse echo loudly between her ears, but she stays where she stands, hairs bristling as that writhing flurry of moths find their way into that incandescent sun—one by one they begin to fall.

There's an inextricable pull for her towards the light, towards the shadow that must be Silas, as the swarm dwindles down with every fallen moth.

Wings singed, bodies charred.

Arm's width away, she's entranced by those reflective eyes hidden beneath a billowing plume of smoke, her gaze finding his heart wrought open across his chest, blood spilling from the wound in a cascade that draws a gasp from her lips. All she wants to do is reach out her hand to feel that wound beneath her fingertips, to spill her suffering into his and ease the agony—but she stops.

She stops when she realizes that it's never for once been where she would find Silas. *The dark,* that's where he belongs, *that's where he resides.*

It's Lorenzo who walks in the light, in the day, in the cold, unfeeling clarity of the sun—and here he is, taunting her with the night she wishes would swallow her whole.

Her skin bristles as the wind picks up once more, a ripple of Lorenzo's laughter brushing against her skin, and with it the realization that this is nothing more than a trick; a demon's illusion, a cruel attempt to stoke the dread welling deep inside her.

Yet Sadie resists her fear, letting her voice act the all the rage she knows is just a flimsy façade. "What do you want from me, Lorenzo!?"

He never replies, the shadow dissipating with the wind, leaving nothing but a pile of dead moths in its wake as Sadie backs away from the streetlamp. Shivering at the inextricable cold, she shakes the sound of Lorenzo's laughter from her thoughts.

She passes the light, rushing onwards down the road, not stopping until she sees the glow of civilization up ahead. She could tell herself it's nothing more than her mind playing tricks on her, that Lorenzo's laughter is nothing but a conjuration of her own dread, but by now—with all that's passed—she knows so much better.

Breathless, Sadie's hair is cast in a veil of candle smoke as she slows down upon the sight of the plaza hugging the church and the dwindling crowd of pilgrims, stopping only when she reaches the foot of Our Lady's pedestal.

Raising her one hand, she brushes her fingertips against the ivory white of a sampaguita garland hanging from the statue's base. Not in veneration, but in melancholy sadness. *Two years ago my mom was here beside me. Last year I buried her, this year I'm alone—and every year after will be the same.*

She crushes a loose flower between her fingers, releasing the sickly sweet perfume onto her fingers, staining her wrists and the blood that beats beneath.

Her eyes follow a small cluster of tourists making their way out of the plaza and into the stall-lined main road that leads to Infanta Bay just up ahead. In their hands sit the hissing glow of sparklers, signaling the impending fireworks that close out the Festival of Our Lady in a celebration of family, life, and the coming of the rain.

Pressing her eyes shut, she hugs her arms around herself, deathly still in her solitude until she hears a voice whisper against the shell of her ear.

"Starling..." It calls out, and her eyes shoot open.

It's him again—Lorenzo and his mocking, taunting tone.

Whipping around for the source of the voice, she sees no trace of Lorenzo, her nerves tangling as she backs away from the statue, dropping the petals to the ground as her heart begins to pace faster and faster.

Balling the length of her skirt up between her fists, she hurries down the main road until the she's standing at the foot of the Taverna, senses soaked through with the bar's blaring music, the din of the gathering crowd lining the beach, and of course the rolling, crashing waves of Infanta Bay.

Making her way across the Taverna's exterior, Sadie looks in through the windows, searching desperately for any trace of normalcy in Lorenzo's wake. With a quickening pulse, Sadie sifts through the sea of people in the dim, finding nothing but unfamiliar faces peering back at her through the noise of the bar. A sinking feeling settles into her nerves as she racks her brain thinking of someplace else Isaiah would rather be than at the Taverna.

Reaching the end of the Taverna's length, Sadie is certain Isaiah isn't inside, and the feeling of eyes watching her from some place unseen sends her away from the windows and out onto the sand where the back alley of the Taverna lies just up ahead.

Shadow lines the entirety of the alley, not a single sliver of light able to penetrate what the night has reclaimed for herself—yet Sadie's pulse skips a beat as she sets her eyes on a distinct shape leaning against the Taverna's exterior wall, a figure of a man with eyes that reflect all the crimson of Hell back at her.

With a strong breeze, the figure disappears into the dark alley in a motion that's as languid as it is unrushed, sending Sadie's thoughts into a spiral. If it is Lorenzo awaiting her up ahead—then why not make himself known the same way he did at the Taverna days ago? There, he relished being seen, he savored acting the wolf in sheep's clothing.

It's not like him to move in the dark, it's not like him to act beneath the cover of night. But up ahead, Sadie realizes it's not just the back entrance to the Taverna that awaits—there's also a secluded little grove behind the dense line of palm trees off to the side, the same spot Isaiah would whisk Sadie away to whenever he could for a stolen kiss.

Sadie narrows her eyes, a strange feeling settling into the pit of her stomach. *He's not chasing me,* she thinks to herself. She stands for a moment on the threshold of the beach, the cricket song loud in her ears as she stares into the darkness beckoning her towards it. *He's trying to show me something.*

And she follows.

The music of the Taverna grows softer as the crowd begins to cheer, no doubt the main event fireworks having just been wheeled out. Sadie peers into the dark, hearing voices up ahead. Carefully, she steps closer, making her way forwards onto the sandy trail until she sees a movement in the darkness.

The whir of the first firework shooting up into the sky fills Sadie's ears, and as a cascade of lights illuminates the night sky, Sadie realizes she sees not one figure, but two.

"This was your idea, so just relax why don't you?"

Sadie holds her breath, listening carefully over the din of the crowd behind her. A louder crackle fills her ears again, signaling what must be a roman candle.

A woman's voice giggles, "God, I missed this, Sai."

"So did I... All these years I never stopped thinking about you."

An array of reds and yellows scatter across the night sky, this one so rich—so vibrant, that for a second it turns night to day. And beneath the light of fleeting day, Sadie sees all her doubts set into stone.

It's Isaiah and Odette, their two bodies entwined, his arms tight around her waist, hers thrown around his neck, lips locked in a kiss. When darkness returns, the soft glow of the Taverna's lanterns light up the two of them just enough for her to see the expression on his face as he pulls away from her; his eyes soft, his fingers wanting.

It's everything you pretended wasn't happening.

Isaiah holds Odette the same way he wrapped his arms around her for all those countless summer nights after her dad's funeral, after his dad's wake, after her mom's empty coffin was lowered into the ground.

Yet it's worse than you imagined.

A wicked hot fire ruptures through Sadie, as she begins to feel the earth beneath wrap around her ankles, threatening to pull her into the depths and bury her in her own heartache—but it never does.

Sadie shifts her weight, spotting a piece of driftwood jutting out of the sand that she stomps down on with all her might, causing a snap of sound that ripples through the air.

Their heads whip in her direction, but it's too late—Sadie steps backwards, retreating into the darkness and back towards the Taverna's back alley.

"Sadie, wait!" Isaiah's voice calls out after her, but the sound of her name from his lips merely ebbs into her subconsciousness as she comes to a stop at the threshold of where the Taverna's back alley meets the beach.

Catching her breath beneath the lantern light, she attempts to steady her rapid-fire heartbeat. Dropping her shoulders, she screws her eyes shut, the ocean wind and her tears intertwining—she's truly alone now, like she always has been. Like she's meant to be.

"Sadie!" Isaiah calls out, coming to a stop beside her with Odette waiting somewhere in the shadows.

She doesn't turn. He doesn't reek of booze, instead he smells of perfume—of *her*.

A fire rises in her throat as she meets his gaze, "Leave me the fuck alone, Isaiah."

"Sara... it's not what you think it was."

Sara. How she hated it when he said that name—it was always *Starling* with playful touches and incessant flirting, and *Sadie* with their breaths mingling, limbs tangled—but never *Sara*.

She snaps her head towards him, and he withdraws his hand. "I'm not Sara. Don't call me that. Don't *ever* call me that."

"Sadie, then." His eyes are soft, reassuring like they always were when it comes to Isaiah Riviera, but this time Sadie sees right through it. He places his hand on her shoulder, one last attempt to coax her back to his side, back into the false promise of everything she so foolishly believed in. "Listen to me... We can still start over, we can still be what we were meant to be."

Sadie presses her eyes closed for a moment before facing him.

"Can't you see, Isaiah? The past is dead. And so are we."

The words rings hollow, suspended high up in the clouds that brew black above them. Removing his hand from her shoulder, she takes a step backwards, motioning to leave. "And if it's still not clear to you now, then it never will be."

He reaches out for her, but she jerks her hand away with a force that surprises even her. "Sadie, wait—"

"—*Don't*. Please don't."

His lips are a thin, straight line. "But it's not what you're thinking, it's not how it seems."

"Hm." Sadie can't help but scoff, "You're right. It isn't how it seems. It isn't how it seems because I can finally see through your bullshit. After all this time, I finally see."

Resorting to excuses was never his thing—it was always him with the clever turn of phrase; the teasing, the subtlety. But this time, it's him that's at a loss for words. This time, he didn't expect her to bite back.

Odette steps forward from where she cowers in the shadows, and immediately Sadie zeroes in on her.

"Sadie, I'm so sorry..." Odette's eyes are downcast.

Sadie scowls, "Don't tell me you're sorry, Odette. Not after what you did at the Hacienda... Pouring ink all over that dress and lighting all those candles in my room like some sort of memorial mass? I never thought you'd be capable of doing something like that."

"*What?* What are you talking about?" Odette shakes her head in disbelief. "I never lit any candles, Sadie. I dropped off your Maria Clara in *my* bedroom and left straight after. I never even went near your room."

Sadie stands firm. "You expect me to believe that?"

"Ask Isaiah, if you don't believe me. It was just *you* in that goddamned house of yours!"

"Odette's telling the truth. I picked her up outside the church and I took her back to the Hacienda. She was in and out in a few minutes."

"I never would have had the time to do anything you're accusing me of." Odette crosses her arms against her chest, and for a moment Sadie feels her resolve sway, a stake of doubt driven deep into her heart.

Isaiah is silent for a moment before he speaks again, his voice no longer soft; no longer warm. "Don't forget there was one other person in the house. I saw *him* when I came over to pick you up, standing in your burnt up room." Isaiah takes a step closer, dark scorn coloring his brown eyes. "Are you just trying to cover for him? What did he really do to you, hm?"

Sadie clenches her fists at her side, hating every wicked accusation that passes his lips.

"Did he hurt you? If you tell me, I can make it all go away Sadie, I can—"

"—He didn't do anything! If anyone's hurt me, Sai, it's you." Sadie flicks her eyes between he and Odette, their figures shrouded in shadow. "And it fucking hurts..." Her voice falters on the last word.

With flaring nostrils, Isaiah only digs his heels in. "You're no saint, either, you know. I know you snuck out of the room that one night after the Taverna. I know you were in his room."

Sadie shakes her head, not believing what she's hearing. "It's not—"

"—Don't deny it." He casts his eyes away.

Sadie's words are a whip of fire against her tongue, "I would *never* do anything to you like you've just done to me!" Her heart heaves in her chest, her voice hoarse with rage as she lets what's been simmering under the surface out into the open air. "After all these years we've been together it's only now I realize you don't know me. Not even a little bit, not at all."

He grits his teeth. "Don't tell me *he* helped you reach that conclusion."

Sadie says nothing, only for Isaiah's anger to erupt.

"Are you kidding me, Sadie? He's using you—why would he pay you any attention without wanting something more in return?"

In disbelief, Sadie shakes her head, fists balled at her sides. "What does he want from me in return then? Tell me."

Isaiah clenches his jaw. "The only thing guys like that want from girls like you."

She wraps herself up in the insult of his every word, absorbing the sting of every reproach to use as ammunition. "Girls like me?"

Isaiah voice lowers for a moment, "Girls blinded by their own grief... come on Sadie, can't you see that he's using you?"

Sadie lets out a sharp, frustrated sigh. "Because you know so well what it's like to use someone, don't you?! *You* of all people! Everything you're accusing him of is everything you've done to me. All you've ever done is take my grief and twist it whenever you needed someone to come back to, whenever you needed someone to keep you in check!" Her last words leave her lips in a hiss of fire, a hiss that's strangled by the chill of the night breeze that passes between them.

"What, just like you used me, after your mom killed herself?"

Her heart falls, and in its absence glows the embers waiting for all these wasted years. This last insult is the final spark needed to fan the flame into hellfire—and how it burns, growing into a roaring fire that spills from her lips in two, simple words.

"Fuck you."

In the silence that settles, Sadie realizes she's no longer looking into the eyes of the boy she had spent all of her grief-stricken teenage summers with; he's not *the one,* just... no one at all.

"I never used you, Isaiah. That's the difference between you and me—I actually thought you cared about me, that we could have been something. But God, I was wrong, wasn't I?" Sadie's voice is barely a whisper, as she lets her words soak through his skin before pushing past him.

She makes her way forwards, away from the din of the beach and the firecrackers and up towards the dense line of palm trees Isaiah and Odette emerged from. Her eyes are vacant, Sadie never allowing the tears to fall as she passes by Odette.

"Sadie..." Odette whispers, voice dripping with regret that Sadie never acknowledges, especially when she catches the smudged corners of her lipstick in the dim light. Odette's fingers wrap softly around the fabric of Sadie's Maria Clara, a quiet plea embedded in her touch. A whistle of wind whips through the towering palm trees behind Odette, the darkness between those old trunks beckoning her towards it.

Sadie keeps her eyes fixed to the dark ahead as she tells her, "Leave me alone."

With the crack and bang of a firework shooting high above the canopy of palms, Odette lets go, Sadie continuing onwards into the darkness between the trunks.

Isaiah doesn't call out after her; and Sadie never bothers to turn back.

She doesn't dare stop—yet with every passing second, the numbness dwindles, the voices of the beach fading until all she hears are the night crickets enveloping her senses. Blood sears through her veins as the wind calls her, the promise of darkness too enticing, so much more of a reassurance than anything here on this lantern-lit beach.

She swears Odette calls out after her again, but whatever she says is drowned out by a thunderous crackle of a firework. In spite of the revelry, the voices, the laughter of the distant crowd, all

Sadie can hear are the crickets and the waves of the sea against the cold, unfeeling shore of Port Cante.

Wrapped up in a sliver of moonlight, Sadie lets herself into the open embrace of the jungle thicket, the rustling palm trees bowing to take her into its dark arms with all the love and promise of a mother to a child that's hopelessly, utterly alone.

18

ODETTE'S VOICE is soon nothing but a whistle of the wind against the trees as Sadie stumbles her way through the dense palms, farther and farther from the Taverna with every fumbling step, deeper and deeper into the depths of solitude.

She goes gladly into the jungle's undergrowth, with only the promise of darkness to guide the way ahead. This way, no one will follow—as long as she keeps moving, no one will ever see her tears, no one will ever hear her cries.

Holding onto the tears brimming at her eyes, she pushes away endless branches and scratchy jungle vines with no care for the twisting mangrove roots tearing at the hem of her skirt, nor the thorns and jutting trunks pricking at her skin. She has no *bolo* knife, no machete to slice through the greenery—all she has is the soft flesh of her arms as she presses forwards, caught in a fevered spell as the numbness recedes with every passing moment.

Desperation urges her onwards as she searches for shelter in an incoming storm, a storm she knows will swallow her whole the moment she unleashes it. The jungle pushes and pulls her onwards, snatching away wisps of her hair, pulling at her ankles, clawing at her cheeks and the fabric of her mother's dress.

This must be what it feels like, she thinks to herself, *this must be what Our Lady of Sorrows feels on the tide of that desperate, hungry crowd.*

Even through the cicada song she can hear the low hum of prayer in the distance. It can only be the remnants of the procession, praying over the statue at the plaza hugging the church, before she's locked away for another year, back to her home, back to her gilded cage.

Wetness laces her cheeks, droplets of tears slipping through the dam she built long ago, the pressure of holding it all back growing unbearable beneath this undergrowth. Speckles of moonlight filter in from the thick canopy up ahead, the moon taking mercy upon her and lighting her path forwards.

Up ahead there's a break in the trees, a fallen tree forming a clearing brimming with dry grass and moonlight.

Unable to suppress the welling sob in her throat, Sadie doesn't stop until she's free of the undergrowth, her body bursting forth from the darkness and into the pale of this grassy clearing where she lands in a heap of ivory and scrapped-up skin.

Her braid has come loose, the pins that secured it lost to the jungle, her hair fanning out against the wild grass, entwined with her fingers splayed out across the thicket. Sadie clutches a tuft of spindly weeds as she lets herself sink into the earth, her bones heavy, heart an unbearable weight as she unleashes the deluge she's been holding back for longer than she can remember.

She cries until she can't feel the tears anymore, until her throat is hoarse, her heart wrung out of everything she's held inside for countless nights and endless days. She hopes to die in this very spot, hidden away in the thicket, her body forgotten, her sorrows finally eased. She'll become nothing but meat for the stray dogs, her upturned veins for the birds. The jungle will feast until there's nothing left of her but scraps of bone, ribbons of ivory, and the glimmer of an opalescent pearl on a golden chain.

She cries, she cries, she cries—until someone listens, until someone hears, until the darkness answers.

A hard wind tousles her hair, a sudden cold against her searing tears as a cloud of smoke emerges from the dark, billowing to form the shape of a man summoned by her agony, a demon hungry for her tears.

"*Solita,*" he whispers, that name from his lips a cruelty, a confirmation all wrapped up in one.

Pressing herself up onto her knees, her hair spills across her shoulders in a veil of silken black as she takes in the sight of him standing so close before her. Crumpled before him, she's ever the penitent Magdalene soaked through the bones with grief, witness to the miracle of darkness that manifests before her. He's proof of resurrection, of immortality, of everything Sadie was taught to believe in—only this time, she can't deny it anymore.

"Silas…" she murmurs, the smoke receding the moment she says his name, his moon-lit features sharply defined as he stands in the center of the clearing, his eyes reflective in the dark in an image that can be nothing else but divine.

"It's him… isn't it?" he asks, voice low, almost inaudible.

It's everything she expects and nothing she desires. His watching, his knowing, it's a horror greater than the grave itself. Tears streak her cheeks, and she makes no effort to wipe them away. "W—what do you mean?"

"Is it him that made you feel this way?"

A glassy film envelops her vision as she holds her breath—not at the thought of Isaiah, but because they are utterly alone in the dark.

His silence is a command, and she has no choice but to answer.

She casts her eyes away, her cheeks burning hot with shame. "No… It's not him. It's me."

He says nothing, only amplifying the heat under her skin, setting a fire on her tongue that cuts her tangled thoughts loose.

"It's all the time I've wasted—all the time I spent wasting away in a dream. A dream of everything I thought I wanted, of everything I wanted to believe. About Isaiah, about Odette... about my mom." Winding her arms around herself, she continues, "My parents, my friends—they all left me behind. *He's* the only one who stayed. He's always been here for me. He deserves to be happy, and I couldn't even give him that. I spent so much time thinking I could—but Odette has only proven that I'm not good enough for it." Her voice grows softer and softer until it's nothing more than a near-whisper as she winds closer and closer to the words encased within her prison of a heart. "Just like I'm not good enough to make my mom happy. I wasn't enough for her in life, and I'm not enough for her in death. She deserved to be happy with the Hacienda she always wanted, but it's a Hacienda I'll never be able to give her." Her head hangs heavy. "How can I ever make anyone happy, Silas? How can I—"

"—What about you?" he interrupts, voice low like the distant tremor of thunder.

She opens her eyes, dropping her hands from her face to meet his piercing gaze. He stands over her, close enough to allow her to hear the sound of his pulse as another breeze rustles through the jungle once more, only this time she feels herself sway with the trees.

"Does your happiness mean nothing?" Silas asks, in his words no malice, no mercy.

She drops her shoulders, eyes focusing on a quick-drying smear of blood on the white of her mother's dress. She wills herself to focus on that droplet of crimson from a scrape against her wrist, but her tongue acts faster than her mind as she whips her eyes up to face him. "What do you know about happiness?"

The shadows chase away the light behind his eyes, the moon retreating behind the clouds. He lingers on a distant thought, and Sadie can't help but wonder what it is that fills his mind. His past, his guilt, his sins, the sum of the life he once possessed now nothing but a faint imagining prescribed to the confines of his memory, his tenuous sanity. A sanity tied to her suffering, a remembering tied to her agony.

The blood on his hands, the blood that stains his past, his life, that distant sea—she can't help but feel it call to her. It lifts her to her feet, the cuts and scrapes that kiss her ankles nothing but a numbness as she carries herself before him, her eyes drinking in all that there is behind those infernal eyes.

"Why don't you just end my suffering?" She lets the words out, no thought for the Hell she invites with every careless word. "Why don't you do what you've wanted to do all this time!? What I know you're capable of!" Balling her fists, she closes the distance between them as she presses them against the width of his chest, heart pacing out of control, sorrow brimming from every broken plea, "Why don't you just do it—why don't you just kill me!?"

But all he does is take a measured breath of restraint before answering in a sigh, "I will not be your suicide, *Solita.*"

Her features twist into hurt, guilt, shame—and it softens her into silence.

In his eyes she can see the fire of his torment, the pyre of his guilt, his breath inches from hers as he continues, "Do you know what it's like to have this wound cursed never to heal?" His jaw clenches, voice dark. "It feels like swallowing the sun—the agony has burned me of my tongue..." His eyes flicker over the planes of her face, as the words stretch out between them. "My taste..." He leans in closer, eyes searching endlessly, "My appetite."

It's with the night wind Sadie realizes what it is the restraint etched into his words is for; restraint for something so much deadlier than death, so much more devastating.

"Yet here I am..." His voice is a near whisper, "Ravenous."

Her heart beats faster in her chest at the thought of being the flesh he sinks his teeth into, the mere image of it sending her cheeks hot, and she doesn't dare look away from the fire.

"Then why..." she trails off, craning her neck to meet his gaze. He's closer now, his hand drawing upwards, his fingers skimming against the drying tears of her cheek, winding through an undone strand of her hair. The braid he set across her crown is all but gone now, yet the imprint remains in the loose curl of her ebony hair. "Why me?" she whispers, the silence between them lasting for but a moment before the crackle of a firework shoots up into the sky, illuminating them both with a fleeting, incarnadine sky. "Why *my* suffering?"

He winds her hair into a curl between his fingers, eyes lidded, brimming with night as he answers simply, "Because it is yours."

The firelight fades, and darkness falls.

"Mine?" she asks, her voice a whisper, heart laid bare.

"Because I have never seen such tears, such sorrow, such sadness wrapped around a human heart the way it is twined around yours... a heart that beats yet wants to die, a heart bruised through yet longs for touch, a heart so lonely yet needs to be anything but."

The cicada song falls to a stuttering silence in this Eden of a jungle, every passing moment drawing her closer and closer towards the black abyss that brushes against her hair, her tear-stained cheeks, her flesh flayed where his darkness trails.

"Sara," he says her name, her birth name—but it no longer feels like the truth. It no longer feels like it's hers as he whispers, "My heart is scarred, but yours is sacred."

"How can I be sacred?" She shakes her head, casting her eyes away, just waiting for him to pull away, to leave her to her solitude, but his hand remains at her cheek, and he makes no motion to let her go.

"In all those years I spent steeped in blood, I never once thought of the scars I inflicted upon those that remained—I never once spared a thought for the living... until now. Until you."

She's rendered silent beneath his words, the cadence of his voice wrapping tight around her senses.

"In my time," he continues, voice low, "sanctity was measured by suffering. Those saints that abstained from the pleasures of life, fasted to starvation, mortified their flesh, drank the blood of the wounded—it was only they who saw the eyes of God, it was only through their agony that they were touched by true divinity, enraptured by their own faith."

"I... I'm not a saint, Silas." Her eyes meet his in a gaze that's wrapped up in the promise for everything she's always denied herself. The promise of temptation for the taste of that forbidden fruit, a single bite all it takes for irreversible expulsion, for an eternal fall from grace.

"I never said you were."

The warmth of his breath is so close to her own, heat mingling, pulses flush close. "Then what are you saying?"

"That *I* am," he answers. "I found God. And I'm looking into her eyes."

Faith is what Father Agustin insisted Sadie abide by—and here, now, this must be exactly what he meant as she lets herself fall. It must be faith as she unfurls her fists at his chest, letting Silas' arms twine tight around her waist. It must be faith as she presses herself into him, winding her arms around his neck, his fingers threading through her hair. It can only be faith that parts her lips and allows him to enter in a kiss that's the communion of all her holy suffering and all his rose-stained, sacred sin.

She falls gladly from grace as another firework shoots up into the sky, committing the weight of his body against hers to profane memory. His taste, this fire lit sky, his hands, and the jungle dark that wraps around them both—it's an intoxication that's stained her blood eternal.

Marked by his fire, his touch, his smoke stained blood.

She can see it all now so clearly; all the demon he is, the ocean of blood at his feet, wrought by his hand. An ocean of blood that threatens to pull her into its depths, into his abyssal soul... the water rises higher and higher, with every knot of their tongues, every ravenous breath—but she has no fear of the sea, for it's an ocean she'll willingly drown in.

Droplets fall across her flushed cheeks, pulling her back to dry land as her eyes flutter open. The first thing she sees is a veil of soft rain. "The first rain..." she murmurs against his lips, a smile spreading over her face at the absurdity of it all. "Of course.... Of course it's now."

Beneath the rain she sees his eyes in a different color as another firework shoots up high into the night sky, a kaleidoscope of light falling far above the jungle canopy. Silas' hand lingers through her hair, and Sadie can't help but be mesmerized at the vivid greens and effervescent yellows, the fiery reds and the dazzling oranges as they light up all the angles of his face, all the planes she's yet to see, yet to discover.

She's lost beneath this rain, but finds beneath his gaze something she's been searching for through countless nights—the reflection of a girl she still remembers, a girl with a smile on her lips, a girl with hope in her eyes.

But a stronger wind blows, turning loose the plumeria flowers from their branches, spilling them out into the clearing and the sheer of the rainfall. Sadie breathes in the scent of the rain and the earth mixing together, the *drip drip drip* of raindrops from the tips of glossy monstera leaves telling of the quickening rain, the passing of the night, this ephemeral moment.

And she lets her tongue loose in a vicious attempt to keep it in from slipping through her fingers.

"Silas..." The moment his name leaves her lips, he knows what's coming next like he knows the veins beneath her skin, like he knows the taste of her tongue. "I need to know."

"What is it?" His voice is the gentlest pressure.

"My mom..." The pulse in her chest beats harder with every passing word, "My mom believed in demons. Before she died, she believed that they were following her—making her life a living hell. She told Father Agustin that she was having these nightmares. One in particular before that storm..."

"*Solita*..." he whispers, an attempt to assuage her grief,

recognizing doubt in the cadence of her voice, her fear in the lilt of sadness that colors her eyes.

"I need to know." She swallows the lump in her throat, voice a quiet accusation, "Are you the nightmare she was trying to get away from?"

In spite of the rain, the fireworks continue—the crackle and snap of another roman candle slicing through the night sky the only answer she gets to her question as Silas' arms stiffen around her, instinctively pressing her closer against him.

There's a crack of noise that seizes her heart, but it's not from a firework, it's not from the sky—it's coming from the jungle. Casting her eyes up to his, he's haloed by soft rain and a sliver of moonlight streaming in from a break between the clouds. Dread fills her every vein as he never meets her gaze, his eyes fixed to the pitch black beyond the clearing, fixed to the path she created.

His fingers dig hard into her skin as she searches his eyes desperately for a reassurance that she never thought she would seek, yet it's an entirely different answer she finds in his eyes instead.

He turns to face her for but a moment, drawing his fingers upwards to brush against the dark of her hair. "Go."

Fear wraps tight around her heart as he tucks a loose strand of hair behind her ear before releasing her from his embrace, stepping forwards and placing himself between her and whatever it is that lurks in the darkness.

"W—where?"

She motions to speak, only for a crack of wood to silence her. Silas tenses, forcing Sadie to peer over his shoulder, where the faint glimmer of a reflective pair of eyes peer back at her. Here beneath the rain, all she hears is the rapid-fire pace of her heart.

It's him.

"Lorenzo..." His name is a gasp from her lips as she draws her hand up to her necklace, gripping the pearl nervously between her fingers in a vain attempt to impart it with the terror seeping quick into her veins.

"Leave now, *Solita.*" His voice is a command, yet she stays firm where she stands. "It's time I settle this business with my brother."

"How will you...?" she trails off, already knowing the answer to her question, knowing exactly what it will take to settle it.

He turns to face her even as Lorenzo's eyes loom in the shadows, a soft smile brushing his lips at her question, "He has his weaknesses."

"And so do you." She casts her eyes to his chest, thinking of the wound that sprawls out across it, and she yearns for him to close the distance once more, to feel his hands through her hair, his lips on hers—but he silences the thought.

"Go to the Hacienda," he orders. "As long as you are beneath that roof, I will be stronger, and you will be safe."

Silas bares his teeth as Lorenzo readies his attack from the undergrowth, his voice a snarl as the shadows reclaim him, a billowing darkness caressing his once moonlit features. *"Go!"*

A shadow strikes Silas beneath a flash of a firework, the crash and tumble that follows soaked in a savagery that beckons forth that ocean of red, that ocean of blood. Yet for as quick as Lorenzo is, Silas is stronger as he rises tall over his brother, his one hand wrung tight around his neck, the other delivering a hook that lands to his jaw in a devastating wave that threatens the very bones beneath.

That crimson tide of rage spills over, filling the clearing and pooling at the hem of Sadie's torn dress, the water calling out for her, vicious and unyielding. Yet her eyes land on Lorenzo's face, and the wolfish smile that pulls up at his lips as he meets her gaze.

Flesh rippling at the contact, Sadie draws backwards, stopping at the clearing's edge. Lorenzo's eyes are wild, flickering crimson as he parts his lips to speak, Silas throwing him to the earth.

"Run, little starling..." He spits the blood from his mouth, staining the grass below as he props himself up to his feet. "Do as he says."

Lorenzo's mocking voice echoes madly in her ears, taking advantage of the lull to drive his fist into Silas' chest, prying a groan of agony from his brother. It's exactly what he did at the Taverna, the same motion, the same smile—only this time, Silas' wound has opened twice in the span of mere days.

Blood dribbles forth from the gash at Silas' chest, the opened wound bringing him to his knees, his fingers clenched tight around the crimson spattered earth beneath.

Without his ties to the Hacienda he's weaker—the pain of his mortal flesh more pronounced, the agony of his scarred heart amplified tenfold.

A hard gust of wind blows Sadie backwards from the sight of Silas brought to his hands and knees, forcing her to focus on Lorenzo as he ambles towards her, Silas' smoke tainted blood dripping from his fingers.

"Run."

The jungle opens its arms out to take her, and Sadie runs terror-struck into the thicket, into those twisting fingers of branches, those root-bound splinters of sharpened nails. Her pulse is loud against her skull, yet she feels an emptiness inside her ribcage that can only mean she left her heart back at the clearing, between a demon's fingers, beneath a demon's teeth, twined tight against a demon's bleeding heart.

19

WITH THE HISS OF A FIREWORK, the explosion of blue light that follows is all the lifeline Sadie has in the darkness as she winds her way through the taunting, jeering undergrowth. Lorenzo is close behind, snapping vine-twisted branches and cracking apart mangrove roots in his wake.

The cicada song has been snuffed out beneath Lorenzo's presence, the moon well and truly hidden beneath the rain clouds, the jungle a dead quiet punctuated only by the sharp staccato of Sadie's heart.

More fireworks resound—bathing the canopy in speckles of vivid yellows and vibrant reds. A jutting branch tugs at the thin cloth of Sadie's sleeve, tearing the fabric clean apart, leaving a stinging scratch that forces her to stop and look over her shoulder.

A pair of red-rimmed reflective eyes stare back at her from the thicket, a face lined in shadow, framed with thorned vines and swaying palm fronds; commanding the dread at her nerves with all the ease of the moon to the tide beneath.

"Is that fear I taste?" His voice is as unwavering as his smile. "It's not me you should be fearful of, Starling."

The wind moves her before her body does, and with a quiver

she throws herself deep into the thicket, staying as low as possible to the ground, hoping the mangrove roots will be enough to conceal her.

A ripple of laughter vibrates through the air, followed by the crash and bang of another firework. It's enough illumination for Sadie to set her eyes on the trunk of an old balete tree up ahead, its vine-laden branches the perfect spot to hide.

Scrambling forwards, she nestles herself behind a curtain of twisting, writhing vines, desperately willing her heart to slow, willing her breath to become stable. Digging her fingers into the hard bark beneath until her nails leave crescent marks, she holds her breath, instinctively gripping her necklace in an attempt to reaffirm the fact that this can't be real, this can't be happening—it's just a nightmare, just another bad dream.

With her heart beating achingly loud in her skull, she darts her eyes across the darkness, just waiting for another firework to light up the undergrowth and reveal Lorenzo's bloodied silhouette standing before her.

Clamping her hand tight around her mouth, she holds her breath as another firework lights up the night, her heart frantic against her ribcage. Tucking her legs tight against her chest, Sadie can do only two things:

Listen and wait.

Time slows to a crawl as her vision adjusts to the constant flood of light and dark as the fireworks pick up in pace, her senses stained with the scent of Silas' coal-smoke blood.

But the splintering of wood plunges her back into the jungle dark, dread enveloping her every nerve as a shadow emerges from the undergrowth. His steps are languid as he comes to stop before the curtain of vines that conceals Sadie beneath, a smirk painted on his lips she need not see to know is there.

It's Lorenzo, and he casts his eyes straight through the spaces between the vines with nothing but brimstone burning behind his eyes.

"Did you like the present I left for you back at the Hacienda? How I've always loved the candlelight..."

Sadie's heart sinks. *It was him,* she realizes, her thoughts spiraling, *not Odette.* She hates herself for the guilt that twines around her heart for accusing Odette—hating herself even more for feeling it in spite of her sick betrayal. She waits for him to act with the light of the next firework, but the firelight comes and goes, Sadie waiting in vivid silence for a demon that never strikes.

Instead, he's listening, and he knows I am too.

"You know, there is adage in our family..." His voice sends a ripple of fear through her, and he drinks it in as he runs his fingers across the cascading vines. "Words passed down with every generation of Espinosas." He takes a step forward, his voice encroaching closer, threatening to pierce through the spaces between the vines. "*Bloom by wrath, wither in love...*"

Sadie holds her breath, hand clamped over her mouth.

"Abide by one, and avoid the other." He leans into the vines, close enough for Sadie to see the wicked red dancing beneath across his irises. "Do you truly think my brother's '*past sin*' was him killing a woman?" A smirk plays on his lips as he's bathed in a waterfall of crimson from a firework that explodes across the night sky. "Countless lives have fallen at his hands... and her life was just one of them. But it is not the killing that brought our father's rage upon him—it was the *why*. Do you want to know why he killed her, Starling?"

The explosion of light catches her off guard, and she draws a sudden breath she knows he hears. Beneath the light of the fireworks, the vibrant colors dancing over the hard lines of his face; she sees a hunger burning behind his eyes.

"Because of love."

Reaching a hand out to part the curtain of vines, Sadie tenses as she's unable to move beneath Lorenzo's eyes.

"He loved her... and she died for it."

Humans have always been his weakness, Lorenzo's words dance over her thoughts, circling around her heart in a thorn-tipped vine that winds tighter and tighter, the threat of severing the organ beneath sending a shiver of terror through her. *And you're no exception, Sadie.*

"That fear in your eyes... the taste is familiar."

A blinding firework scatters light across the canvas of night, and in the deafening roar of its explosion, her heart races faster at the fact that it's her fear he's hungry for. It's what he feeds from, what nourishes him, the dark sustenance that's kept him alive for as long as it has.

She expects him to rip the vines apart, to throw her down against the balete roots and drag her out into the light—but he makes no motion to move. Like a predator toying with its still-breathing meal before he crushes her between his jaws, he waits; supping on her fear, and the dread dripping from her pores.

"Yet it's sweeter than hers."

All she can do is stare wide-eyed in horror as he peers down at her through the part in the vines with nothing but death in his eyes, his words ringing between her ears.

Sweeter than hers.

Sadie gives herself away as she asks, "W—what did you say?"

But he never has the chance to answer as a rustle of movement resounds from the undergrowth, followed by heavy footfall heading straight for the balete tree. Her heart rises at the sound, yet Lorenzo keeps her attention firmly in his grip as he whispers, "You want nothing more than truth, don't you Starling?"

The question catches her off guard, along with the figure of a man rising tall behind him, a shadow darker than night itself, eclipsing all that remains of the light.

"Go to the cliffs," Lorenzo commands. "You will find everything you've ever wanted." Lorenzo reaches out to grab her, eyes burning as he wraps his fingers vice-tight around her wrist, willing her to listen to his words. "Forget his heart," his voice is a menacing quiet as the thought of those dark cliffs come crashing over her senses. "Look to your own," he whispers, his voice laced with a softness that almost feels like mercy.

And he releases her, only for the shadow of black to rise up behind him in a billowing plume of smoke, the wind stealing away the darkness and revealing the crimson eyes of a raging demon.

It's Silas.

And her fears are silenced when Lorenzo begins to levitate.

Silas lifts him up off the earth, and all Sadie can do is raise her eyes to Lorenzo as he struggles hard against his brother's hand gripping the back of his collar.

"Leave her," Silas orders as his brother sputters for breath, his nails digging hard into Silas' fingers against his throat. "This is between you and I—no one else."

Lorenzo's eyes bulge at the force, before Silas casts him against the trunk of a plumeria tree, the wood snapping at the force in thunderous cacophony.

Falling to the rain-soaked undergrowth, Lorenzo claws at his throat, marked red raw as he sputters, "You really have no idea, don't you?"

Silas ignores him, instead turning to Sadie, his eyes hard but far from distant. His jaw clenches as he reads what's written plain on her face, a flicker of red flashing over his eyes—a familiar shade she'd only seen in the sin of his past, in that distant, blood-soaked memory of his life before her.

The tide of his past threatens to drag her under its current, yet the call to the cliffs is so much stronger, the pull towards the truth Lorenzo promises an inescapable force.

Rising to her feet, she presses herself up against the trunk of the balete tree, pinned to the bark by Silas' gaze as he draws ever closer, his fingers laced with his own blood.

"*Solita*," he commands, that name on his tongue an insult, a humiliation, a chain that tethers her back to everything she hates in herself. "Go back to the house."

Silas draws closer, reaching out to touch her—but she draws away, retreating into herself with a voice wrapped up in steel.

"No!" she cries out, forcing him to stay where he stands. She shakes her head, fire burning in the pit of her belly with the hunger for the truth, for its tide, for the sea she's been avoiding for a year since her mother died. "Don't... don't call me that." The light of a firework passes between them both, a cascade of silence, a cascade of fiery yellow that illuminates the blood seeping out from beneath the fabric of his shirt. The scar is now a gash, a wound as fresh as the day he earned it, as vivid as the color of his sin, the color of his guilt. "It's not my name."

And she never lets the cascade have the chance to settle before she runs. Out from beneath the vines of the balete tree and into the thicket, she runs and she runs and she runs until the trees grow sparse, the dense canopy opening up overhead. She runs until she's found the jungle's edge, the Hacienda staring back at her with merciless eyes.

Clambering out from beneath the drooping gumamela flowers lining the boundary between jungle and Hacienda, Sadie rests breathlessly at the edge, panting for desperate breath. The Hacienda is a sentinel in the night, as dark and watching as it's ever been, an offer of refuge in this nightmare, in this insanity.

One step at a time, she makes her way forward. Across the last of the thicket, across the rain-soaked dirt driveway, fumbling forward in the direction of the front doors in a haze of tangled thoughts, her hair streaked with twigs, skin littered with scratches, dress marked through and through by the hands of the jungle.

She's so close to entry, so close to those comforting walls—yet she stops before the doors. Twisting the handle beneath her fingers, she pushes open the front doors, finding a moment's reprieve as she's greeted by an overwhelming presence. A presence written in every black narra wood column, entwined with the twinkle of every capiz shell window, carved into the inlaid panels itself, an oppressive shadow darker than any demon, worse than any Hell.

It's the presence of her past.

Every feature, every edifice of this house from the torn up floor boards to the charred remains of her bedroom—all of it forms the bars of a cage she'll never be free from as long as she returns to the false safety it promises.

The Hacienda is her cage, gilded with her grief, adorned with her sorrow; and freedom means nothing to a captive that never wants to be free.

Forget his heart, Lorenzo's words ring in her ears.

She knows where freedom lies, and it's now or never. Leaving the front doors hanging open in the wind, she backs away from the entrance, the need for truth coursing through her veins.

Look to your own.

Saint or demon, God or monster, Sadie no longer cares to draw the distinction between the two. Here, alone in this fevered night, freedom tastes of first rain and firelight, of a demon's kiss and a demon's promise for truth.

She turns her back on the Hacienda, disappearing into the dirt road, into the velvet night—towards the maker of her nightmares, the mother of her grief.

20

THE ROAD that stretches up towards the limestone cliffs is as overgrown as it is unused, the same route her mother used a year past in her pilgrimage to her own demise.

The tension in her shoulders is impossibly tight as she nears the road's end, where the fine dirt road morphs into the loamy, dark jungle path that snakes its way up and over the cliffs. With the hem of her skirt gathering up flecks of mud and grass, she stops at the base of the cliffs, where the road transforms into a steep incline— leading only to a dead end.

She draws her gaze down to her wrist, where purple-red marks snake around her skin from Lorenzo's grip. The pain throbs through her nerves, but she never gives herself the chance to linger.

Just like her dream, just like her nightmares; it's all rushing through her senses, winding through her nerves and wrapping around her heart as the jungle canopy envelops the sky above her, the path before her twisting like a serpent's flesh, writhing endlessly towards her final destination. The cicada song is loud in her ears, softening the sound of the fireworks from the beach, leaving only the firelight; as clear and plain as day.

With the adrenaline quickly fading, the bruising marks Lorenzo left behind on her skin grow sharper into focus—but she presses on, bunching up her skirt between her fingers as she crosses the boundary between the road and the dark jungle path.

The way ahead is one she knows well. Her memories stir with the feeling of her mother's hand in hers as she led her carefully up the narrow path that snakes its way up to the highest point of the cliffs that hug Infanta Bay, a pang of heartache shooting through her at the phantom warmth of her mother's beaming smile from that first time she saw her daughter's reaction to the view.

Ever since she could remember, this would be *their* escape. A treasure of a view yet untainted by tourists and foreigners, where one can see the entirety of Port Cante and the rolling green hills enveloped by dense jungle stretching out endlessly around it. It's a place only her mother knew of, a place she shared only with her blood, only with her daughter.

The incline grows sharper; steeper—and Sadie's thoughts follow suit. The answers are so close, just within her grasp, yet she can't help the sting that cuts through her at the thought that they were never in Silas' hands—but Lorenzo's. She can't keep his words out of her head, the seeds of doubt taking root; growing and growing into twisting vines constricting around her mind, around her heart.

Scrambling up along the path as the undergrowth pokes and prods at her already tender skin, the scratchy roots and the sharpened branches paw at the remaining fabric of her dress as if even the cliffs are trying to reclaim it; rip it from her body and leave her bare. Her stomach twists at what's left of her mother's memory being torn to shreds—yet the call of the cliffs is louder than the ache in her bones.

Up ahead she can hear the crashing of waves at the base of the cliffs, the melody of that angry, violent tide lulling her to the heart of her nightmares. Clambering up and over the sharp limestone rocks, Sadie's Maria Clara is all but tattered by the time she can hear the swelling waves of the sea loud and clear against her senses.

The moment the night sky and all her cloud-veiled stars open up above her, she knows she's made it, she's here. Not in a nightmare, but in reality. The winds carry the rainclouds across the sky, obscuring the starlight once more as she sets her eyes over the narrow clearing before her, sprays of wild moonflower twisting around the trunks of the sea-battered mangroves hanging over the cliff's edge.

The silence is interspersed only with the distant sound of fireworks, casting a kaleidoscope of color against the rain streaked sky—no amount of rain a reason to stop the festivities of Port Cante, nothing enough to stop this celebration of family, of faith, of *life*.

Yet here Sadie stands, with only death on her mind as she takes in the sight of her mother's grave—from the vastness of the sky above to the sea spray from the crashing waves below, Sadie wishes she could be swallowed up in the same black waters her mother plunged into.

The ocean wind is cool, but the blood in her veins is simmering, and she lets it carry her into the heart of the clearing. It's been a year since her mother died, a year since she could bear to look at the sea she once loved, a year since she had the courage to stand before it.

Sadie takes a step forwards, sharply aware of the precipice looming before her, the crashing waves below seeming more and more like a melody than a roar. But the sound of a voice pulls her from the edge, and Sadie turns to see Lorenzo standing at the entrance of the clearing. He's worse for wear, body marked with Silas' hand, his neck wrung red—yet on his bloodied lips is still that same, wicked smile.

"Be thankful for your mother." His voice clings to her shoulders with all the chill of this eerie night. "Be thankful she lived past your birth."

Sadie's thoughts tangle at the idea of Lorenzo and Silas' family, at the image of them having a mother, a woman to call mom, just like she did.

Lorenzo ambles forward into the clearing. "Whatever remained of my mother's strength after the devastation of Silas' birth was destroyed the day I was born. I killed her... and I was mere minutes old." His eyes grow distant beneath the weight of his past, just as Silas' eyes do—yet the lull lasts only for a moment before that vivid crimson returns to reign supreme. "Perhaps it was written in the stars... the day I was born was marked by blood and death. A sign of all the death to come by my hands, of all the suffering I was to reap." Lorenzo wipes a dribble of blood that escapes his lips, "And how I rose to meet that destiny... and how I enjoyed every minute of it. All these centuries spent watching empires rise and fall have taught me one thing." He stands arm's width away from her, continuing, "Your kind wants pain. Your kind *needs* it. Just as demons find nourishment in your tears, humans find pleasure in all the agonies this world has to offer... and for that, can we truly be blamed? To take from the well of woe you so freely offer?"

Sadie's eyes are fixed to the depths of the dark ocean beyond, beckoning her into its arms for but a moment before she whips around to face Lorenzo's red rimmed gaze. "I blame you when you cause the agony that you feed from. I blame you when you tip the scales in your favor—all so you can *drink*."

Lorenzo steps closer, his voice rising over the sound of the waves as something wicked passes beneath his eyes. "You know... you should be thankful for that storm."

Sadie clenches her fists at her side. "What storm are you talking about?"

"You know exactly what I'm talking about—it was a typhoon like no other. I came here to these shores to awaken my brother from the sentence he's served, yet I found interference."

Digging her heels into the rocky earth, the wind whips violently at Sadie's hair.

Lorenzo's voice is laced with assurance as he upturns all that's passed with an ease that sends Sadie's blood boiling. "The spell your ancestor cast on my brother plunged him into an eternal slumber, a nightmare of a curse that I sought to sever in spilling your mother's blood and ending your line... Yet how was I to know she had a daughter? Hidden away at the Hacienda, protected by that monster of a storm. Providence it may have been, I decided to watch and wait as your grief ate you up from within, watching in the shadows of your nightmares."

"No..." Sadie shakes her head, unable to bear the weight of his revelation. "This can't be happening," she mutters, voice growing hoarse. "This can't be true."

Yet Lorenzo assuages her doubt as he raises his voice in triumph, "When you woke Silas, I thought to see what my dear brother would do. After all, it's the taste that's my temptation—and how can I ever resist the promise of true, pure suffering?" A grin pulls up at his bloodied lips as Sadie backs away from him, her thoughts unraveled, memories brewing like the sea below.

The sound of the winds battering the Hacienda that stormy, dark night as she waited for dawn to break, as she waited for her mother's return engulfs her senses. Digging her fingers into her flesh, a quiet dread simmers through every vein in her body.

Lorenzo takes yet another step closer, his voice edged with satisfaction as he reaches his hand out to touch her shoulder. "Here —let me help you remember. Just close your eyes for me."

She resists him, yet as his fingers wrap tight around her, he leaves her with no choice as he pries into her very subconscious, a bright beam of light consuming her whole, forcing her to shut her eyes at the intensity. Instinctively, she draws her hands over her face to shield herself from the sting of the ocean and the whip of the merciless wind that washes over her—but it never subsides.

Once the light fades, sea spray washes over her, the low howl of the wind gripping her senses, leaving her momentarily stunned. The gusts are gale-force, her skin soaked to the bone in a rain that has no mercy. She's back in the dream of her mother's last moments—but this time is different.

The clouds are darker, the air colder, the sea wailing with the wind in a cacophony that Sadie fights hard to endure. The necklace between her fingers is the anchor that weighs her down in this place, keeping her from being cast adrift as she's cast into the truth of that dark day.

She finds herself back at the start of the path that leads to the cliffs, the precipice just up ahead, leaving her no other option than to run.

Running against the wind, against the roar of the sea, against the voice of reason that wills her to turn back, Sadie presses onwards, her blood running hot as she finally reaches the rocky clifftop and the clearing decimated by the ocean gusts.

The winds are harder here, and she digs her heels hard into the sodden earth, trudging forward against the daggers of rain falling over her skin. Squinting into the storm, Sadie sees a dark figure standing by the precipice—exactly where she's stood in her nightmares every night for a year past.

Moving closer, Sadie reaches her hand out, yearning to touch her, to feel her alive one more time beneath her fingertips.

"Mama..." Sadie whispers, the rains letting up as the word leaves her lips.

She's mere inches away, about to touch, about to meet—but this time, she turns around. "It's me." Sadie's heart pulses quick as she lays eyes on a face that she's been searching for every night in her nightmares. She waits for the spark of recognition to wash over her mom's face—but it never does.

It's not her she's seeing; it's someone else.

The lines around her eyes deepen as her mother frowns, fury filling her eyes. "You..." her mother spits it out in accusation as a pair of hands dig hard into her shoulders, eyes wide and unflinching. "It should have been you." The knuckles holding her in place are white hot, fingertips leaving an ashen trail that's washed away, out of sight by the rains.

Sadie tries to reach out, to stop it—but she feels nothing

beneath her as those phantom hands push her mother backwards, and she begins to fall.

"Mama!" Sadie cries out, lunging forward, her fingers brushing against the fabric of her mother's clothes just before she falls out of reach, a single whisper leaving her lips.

"*Sara...*"

And those are her last words as she falls into the depths.

The sea gust returns, forcing her to cover her face from the typhoon winds threatening to hurl Sadie into the sea along with her mother—but when she opens her eyes, she sees the nightmare snatched away by the storm, returning her back to the present where a demon awaits her.

Sadie's heart sinks into the depths of her soul, falling deeper still as she twists around, seeing a towering figure standing over her.

"Lorenzo." His name falls from her lips in a deadened whimper. "You... you killed her." Her blood burns as she snaps her eyes up to the man who murdered her mother. "You killed my mom.*"*

She motions to lunge forward, to make contact—anything—but the image of her mother's final moments keeps her anchored in place. Sadie clenches her jaw hard, teeth grinding together as she attempts to still her raging heart.

"*You killed her!*" Sadie screams until her voice runs hoarse. Dropping to the earth beneath her feet, she hangs her head as her veins fill with fire. The anniversary of her mother's death was marked with that desperate, longing question: *why did she leave?*

And here her answer stands before her.

"I did." Lorenzo answers, satisfaction soaking his every word, just like a shark caught in a bloody current, his prey so close, fast bleeding out. "But her spirit is strong, I will give you that."

Sadie shakes her head, fighting away the thoughts of that fateful day she found her necklace wrapped up in a demon's grave. Racking her brain, she dredges up the pain, the heartache, the emptiness gnawing at the pit of her belly as she laid in her mother's sheets—alone in the house.

"Who do you think led you to my brother's grave?"

Footsteps—that's what she heard, that's what roused her from her sleep. Descending the staircase in her mind's eye, she hears a low, dull *thud* coming from deep within the house; behind a sealed door.

"Listen closely—that *thud*."

The courtyard—there's another entrance, and it's swinging wide open in the breeze. The night is hot as it is dark, and that *thud*; it's coming from within. Deeper she goes, and beneath the twisted wood she finds a pit in the floor; something unearthed and never exhumed. A moth flutters into the darkness for but a moment before disappearing completely.

"Do you think that can come from a slumbering demon?"

Thud.

Sadie can feel the vague pressure of Silas' arms wrapped around her—*he's the demon she wanted me to find.*

Thud.

Sadie's thoughts surge, the *thud* resounding from her memory now one and the same as the pulse of her heart. That moth—*of course,* it's her spirit, a messenger, one last gift.

"It was my mom..." Sadie whispers, touching her necklace, the realization falling from her lips as she runs her fingers over every bump, every striation written on the surface of the fresh water pearl. "She led me to Silas."

Lorenzo draws closer, just arm's width apart—but there is no escape from his searing gaze, not when the precipice looms behind her. His voice is a lick of flame, as he lets it all loose, "She knew that the only chance you'd have against me... is with him."

Her blood turns to ice in her veins.

"How sweet it was..." he continues, his eyes flickering the color of an inferno. "The realization that it wasn't my brother she should have been sealing away—it should have been me."

Sadie's mind is a brewing storm, with each passing second the surge of her thoughts grow more uncontrollable. "She unearthed Silas when she was renovating the house... and in doing so she woke him." Sadie shakes her head, fingers digging hard into her sides. "She thought he was the cause of her grief... *he* was the root of her suffering—so with her necklace, *this* necklace she put him back to sleep. Just like our ancestor did..." Images of that smoke stained day centuries ago flit through Sadie's mind, along with the stench of burning flesh and the familiarity of that woman's features as she recited an incantation that would ensure Silas' sleep until the sky fall into the sea, until Judgment Day come, until he turns to rot and stardust. "She did it all for me. She did it because she thought she would save me from the same fate... but she was wrong." Sadie drops her hands to her sides, fingers limp, veins filled with lead as she rakes her eyes over Lorenzo. "She was wrong, because the man —that demon—in her nightmares wasn't Silas. It was you."

Lorenzo smiles, and it's all the confirmation she needs to hear. Swiping his tongue against his teeth, ecstasy winds through his features as he drinks in the ache that surges through Sadie's heart, the sting of her pain like ambrosia to his lips. "For all the pain I harvested from her final, fleeting nightmares..."

Sadie's chest constricts, his thorn tipped words purging the blood from the quick-beating organ beneath.

"For as filling as her suffering was, it's nowhere near as sweet as yours," he whispers, his eyes brimming with crimson malice. "Go on..." he gestures behind her, flicking his eyes over to the monstrous sea over her shoulder. "Why don't you end it all yourself? Do what your mother couldn't... Do what I never gave her the chance to do—jump."

The great, heaving waves of the sea below threaten to swallow Sadie so easily—all she needs to do is take a step backwards. But as Sadie feels her heart inflame, she becomes aware of the strange weight pulling at her side. Slipping her hand behind her back, she reaches into the pocket of her dress, her fingers wrapping around cold metal. Pulling it out she unfurls her palm, and she sways at the sight.

It's the coin Silas gave her; wrapped up in that dream of Italy, the one destined for the Trevi Fountain.

Lorenzo spies the coin, his tongue moving faster than she has the chance to process its meaning. "Yet another false promise my brother has given you... a dream that will remain just that," he hisses, pressing ever closer. "Nothing but a dream. And tell me Starling, what good are your dreams now?"

The coin glints back at her, waiting for her to realize that its weight against her palm is no burden. *No,* Sadie drops her shoulders, thinking of all those years she spent waiting for the right words, the right moment—and here, she's finally found it.

It's not everything that could have been... It's everything that can be.

The night twists around them both, conjuring up a shadow darker than sin.

Everything that is.

A merciless wind brings Sadie to her knees, and she clutches the rocky earth beneath for stability as she watches a shadow emerge from the undergrowth behind Lorenzo, and she smiles at the sight.

Everything that will be.

"You're wrong," her voice is hard, eyes flickering to the writhing dark looming over Lorenzo's shoulder, as she drops the coin into the raging sea below, where it's swallowed up by her mother's grave in a promise of hope, a promise of life. "They're all I have."

The shadows recede, spitting out the figure of a demon rapt in wrath, a sight she never thought would be a balm to her fear, an ease to her tangled nerves.

Yet it's all he is—Silas, his eyes a flicker of crimson, his heart bleeding black blood, the sight of him all she needs to know that her one and only wish has come true.

SADIE STANDS AT THE PRECIPICE, alongside the trailing moonflowers that cascade over the cliff's jagged edge as Silas rises from the undergrowth in a shadow larger than she's ever seen him, the wind bowing to his presence.

The rain recedes just enough for Sadie to see the damage the two brothers have wrought upon each other—Lorenzo's face courting red with a swelling cut across his cheekbone, Silas' brow bone sporting a black gash, his jaw adorned with a serpentine black bruise. But for all the pain of the flesh, there is none as threatening, as agonizing, as painful to look at as the quick bleeding slit in the center of Silas' chest.

"Here he is..." Lorenzo turns on his heel to greet his brother with a faux bow. "The Espinosa Infante. The heir, the prodigal son, the only Espinosa that ever mattered." Lorenzo's voice erupts like a lick of fire; ever bitter and laced with the scent of ash.

Silas takes another step closer, and Lorenzo continues without a trace of fear. "And look at you now—everything father said you could have been... I've seen it in the fire. Everything you still *can* be."

One step closer.

Lorenzo clasps his hands together, assuming an air of lightness that matches the wolfish grin on his lips. "Father was right, you know... what he did to our sisters—it was not enough. Nothing will ever be enough for you to realize the depths of what he has done for you. Always for *you*."

Silas stops arm's width away from Lorenzo, a miasma of smoke surrounding him, sputtering plumes rising from his skin, growing fiercer with every passing second.

"Do you remember, brother? Not a single cry escaped their lips as they burned." Lorenzo knows exactly what to say to conjure up the monster in Silas, the mention of his sisters bringing to the surface an anguish that has lay sleeping for centuries—an anguish that manifests in plain as the hellish shadow of who he truly is takes form before her very eyes, Sadie's stomach twisting in knots as Silas' eyes flare ruby.

Lorenzo's voice is a quiet hum, his words sharp, tipped with poison. "And what's worse, I wonder... their silence? Or *yours,* brother?"

And without a breath between them Silas strikes, his fist connecting with Lorenzo's temple with a force that sends him tumbling into the sodden earth.

With a gasp on her lips from the impact, Sadie backs away, retreating into the arms of the twisting moonflower vines, their vespertine blooms as fragrant as the petrichor, as potent as these two brothers' smoke wrought blood. She can only watch as the inferno crackles between them both, her heart beating impossibly fast.

Lorenzo presses himself up onto his feet, stumbling beneath Silas' impenetrable gaze. Lorenzo ambles forward before pulling his arm back to land a hook that Silas catches with his other hand. The crackle of the fireworks lighting up the night sky overhead is all that passes between them before Lorenzo takes the distraction and digs his free hand into the depths of Silas' chest.

Silas' body buckles at the impact, yet he never allows a sliver of agony to pass through his lips as Lorenzo twists his fingers into gushing blood of his wound, using his fingers as the knife that cleaves the scar tissue apart until his chest is a bleeding, black void.

"You will never escape our father's will, Silas." Lorenzo's teeth are stained with blood as he grins through the gore, only for Silas' fingers to dig hard into Lorenzo's fist, twisting his arm with enough force to pull it from its socket.

"*Argh!*" Lorenzo cries out, his piercing shriek covered up by the din of the rain and the fireworks.

"Father is *dead,* Lorenzo." Silas' voice is even, measured—in spite of his wound, in spite of the pain. He rises tall over his brother, eyes blazing, "Yet he still has his claws on your mind. On your soul. There is no escape as long as you act as his will."

"Don't you understand?!" Lorenzo's voice drips with fervor for a man long dead, as he clutches his limp, twisted arm. "His will is our freedom."

Silas shakes his head, "We are all that remains of our family, Lorenzo. The Espinosa name is *dead.*"

"No..." Lorenzo's voice grows quiet, "As long as *you* are alive... we will live forever."

The stench of smoke begins to permeate through the air, rippling through Sadie as hellfire begins to spark from between Silas' fingers, rage engulfing his senses.

"Isn't that what you want?" Bitterness clings to the scowl on Lorenzo's face, yet his words are laced with a melancholy that lasts for but a moment before Silas closes the distance between them once more. The winds whip hard against the cliffs as Silas' countenance begins to change—*no,* revert to what he truly is.

"I spent centuries in a casket, unable to die..." Silas' voice is hard, faltering as the blood from his wound pours out in a cascade of crimson. "Is that what father wanted? His *will* means nothing more to me than the ashes at his pyre. He burned long ago, Lorenzo. He is gone from this world."

"But his heart beats, still. Just as you said—not in this world, but another." A wolfish grin spreads over Lorenzo's features, a flash of white against his mangled face. "He lives on in me... and forever in you. Forever in that wound. It's cursed never to heal for a reason, brother."

Silas motions to close the distance between them, but Lorenzo acts faster, darting backwards in a haze of shadow. He takes the opportunity to collect his insurance in the form of Sadie's arm as he lunges to grab her. The sudden impact jolts her senses as she screams, "Let me go!"

His fingers dig into her forearm with monstrous strength in spite of his twisted arm, just above the purple-black bruises he left at her wrist as she pounds her clenched fists over his grip, but to no avail. Flicking her eyes down to the shreds of skin clinging desperately to Lorenzo's knuckles, Sadie knows that this can go either way as Silas draws closer, visibly weakened from the toll of the fight.

"That wound is there to serve as eternal remembrance." Lorenzo warns, yet Silas says nothing in response, his eyes aglow with hellish red as he steps closer, trailing black blood across the rocky clearing.

The wind whips hard at Sadie's face as Lorenzo continues, "That wound is there so you do not forget who you are..." Sadie bites down on the inside of her cheek at the thought of the carnage that's passed between them both. "So you do not forget the ocean of blood you have spilled..." Lorenzo and Silas, the last two sons of a demonic legacy soaked through with the suffering of infinite souls —the abundance of suffering that's kept one alive, the lack of suffering that's kept the other from truly living. "So you do not forget the name that binds you to that tide."

Lorenzo pins Sadie's arms down as he forces her back against his bloodied chest, drawing her closer to the moonflower vines and the precipice just out of reach.

"I know just what you need to help you remember..." Lorenzo's fingers wind through Sadie's tangled hair, pulling taut and forcing her down onto her knees. "I know just what you need to remember how sweet true suffering tastes."

Lorenzo crouches down over Sadie, encasing her in his iron grip, desperation thrumming through his fingertips, through the vibration of his heart against his chest—this is his last resort, his last chance.

"Don't you want to ease that gash in your chest?" Lorenzo's voice grows darker, "All those nightmares you've been feasting on beneath the ground... they're nothing but vague agonies." Lorenzo yanks harder against Sadie's hair, the tender flesh of her scalp stinging like the tears forming fast at her eyes. The urge to cry out claws at her throat, but she keeps it to herself, never allowing it the chance to resurface, for it's exactly what Lorenzo wants. "Don't you want to taste it in full? Slit her throat and splay her heart open... What is another few droplets to the ocean that you've already spilled?" Lorenzo pulls Sadie into him, forcing her to sit across his lap where the scent of Silas' blood is strong on his fingers. "Come... come and bleed her dry."

She doesn't struggle, she doesn't wrench away from his grip for there's no use—no use when it's not Lorenzo who holds her life in his hands, but Silas. Like Andromeda chained to the raging cliffs, she's nothing more than the offering to the waves, to the crimson tide, to the monstrous demon that commands it—yet there is no Perseus, no saving grace, no hero with a sword to act as her salvation.

It's only Silas.

And he makes his way to where she's heaped up against Lorenzo, bound by his hands and the rope of her hair. Silas drops to his knees before her, the fatigue of this fight taken its toll, the blood pouring from his heart nothing but a trickle of what's left within. Caught beneath his gaze as he draws closer, the stench of blood and smoke wraps tight around her senses in a perfume of all the dark devastation Father Agustin has ever warned her about.

Silas is the inferno, the monsoon sea, the master of her fears.

He stops arm's width away, the moonflower vines encasing them three in bloody union as Lorenzo yanks her head back forcefully, allowing Silas access to her neck and the coursing fear she keeps concealed within.

"Taste her." Lorenzo orders, and Silas motions closer, his one hand digging into the flesh of her thigh to keep her still as he slices through the rain and the silence, his eyes glazed through and through with blood and something else.

Hunger, Sadie realizes. *Hunger for my suffering.*

Lorenzo pulls tighter at her scalp, Sadie never releasing a sound as she's fixed beneath Silas' unreadable expression. She searches desperately for any semblance of the demon she's come to know beneath the reflective film of his eyes, yet all he gives her is impenetrable silence before he leans down to deliver her to a fate that's long since slipped from her fingers.

Even the moon turns her eyes away from this dark convergence, away from these three tangled bodies. She's trapped between Cain and Abel, an unholy trinity of suffering and hunger, of sin and guilt, of blood and want. Sadie can do nothing but screw her eyes shut tight at the feeling of Silas' lips brushing against her skin, his one hand tracing over the pulsing vein at her neck as he positions himself above her, pinning her back against Lorenzo until there's not a single breath for movement, not a single chance for escape.

Yet her heart is an eerie stillness in her chest—a silent calm as she hears a whisper of a name escape from his lips, a whisper for a girl named *Solita.*

Opening her eyes, she sees Silas' eyes so close to hers, yet there's a plea in his eyes. Her mind races, as firelight dances above them three, and she realizes in this suffocating embrace that it's a plea for her tears, for her sorrow, for her anguish.

It's a plea for her to let her tears loose.

"*Dame tu angustia,*" he says in that same desperate whisper he did that first night she allowed him into the Hacienda, her heart constricting at the memory. As the firelight fades, Sadie understands exactly what it is he wants.

Give me your suffering.

And with a whimper, she lets her tears fall free.

She cries, rage and sorrow twisting into one, hate and grief spilling from her eyes in saltwater droplets that sear her skin as they trickle down her cheeks, dripping from her chin, trailing across her neck and down towards her chest. It's a divine expulsion; the sum of a lifetime of loneliness soaking her lashes, her mother's murder, her wasted guilt—she rages against it all as she lets the rain upturn the earth and sorrow she buried deep inside her body.

Silas drinks from the font of her tears, his lips brushing against the underside of her jaw, his tongue collecting the droplets of sorrow in a motion that sends a fire through every nerve in her body. The purging feels almost like ecstasy as she allows him her torment, prying herself apart for him to enter and take what he needs.

"Doesn't she taste like everything you've ever wanted?" Lorenzo's voice brushes against the shell of her ear, his words brimming with satisfaction as he holds her impossibly taut against his chest, pinning her arms to her sides as Silas pulls away from her lips.

"Everything you've ever needed?"

She misses his warmth instantly, yet even in the darkness Sadie can see something in him has changed, something in him stronger.

"She does," Silas answers as a burst of vivid green lights up the night sky, illuminating the disappearing bruise across his jaw, his brighter pallor, the renewed light behind his eyes. Sadie's heart skips a beat as Silas traces the trail of her grief, wiping away a tear with a sweep of his thumb, the motion belying a gentleness that can only mean one thing.

"You've always been blind, Lorenzo." Silas casts his eyes up and over Sadie's shoulder, his voice dripping with abyssal dark. "Let me show you just how blind you've been," Silas murmurs, his hand slipping up from her cheek towards his brother's face with a speed Sadie hardly has the chance to process. Silas' other hand grips the back of Lorenzo's head until his hair is pulled taut, keeping his face staunchly in place with hellish force—leaving Sadie no other choice but to simply watch.

Watch as Silas' eyes flare crimson, watch as his fingers dart to Lorenzo's eye with an intention that can only mean one thing.

The chance to get close is all he needed.

"What are you—" Lorenzo starts, but the words become a tangled knot on his tongue as Silas pierces through the skin of his eyelid. Terror claws at Lorenzo's throat as he lets out a scream of agony against the shell of Sadie's ear, eliciting from her a gasp that she keeps taut in her throat as Silas drives his fingers deep into the socket of Lorenzo's skull. Sadie focuses hard on maintaining the tremble in her bones as Silas stops briefly, his fingers finding purchase against what can only be the thick meat that lines the back of the eyeball.

With her eyes fixed solely to the bloodlust etched beneath Silas' focused eyes, the sound of his fingers inside his brother's eye socket is amplified tenfold, his breath hot against her skin, Lorenzo's grip still wound tight against her hair.

She waits, she listens, knowing what's coming next, knowing how this has to end—and with a jolt of a shiver, she knows it's come.

Lorenzo's agony rings loud in her ears as Silas pulls, pulls, pulls —the thread of his optic nerve stretched to its very limit, the thick underside of his sclera bulging beneath the force of Silas' fingers. That sting of acidity permeates her nostrils, along with the *drip, drip, drip* of searing blood over her shoulders, pooling at her collarbones and dripping down between the valley of her breasts. A tremor ripples through her spine at the sensation, yet Silas never allows her the chance to resist it as he pulls at the optic nerve a final time, with a force that ensures he need not try again.

With a gurgle of pain, the nerve snaps, severing the eye from its owner—and Sadie releases the breath she's been holding.

She twists and turns from beneath the weight of his body, watching in horror as the stub of a thread that hangs out from the bloodied hollow of Lorenzo's eye untwines, like a gnawed end of a piece of yarn. There is no saving it, no re-attaching, no going back.

Lorenzo slumps forwards, releasing Sadie from his grip, her hair spilling across her shoulders as his bloodied eye socket drips out across the torn fabric of her dress. Lorenzo clutches at his now hollowed eye with both hands, the blood flowing fast from the emptied socket as his silver tongue struggles to find the words for the first time since she's known him.

Silas looms tall over his brother as he claws at his face in crippling agony, the searching motion of his desperate fingers a tell of stark disbelief. Lorenzo pulls at the now loose, pathetic skin that once covered his left eye—now hanging limply over a bloody black void and the hanging, fleshy remains of his optic nerve.

He drops his hands to his sides, a surge of rage bringing him up to his feet with renewed speed. He dives to lunge forward for Silas, only for a flutter of black to slice through the rain, zeroing in on Lorenzo. He swats at his face, staggering backwards as what can only be the glossy plumage of a bird—a starling—aims straight for his face, pecking at his empty eye socket, forcing him back to the earth in a stuttering pain.

It can't be the same starling Sadie patched up, he's back at the Hacienda, back in her bedroom—but with a breath she lets all doubt go as she recalls the image of the Hacienda's front doors splayed open against the rain and the wind. It was her who left the doors open, she the reason for the starling's presence.

And of course here he would be; freed from his cage, freed from his prison.

Lorenzo knocks the bird away from his face, Sadie's heart lurching in her chest at the impact only for the bird to hop back up onto his feet, his crimson eyes bright even under cover of the night. Silas turns towards the starling's direction, holding his arm out, beckoning him to perch.

The starling obeys, landing upon Silas' wrist. "Here," he says softly, unfurling his bloodied fist, where a deflated mass lays across the flat of his palm, at its center a dimming, wicked green. The starling hops forward, his crimson gaze taking in the sight of the severed demon's eye offered up to him.

The starling flits closer towards the grotesque eye before finally pecking at that glassy, molten cornea. He pierces through the thick outer layer with the tip of his beak, again and again and again, supping on the liquid, tearing at those pink tendrils of nerves as if it's nothing more than one of the honied figs Silas gave him to eat back at the Hacienda.

Snatching up the eye by the base of the optic nerve, the starling steals away into the night, flying away on mended wings with a demon's eye in his beak and a demon's phantom pain in the pit of his belly.

Silas drops his hand to his side as he strides forward, looming tall over Lorenzo and his one-eyed gaze. Sadie's eyes dart between them both, her nerves tangled as she realizes Silas is far from finished. He crouches down before his brother, fingers wrapping tight around the skin of his throat with nothing but fire in his eyes.

Holding him upright, Silas's fingers dig into his jugular as he strikes him again and again, unleashing centuries' worth of fury upon his body. Blood mixes with the rain, teeth with the dirt, and flecks of skin with the rocks and roots and moonflower vines entwining the cliffside. The shadows rippling from him grow darker and darker with each passing second, and Sadie's skin prickles at this carnage.

The crunch of bones, of teeth, of rupturing flesh; both are steeped in a sea of blood. His, or the other's, the crimson intermingles with not a single distinguishing mark. The same wrath runs through them both, the same name, the same inferno.

And Sadie can't look away—not when it's the demon who killed her mother facing a death he so justly deserves. Lorenzo's one-eyed face contorts in agony as Silas' fist connects once more with his cheekbone, and the blood rush that follows fills Sadie with a twisted satisfaction. The hate burning through her veins is bitter as it is sweet; the taste on her tongue as mesmerizing as the fire licking her skin, a fire that grows hotter and hotter until it's near unbearable.

It's poison, she decides—it's all it is.

"Silas..." Sadie calls his name over the din of the sea, the heat running through her veins burning her alive. *"Silas!"* Her voice should be nothing but a whisper against the inferno cast between these two bloody demons, but as Silas pulls his fist back to land another blow—he never delivers it.

Heart racing, she draws her eyes up to his, a bolt of lightning shooting through her at the sight.

Blood and rain cling to Silas' face, the cuts on his knuckles a stinging red that matches his brother's mangled face, but his eyes are fixed on hers.

He heard her.

Silas' fist drops to his side, and he rises like a stack of smoke above his brother's broken body. Rain veils the cliffs, shrouding Sadie's vision in a cast of white as the droplets wash away the gore and the violence, carrying it back down into the parched earth below, feeding the bone dry soil with all the decadence of demon's blood.

Lorenzo's blood caked brows furrow, prompting the deep gash running across his eyebrow to ooze black blood. "Y—you..." he sputters, eye fixed on the girl he's all but underestimated.

Sadie rips her eyes away from Lorenzo's cracked lips, the sight, the taste of his suffering leaving nothing but an emptiness in the pit of her belly.

Sadie steps aside as Silas hauls his brother's gored body to the precipice, his fingers wrapped taut around his throat in a grip vice-tight. Whatever second wind he gained from the taste of her tears, must be well and truly on its last legs by now, his heart blood-drained and body utterly battered. Hoisted up above the ground, Silas holds Lorenzo at arm's length, taking another step closer towards the edge.

"You're all I have left, Silas." Lorenzo's voice is devoid of the cruelty that so usually clings to him, yet Sadie doesn't believe for a second that it isn't just another mask, a façade of defeat. "You're my brother."

Sadie can already feel the rain begin to dissolve the blood staining her skin, yet even through the lull of the rain, Lorenzo's remaining eye flickers crimson as he sets his gaze on her, and the pearl at her neck.

Silas' voice is unwavering as he answers, "And I am not your keeper."

And with the howl of the wind, Silas lets go.

But it's not fear that's written on Lorenzo's lips—it's a smile. In the haze of a heartbeat, he reaches out for the pearl around her neck, tearing it from her body in one last infliction of agony. Clasp broken, chain torn, pearl between his fingers as he falls over the edge, disappearing into the rain and the waves beneath along with the last tangible memory Sadie has of her mother.

Falling to her knees, all Sadie can do is watch helplessly as she clutches the edge of the clifftops, staring down into the depths of the abyss below—waiting for the sound of his body to hit the water.

But she never hears it.

The feeling of a bloodied hand at her shoulder and all the darkness thrumming beneath it grounds her back to the present, back to this place that's the cradle of her dreams and nightmares twisted all into one.

"*Solita*..." Silas' voice wraps around her, easing her heartbeat back to a stillness at the mere feeling of his touch—yet it's short lived as he collapses to the ground behind her.

With a gasp she turns, scrambling onto her hands and knees

towards the pool of black blood seeping from Silas' heavy body, hunching over his face to shield him from the rains falling hard above them both.

"No..." Her pulse is deafening as she pulls him up onto her knees with all of her strength, cradling his head in her arms like a blood stained *Pietà,* an unholy embrace. Her tears could only do so much it seems—his face a paler shade, drained of color, the cursed wound in his chest gored, wrought open wider than she had ever seen before. "No, Silas..."

Pressing her palm into the depths of his upturned flesh, she wills the wound to close, to heal over like it did that first night he pressed her into him—but it doesn't work.

"No, no, no!"

Leaving streaks of blood across his chest, up to his neck, his cheeks, and his pallid complexion, she listens in a panic as his breathing slows, the tether that binds him to his sanity, to himself, growing thinner with every passing second.

"Silas..." she pleads, her voice a whisper against his cheeks.

Taking his face in her hands, she leans into his body, winding her hands through the black waves of his hair as the ocean crashes below them, a melody and a deafening cacophony all at once.

For all this time being the vessel, the prey, the victim, the perpetually suffering Virgin—this time, she wants to know exactly what a demon's suffering tastes like.

"Wake up," she commands, kissing the death on his lips, denying him the darkness.

Cold rushes over her in a shock of stinging brine water as her vision floods over with the weight of everything she's held back all these years. Her monsoon nightmares meeting the tide of his blood-soaked sin captures her in its dark embrace, unleashing upon her the full force of his countless memories, his countless dreams, of a life once lived, and a life he's yet to claim. Sadie clutches the ruined fabric of Silas' shirt, knuckles wicked hot as a raging current flows from her and into him, from him and into her in a reciprocity that feels like forever beneath the night sky.

Don't leave me, she commands, tears stinging at her eyes.

But there's a twitch beneath her, a twin pulse she feels beneath hers.

Don't leave me alone.

He stirs.

In a heartbeat she feels his hands on her body, the warmth returning to the veins beneath his skin, as his wound begins to ebb away—but he breaks the kiss first.

He blinks. Once, twice, and then he sees her.

The ghost of a smile forms at his lips before faltering into a grimace, tension wreaking havoc through his nerves as the gash yawning out across his chest begins to close over, the flesh reforming, twisting, writhing, becoming whole again. With a gasp of a breath he feels his strength return to him, and he exercises his movement the only way he can—by wrapping his arms around her waist, pressing her tight against him.

"Y—you're..." she stutters, exasperated as a smile brushes her lips. "You're here."

He closes the distance between them again, returning her kiss with equal force, like a wound to a knife that never wants to close; never wants to heal.

He winds his fingers through her hair; and despite the darkness he marvels at her as if it's starlight that drips over her skin instead of the rain that it is.

What must be the final firework launches high into the air, the clouds breaking above, the rains dying out. And she realizes—amidst the vivid crimsons, the greens, the vibrant yellows—her favorite color of all is the starlight on his cheeks, the reflection of the moon in his eyes.

"I'm here." His voice is a soft caress against her twisted nerves, yet a trickle of blood catches Sadie's attention.

It's a droplet of ruby trailing across his bruised face, and she draws her hand over his skin to wipe the smoke-tainted stain away from his eyes, the gash at his brow bone as deep as it dark. She lingers at the wounds embedded into his flesh, bruises—all the adornments that belong to a demon's kind.

"Are you afraid?" he asks, his voice slicing through this rain-soaked night, his fingers brushing against the shell of her cheek.

Sadie casts her eyes away, down at her lap at what remains of her mother's Maria Clara, inhaling a shaky breath. She runs her eyes across the ivory fabric, illuminated by a fire lit sky—once part of a dress she couldn't bear to touch, now torn and irreparably bloodied.

"I am," she whispers as she takes the dress between her two fists, tearing the skirt apart, the threads irreparably broken, the seams split in two to form a strip of fabric that she presses to Silas' brow bone. "I'm afraid like I've never been before."

He doesn't for a second flinch at the pain of contact, responding only by closing this distance between them as he lifts himself upright, enveloping her completely in his arms as he buries his face in the thick of her hair, the tip of his nose brushing against the line of her jaw.

"Mm," he replies. "I can taste it."

"What does it taste like?" she asks softly, anything to lull this newfound feeling welling deep inside her.

"It tastes of a curse I'll never be free form." Silas' hand closes over her wrist, pulling her hand away from the gash at his brow as he presses his lips to the underside of her jaw. "It tastes like you, *Solita*."

With the softest of smiles, she allows this unfamiliar agony, this strange new pain to wash over her like the night rain as she winds her fingers through his hair, giving him freely the fear and the faith she never thought she'd have to give.

Without a thought she moves her other hand behind her back, untying what remains of her Maria Clara's torn skirt, leaving her with nothing else but her silk slip fluttering in the wind as she takes the bundle of bloodied ivory in her arms.

She breaks away from Silas for but a moment, rising to her feet and meeting the rain soaked wind as a hard gust tousles her hair. She stands over the cliff's edge, holding the fabric of her mother's dress over the precipice.

Sadie is filled with a sense of peace standing where her mother died; standing in the same place she drew her last breath, the last time her mother said her name in a desperate attempt to let her daughter know that she was loved right to the very last.

Her heart aches, and with an exhale, she lets go.

A sea gust catches the fabric, and for just a moment she sees a shape of a woman in the fabric—but she's only a specter, a ghost that falls and drowns below in the waves of that swirling, starlit sea.

This feeling, a smile pulls up at her lips, *I never thought I'd feel it again.*

"What is it?" Silas asks, voice impossibly soft.

Sadie drops to her knees, winding her arms around his neck, pressing her forehead to his with a lilt of laughter rising from her lips in response.

"You're not a dream," she smiles, speaking the words aloud in a final act of manifestation, "and I'm awake..." She feels no need to shut her eyes, to shrink away beneath the words, instead she wants nothing more than to melt into him just as she is, through his skin, pierced by his ribs, devoured by his demon heart. "I'm finally awake."

SADIE AND SILAS' STORY
CONTINUES IN BOOK 2 OF THE
SOLITA SERIES:

SILENCIA

SADIE'S ONCE GRIEF-RIDDEN NIGHTMARES HAVE TWISTED INTO DREAMS DARKER THAN SHE'S EVER KNOWN NOW THAT HER LIFE IS FOREVER ENTWINED WITH THE DEMON NAMED SILAS WHO BEARS THE WEIGHT OF COUNTLESS SIN.

SIN SHE LONGS TO UPTURN.

SIN HE LONGS TO BURY.

FOR EVERY SECRET OF HIS PAST HE REFUSES TO SURRENDER, SADIE IS DRIVEN DEEPER INTO THESE SINISTER DREAMS. DEEPER AND DEEPER SHE DELVES UNTIL SHE FINDS THE GREATEST TEMPTATION OF THEM ALL; THE OPEN ARMS OF THE ONLY SOUL WHO KNOWS THE TRUTH.

A PHANTOM. A WOMAN. A MURDERED LOVER.

SHE OFFERS SADIE EVERYTHING HER HEART DESIRES TO SEE, AND NAMES ONLY ONE PRICE:

LET ME IN.

THE TEMPTATION IS TOO GREAT, AND SADIE ENTERS INTO THIS GARDEN OF EARTHLY DELIGHTS, TASTING, DRINKING, FEASTING UPON ALL OF SILAS' SIN UNTIL SHE IS BLINDED BY FRAGRANT BLOOMS—BUT SHE MUST BEWARE THE SERPENTS COILED BENEATH.

FOR A SNAKE CLEAVED IN TWO CAN STILL SINK ITS FANGS DEEP INTO THE VEINS; AND ONCE THE VENOM OF DESIRE HAS SPREAD THROUGH THE BLOOD, A DEADLY DANCE FOLLOWS SUIT.

AND THERE IS NO CURE, THERE IS NO BALM, THERE IS NO ESCAPE FROM DEATH'S DESIRE.

AFTERWORD

The poem recited in the prologue was written by Abu Muhammad
ibn Hazm (994-1064 CE), an Andalusian scholar born in the then
Caliphate of Cordoba, now present-day Spain. The words and
sentiment of a man who lived and died a thousand years ago is
what gave me the spark of inspiration that started the Solita series
—yet can the dead truly die when their words stretch out and yawn
across the page before you?

I would split open my heart
with a knife, place you
within and seal my wound,
that you might dwell there
and never inhabit another
until the resurrection and
Judgment Day—thus you
would stay in my heart
while I lived, and at my death
you too would die in the entrails of my core,
in the shadow of my tomb

ACKNOWLEDGMENTS

To Robin, my heart, my home, my endless support.

To my mother in law for her persisting encouragement and belief in the girl who at times barely even believed in herself.

And to my dearest dad for his unwavering, unconditional faith in my dreams and everything he knew that I could become—I would not be the woman I am today if it wasn't for you.

ABOUT THE AUTHOR

Writing the stories about those who were never represented in the
gothic literature she consumed as a child is Vivien's life's goal—for
to pick up a book and see someone like yourself be the hero of
their own story is all it takes for others to know that they can be
the masters of their own fate, too.

@authorvivienrainn

Printed in Great Britain
by Amazon